Designs on
the Dead

Also available by Emilia Bernhard

The Death in Paris Mystery Series

The Books of the Dead
Death in Paris

Designs on the Dead

A Death in Paris Mystery

EMILIA BERNHARD

CROOKED
LANE

NEW YORK

Published in the United States by Crooked Lane Books, an imprint of The Quick Brown Fox & Company LLC.

Crooked Lane Books and its logo are trademarks of The Quick Brown Fox & Company LLC.

Library of Congress Catalog-in-Publication data available upon request.

ISBN (hardcover): 978-1-64385-454-0
ISBN (ebook): 978-1-64385-455-7

Cover design by Lori Palmer

Printed in the United States.

www.crookedlanebooks.com

Crooked Lane Books
34 West 27th St., 10th Floor
New York, NY 10001

First Edition: September 2021

10 9 8 7 6 5 4 3 2 1

For Roselyn Farren

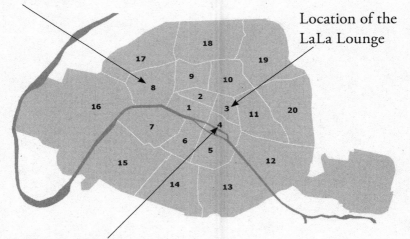

Location of Sauveterre
headquarters and the Holiday
Inn Elysees

Location of the
LaLa Lounge

Location of Cyrille
Thieriot's apartment

Arrondissements of Paris

Chapter One

❦

On a gray Saturday morning in Paris, a woman sat alone and mourned the death of a man who made clothes.

Roland Guipure Dies

read the headline on the front page of *Le Figaro*. The obituary continued,

Designer of Artful Power Found Dead
16 avril 2016
Roland Guipure, the fashion designer who consistently broke ground and raised the stakes as head of Sauveterre, the fashion label he founded, died on Thursday night. He was 40.

Guipure was found dead yesterday morning near the LaLa Lounge in the third arrondissement, where he had been celebrating his birthday. He had recently completed treatment for heroin addiction at a rehab facility in Greece. His death has been confirmed by the House of Sauveterre.

Roland Guipure began his design career at age 24, when he showed his "Nereid" collection during Paris Fashion Week in 2000. Critics called the collection "revolutionary" and "a challenge to anyone who thinks they know what fashion means." Over the years that followed, Guipure's rise was meteoric. He funded Sauveterre with an inheritance from his grandfather Maximilien Sauveterre, the much-admired art dealer, but the label soon became self-supporting under the financial management of his twin sister Antoinette. Sauveterre's trademark double *S,* surrounded by guillemets—»§«—became a familiar sight on pieces worn by chic women. As the house became more established, Guipure's designs became more serious, known for clean lines that were almost sculptural and often startling.

Although Guipure never had formal fashion training or worked under another designer, he apprenticed to a tailor after his graduation from secondary school, and this may account for his lack of interest in standard fashion expectations. His prêt-à-porter was as likely to feature square-cut suitings with peplums of burlap and leather as his haute couture was to feature a bridal gown created from gold-pinstriped red flannel (both feature in the house's autumn/winter 2007 collections). His *Ne Touche Pas* dress, with its elaborate lapels of pleated organza and wired-back collar reminiscent of antlers or tentacles, is currently on display in London's Victoria and Albert Museum.

Over the last two years, however, Guipure became increasingly dependent on heroin. His health suffered, Sauveterre's sales began to drop, and his 2015 collections were poorly received. Last year he entered a rehabilitation facility in Greece. Sauveterre showed no collections for spring/summer 2015 and no haute couture collection this January, but for spring/summer 2016 prêt-à-porter they presented looks Guipure designed while in recovery. Reactions were positive, with *WWD* calling it "a fresh revisioning that promises a strong future."

Guipure's recent autumn/winter 2016 prêt-à-porter collection, his first completed after emerging from *désintoxification* last November, was greeted rapturously. Based on this success, the house had decided to recommence showing haute couture next season.

The fashion world is reeling from this unexpected tragic afterword to what had seemed to be a happy ending. "Roland was a bright beacon," said Marianne Faubois of French *Vogue*. "His death leaves a gaping hole in the future of couture."

Roland Guipure was born on 12 April 1976 to Genevieve (née Sauveterre) and Paul Guipure, and died on 15 April 2016. He is survived by a sister, Antoinette Guipure.

It was silly, Rachel Levis knew. She had never met Roland Guipure. She couldn't afford any of his haute couture fantasies, and at five foot two and a hundred and thirty pounds she wouldn't have fit into them anyway. Yet she knew and loved his designs. Every woman in Paris with any kind of interest in fashion knew them: the early miniskirts and shirts that looked like Chanel jackets ripped apart and stuck back together at random; the combinations of angles and flow that made up his more recent collections. And a month ago his prêt-à-porter collection, the first he'd staged since finishing rehab, had made critics reach for new superlatives. She hated clichés, even when she only used them to herself, but Guipure genuinely *had* been full of promise, a talent that made fashion both surprising and significant.

Normally, she would have pointed out the obituary to her husband, Alan, but he was on his annual visit to his parents in Florida and wouldn't be back for another month. As a poor substitute, she bit into her croissant and remembered the previous spring when, during a visit to London, she and her best friend Magda had seen the *Ne Touche Pas* dress in the Victoria and Albert Museum. The tight column of heavy marigold-colored silk had been lit from above, making its red organza ruffles and huge wired collar almost iridescent. They looked like the wings of a bold Elizabethan insect or the petals of an enormous glass poppy balanced on a golden stem. Although she had loved clothing for as long as she could remember, her encounter with the dress was the first time that she understood how fashion could blend nature and artifice to enhance life in the ordinary world.

The ring of her *portable* cut across this memory. The screen told her Magda was calling. She swiped at the green icon and took the call.

"Roland Guipure—"

"I know," Rachel said, cutting her off. "I'm just reading the obituary now."

Magda sighed. "Remember when we went to the V and A?"

For a few minutes they rehashed the day Rachel had been remembering, reminding each other about the dresses in the exhibition and the glossy hardback catalogue neither of them had felt rich enough to buy. Then Magda said with finality, "Well, it's the curse of rehab, isn't it? People seem great when they get out, but wait a couple of weeks and they fall right off the wagon."

"You can't be sure it happened that way," Rachel protested, although she'd been thinking much the same. Still, she hated to think of anyone she admired, no matter how far removed, dead in an alley from an overdose. "The obituary just said he'd died, not how he died."

"Oh, please! Dead outside a nightclub after his birthday party? If you say that, you don't need to say *overdose.*"

What can I say? Rachel thought. She couldn't disagree; she was as familiar with the clichés as Magda was. So instead of responding she moved the conversation onto another topic. After all, like all people who speak to each other daily, they had plenty to talk about.

Chapter Two

The rest of the week passed as the first weeks of spring do, with an overwhelming sense that change is coming and a corresponding sense that it isn't coming quickly enough. Rachel noticed that the trees had begun to put out the little yellow leaves that would turn dark green in summer. Spring was her favorite season in any country, but here it almost made the late Paris winter, with its drizzle and its slushes, worthwhile. In the mornings she watched the new leaves from the window of her *séjour* as she drank her tea, marveling, as she did every year, over their combination of tenderness and precision, the way their bright edges seemed perfectly etched against the blue of the newly sunny sky.

She had the same thought on Thursday afternoon as she walked home after meeting a friend for lunch near the Place des Vosges. The crisp square of the Place, neatly bisected on each side by paths that met in the middle, always soothed her, and walking under the trees now she saw that their leaves had already shaded into a firmer green. The air on her cheeks was fractionally warmer than it had been two hours before, and as she breathed in, she smelled the faint scent of earth from the thawing ground. Spring was staking its claim. She would walk home in it.

As she crossed the Rue de Turenne heading toward the Rue St. Paul, she saw that the corner news kiosk fluttered with the latest issues of the weekly gossip magazines. All the cover headlines were about Roland Guipure: "Twenty-First-Century Dior: We Will Not See His Like Again," the cover of *Paris Match* mourned; "Sad Day for Fashion!" bellowed *Closer*. She thought about the rituals of death in the celebrity age. These same headlines would be used with slight changes when the next famous or semi-famous person died, and in a year—or less—Roland Guipure would be just a name.

My God, she said to herself. Such mournfulness on such a day! The sun was out; the air was soft; she would Skype her beloved husband that evening . . . Cheer up, she told herself.

She became aware of a male voice shouting behind her.

Any woman in Paris quickly learns to ignore the sound of a man yelling on the street. Keeping her head down, Rachel sped up into a brisk speed-walk that usually outran any street harassment. But the voice only seemed to come closer. Now it was saying, "Father's friend! Hey, father's friend!"

A hand landed on her shoulder.

She spun around, tensed for action. At first she didn't recognize the man in front of her, tall and thin, skin stretched tight over his cheekbones. Then she remembered an elevator door opening onto a landing, a snaggle-toothed smile, and this same skull-like face asking her if she'd ever seen *Scarface*. Matthieu Mediouri, drug dealer and briefly a suspect in the murders of Rachel's former boyfriend Edgar Bowen and his son David two years earlier—murders that she and Magda had solved. When she and Mediouri had first met, on the landing outside that open elevator door, she'd identified herself only as "a friend of David's father." Mediouri had decided this would make an excellent nickname, and now he stood there smiling, as if the irritating phrase were a delightful shared joke. She felt her stomach tighten.

"You don't remember me," he began. "I am—"

"Monsieur Mediouri. I remember you."

His smile widened. She saw that he'd had his teeth straightened. "Well, well! Good to know I am not forgettable. Just like you were not forgettable to me. I recognized you right away. What are you doing here, father's friend?"

"I might say the same to you. Or do you have a lot of customers in this area?" Let him see that she remembered what he was.

He laughed, a sharp bark. "*Absolument!* But not in the way you're thinking. I'm a legitimate businessman now." He pointed behind him. "I own that *pressing*."

Rachel could just make out a storefront halfway down the street with *Pressing Saint Paul* written on it. Mediouri had left drug dealing to become a dry cleaner?

He must have sensed her disbelief, because he said, "Come see my premises. I invite you for a coffee."

"I don't drink coffee."

He shrugged. "Tea then. Moroccan mint tea. I make it in a special way." In the heavily accented English she vividly remembered he said, "It is *de*licious!"

It didn't seem wise to leave a public location with a known criminal, even one who claimed to be reformed. On the other hand, it didn't seem wise to refuse a known criminal's invitation either. And she was curious. Squinting down the street, she saw that the *pressing* had a large plate glass window, easy to see and be seen through. She would simply refuse to go into any back rooms.

The tea was good: hot but not too hot, and sweetened with sugar that Mediouri added in careful increments with a tiny brass spoon. Its mint taste was bracing; the silent ritual of mixing, oddly soothing. She took a few silent sips and rested her elbows on the *pressing*'s front counter.

"You are surprised, eh?" Mediouri's words blew steam off his miniature gold cup. "You thought I would be in jail, or dead."

Embarrassed at being so easily read, she blushed.

He laughed again. "The movies and the TV, they make you think we all die in a shoot-out or with a needle in the arm. And that does happen. But more often one just . . . moves on."

Rachel couldn't help herself. "But dry cleaning?"

He shrugged. "It's the family business. My grandfather was a tailor in Morocco, and my father owned a laundry out in Clichy sous Bois when he first emigrated. Besides"—a quick flash of gleaming teeth—"this business isn't completely unconnected to my old work. I let some of my old friends use it as a kind of laundry too."

Rachel smiled back at him before she could stop herself. Warm, witty, frank: he was completely different from the sinister lounge lizard she'd encountered outside Edgar's *appartement* all those months ago.

"And your friend? Uh . . ." She could see his stubby sidekick in her mind's eye, wearing his baseball cap and puffa vest, but she couldn't remember his name.

"Laurent. L-Brah. He died."

"Oh, I'm sorry."

"That *was* a cinema death. He was shot. And that made me realize it was time. If you stay too long in the business the police come to recognize you. It gets harder to do your work. And kids coming up want to use you to prove something. And all the hustling for customers, running around making the deliveries—it's a young man's job." He shrugged again. She concentrated on her tea, stirring its green depths with her tiny spoon.

"And you?" he said after the pause had lengthened into a silence. "What are you doing here on the Rue St. Paul?"

She might be warming to him, but she still wasn't going to tell him the specifics of her life. "Just walking home from a visit to a friend."

"In between catching murderers?" Again he clearly enjoyed her shock. "Yes, I heard you caught the killer of the father. And then another one last year." He must have seen that she was trying to figure out his source, because he gave a little smirk. "I have some *flic* friends too. So now you are a *detective privé*?"

She forced herself not to imagine him sharing tea with Capitaine Boussicault, her police connection. "Yes." She made her voice firm. "I am a private detective."

It was almost true. Eight months earlier, she and Magda had solved what Magda liked to call "our second murders," two employees of the Bibliothéque Nationale killed to cover up thefts of priceless engravings. Feeling that unmasking two murderers in a row must mean they had some kind of talent for detection, they'd decided to set up as private investigators,

Rachel handling what Magda defined as "the more material aspects of investigation," while Magda, who ran a successful online business, appointed herself "the digital division." Still filled with American optimism, no matter how long they lived in France, they'd assumed the process would be relatively simple given their experience. But they had forgotten to factor in the French love of bureaucracy and documentation. There were courses they had to enroll in and exams they had to take, and only after could they submit the long and complex form that, along with a description of their experiences and attached affidavits from reliable witnesses, might result in certification. *Still*, Rachel thought, *If you can't try out a new identity with a drug dealer turned questionable dry cleaner, who can you try it out with?*

Indeed, Mediouri didn't seem surprised by her confirmation. He just gave a second shrug and nodded. "Makes sense. You solved two already; why not make a job out of it?"

Having been so easily accepted, she now felt she needed to be completely honest. "Well, I'm not quite there yet. At the moment I'm—"

The bell over the door rang, and a harried-looking woman came in, her arms full of silky fabric. She paid no attention to the teacups or to Rachel, just dropped the pile onto the countertop. "Can I have these by Monday morning?"

Instantly Mediouri became a smooth service professional. "Of course, Madame. Any spots we should know about? Special care instructions?"

As he groped under the counter for his receipt book, a magazine flopped out. It was a copy of *Oops!*, its cover decorated with a picture of Roland Guipure frowning as he altered the pleats on a gown. The huge headline read, "Sad Last Days of Fashion's Comeback Kid." Rachel picked it up.

"You can have that. I'm done with it." The door closed behind the customer as Mediouri spoke. The woman's entrance had broken their spell of intimacy, and now he picked up the pile of clothes. "I better start on these. But"—his tone softened; he groped in his pocket—"private detectives, they need connections, yes? And you and I, we have a connection." He leered, a touch of the old Mediouri. "So please . . ." He held out a business card. "In case I can ever help."

Rachel looked at the card. The only connections her previous investigations had given her were a society matron and a book restorer, and while both had proved surprisingly useful, they weren't exactly links to the city's seedy underbelly. She slipped the card into her bag.

Outside, the air had changed again, and it was too chilly to continue walking. She headed down into the Pont Marie métro. Once on a train, she opened the magazine.

Designer to the stars Roland Guipure seemed to have pulled his life back from the brink. He had completed désintox last autumn, and his most recent collection for the Sauveterre label was hailed as a perfect return to form. On top of that, he had just signed a licensing deal that would earn him up to €100 million a year.

But behind closed doors all was not well with Guipure.

"Roland was tense about the licensing deal," says a source speaking exclusively to *Oops!* And it seems that, despite the good reviews, Guipure was also concerned about his future: "He was worried that without heroin he would have no creative stimulus. He wondered if this most recent show was just a fluke."

Then there was his upcoming milestone birthday. "Getting older is difficult for anyone in fashion," said a friend close to the designer. "And forty is a big number. You could see he was bothered by it."

So maybe it's not so surprising that three days ago, this once-confident fashion genius was found dead of heroin overdose—

So *it* had *been an overdose.*

—a heroin overdose outside the exclusive nightclub LaLa Lounge, where he had been celebrating his birthday with a lavish party. The left sleeve of his €300 white Armani shirt was dotted with blood where he'd stuck the needle in his bicep.

While patrons can pay as much as €35 for a cocktail at—the LaLa Lounge, it's also in an area known for its access to street drugs. "It would have been easy for Roland to buy heroin there," said one of last night's gue—

Wait. What was that about the injection? Rachel moved her eyes back up the page.

—the LaLa Lounge, where he had been celebrating his birthday with a lavish party. His €300 white Armani shirt was dotted with blood where he'd stuck the needle into his bicep.

As part of her education in detection, Rachel had been reading *Knight's Forensic Pathology*, and she half-remembered the section on death from an overdose. There was something about the *antecubital fossa* and the *dorsum of the hand*, but what was clearest at that moment was the book's assertion that no matter how hard it was to find a vein, addicts preferred not to inject into muscle because it slowed the effect of the hit. What was Guipure doing injecting into his bicep, then?

"Nôtre Dame des Champs," announced the metallic voice of the métro. She stuffed the magazine in her bag, stood up, and when the doors opened, nearly ran down the platform to the escalator that would take her to street level and a cell phone signal. She needed to talk to Magda.

Chapter Three

⁓

They sat across from each other in Rachel's kitchen, the creased copy of *Oops!* between them. Although the *séjour* had begun to look a little the worse for wear, Rachel had made an effort to keep the kitchen clean, so the oilcloth on which their mugs rested was freshly wiped, and behind Magda's curly head the olive oil and spice jars gleamed when the light hit them. It would have been a cozy scene if they hadn't been discussing a murder.

But it became clear that as far as Magda was concerned, it was only a possible murder. She was normally the more excitable of the two, with cautious Rachel trailing behind her warily, but when it came to murder, Rachel had noticed before, they seemed to change places. This had happened with their first case, when she'd refused to believe that Edgar Bowen's death was murder, and here it was happening again now.

As if to prove this point, Magda said, "I did the background research you asked for. But I have to say, I don't see anything."

Rachel wrinkled her nose. "I hate it when people say they have to say. What they really mean is they *want* to say."

"Okay, I *want* to say I don't see anything." Magda pursed her lips. "Because I *want* to say that, as you will see, this has accidental overdose written all over it. The man was an addict. Less than six months out of rehab. On his birthday. It would be more surprising if he *hadn't* shot up. But he did, and he misjudged the effect that four months of being clean would have on his tolerance, so he overdosed." She mimed dusting her hands. "Case closed."

Not for me, Rachel thought. Aloud she said, "Except that he injected into his bicep."

"Again, he was an *addict*. Their veins collapse all the time, and they need to find new places to inject. Between the toes, into the thigh . . ."

But while waiting for Magda to arrive Rachel had re-read her copy of *Knight's Forensic Pathology*. "The obituary said he'd used heroin for two years. That's nowhere near long enough to use up your veins. And anyway, veins turn unusable because they're clogged with whatever the heroin's cut with, but given the kind of price he could pay, his heroin would be pretty pure. And even if his other veins were clogged, the vein in your groin never collapses. He could have used that before his bicep."

"Yeah, but would he have wanted to risk being photographed shoving a needle into his groin? That's exactly the kind of thing someone would sell to the tabloids. He'd want a more discreet way of getting a rush."

Rachel sighed with exasperation. Magda's stubbornness could be useful, but now that it was holding her back, it was just irritating. "Yes, but he wouldn't *get* a rush. Intramuscular injections enter the bloodstream more slowly. He'd get more like a slow-building reaction."

"He was at his birthday party. Maybe he wanted a nice relaxing buzz."

She sighed again. "Let's leave aside the fact that, according to what I read, heroin doesn't give you a nice relaxing buzz. You take it because it makes you feel fantastic, and you shoot up because you want that feeling as soon as possible. And all right, I'll imagine that an addict who's so driven that he decides to shoot up at his birthday party also cares about being caught doing it in an ungainly position. That still leaves the fact that injecting your own upper arm is very awkward. Try it."

Magda mimed holding a syringe in her right hand, reaching it over to her left bicep.

"Look at your hand."

Her fingers were curled into a fist. She relaxed them, but even so, the best she could do was hold her imaginary hypodermic flat against her upturned palm and depress her imaginary plunger with a cramped thumb. She grunted. "Okay, it's hard. But it's not impossible. And if it's hard to inject yourself in the bicep, it's also hard for anyone else to do it. You can't stab someone with a syringe in public without other people noticing."

"It doesn't need to have happened in public. He died outside, but he could have been injected inside. Especially since it would take a while for the dose to kick in."

They stared at each other for a long moment. Then Magda exhaled and reached into her bag. She pulled out a sheaf of papers. "Just read these, okay? Then see how you feel." She handed them across the table.

The first sheets were printouts of photos, all showing a man Rachel recognized as Roland Guipure. In most of them, he was with a woman, and from the way she shared his dark hair and wide, full mouth it was easy to guess she was his twin, Antoinette.

Guipure was one of those people who would always have—*had always had*, she corrected silently—a boyish face, and the progression of the photos could be charted not only by the date Magda had written at the top of each but also by the gradual wear and tear that turned him from an actual near-boy into a disconcertingly fresh-faced, middle-aged man. There was *Roland Guipure, recently named Best New Designer by* Nouveau *magazine, with his sister Antoinette Guipure*, with dark hair flopping in his face in 2001; there were *Roland and Antoinette Guipure, the twins taking fashion by storm, at the Met Ball*, Roland rake-thin in an electric blue tuxedo, in 2002; there were *Designer Roland Guipure and his sister Antoinette, with Alexander McQueen at the launch party for McQueen's collaboration with MAC cosmetics* in 2007, Guipure's face leaner and his features more defined; there was *Roland Guipure at his company's induction into the Fédération de la Haute Couture et de la Mode, France's exclusive club for the best haute couture houses in the country* in 2010, gray just beginning to show at his temples. Last in the pile were two photos of Guipure with a young man. Both were dated 2015, and in both the younger man's face was beautifully made up, first (*Roland Guipure and a male companion at Nüba on Thursday)* with smoky eyes and black mascara, and then (*Roland Guipure and a friend at Paris's exclusive Le Montana club*) with aquamarine eyeshadow and carefully applied cosmetic glitter, set off by pale peach lips.

In both Guipure looked tired, his face pasty and the beginning of bags under his eyes.

"Male companion?"

Magda shrugged. "Presumably a boyfriend. I couldn't find a name."

Rachel put the photos to one side and began to work her way through the pages beneath. They were a collection of articles from various sources, the first from fifteen years before.

Elle, July 2001

Fashionistas of all ages are hearing about newcomer House of Sauveterre. Designer Roland Guipure's first prêt-à-porter show two months ago was bought out after an hour, and now his A/W haute couture is creating the kind of buzz we haven't seen since Galliano. *One to Watch.*

"Why is he showing winter clothing in July?" Rachel asked.

"Ah!" Magda held up an index finger. "You ask that because you don't know fashion." She shook her head. "You and I might think we know fashion because we know the names of designers and famous models and read the reviews of collections in the papers, but we do not know fashion. It's a world all its own, and that world has its own calendar. If it's snowing, it's spring; if it's hot out, it's winter. Haute couture runway shows happen the season *before* the season for which the clothes were designed—so spring/summer shows in January, and autumn/winter shows in July. Prêt-à-porter shows happen two seasons before the season they're designed for, which means that spring prêt-à-porter clothes are shown in the winter of the previous year and autumn ones are shown in January." Seeing the look on Rachel's face, she reached into her bag once more and produced a piece of slightly wrinkled, lined notebook paper. "I know. This will help. I had to make it to keep the dates straight."

"SCHEDULE," the page said at the top. Then neatly spaced out underneath:

January
Spring/summer haute couture shows

March
Autumn/winter prêt-à-porter shows

July
Autumn/winter haute couture shows

October
Spring/summer prêt-à-porter shows

Armed with this, Rachel turned her attention back to the printouts.

The BoF: Business of Fashion, 7 January 2002

First Time's the Charm
Paris, France—Roland Guipure may be a new name on the catwalk, but his label, Sauveterre, is already having the kind of impact more established designers would kill for. Sauveterre's wittily deconstructed dresses and impressive Lognon pleating appeal to both the youthful customer looking to move toward

more sophisticated pieces and the older woman who knows her style but wants to enliven it with unexpected fabrics and quirky details. As a result, Sauveterre had a net income of €500,000 at the end of the last fiscal year, its first as an established house.

Style Magazine, The Sunday Times, 26 October 2006

Fashion's Wonder Twins

Antoinette Guipure wasn't known for taking gambles. A graduate of the London School of Economics and a vice president of Major Finance at BancFLAN, she had a reputation as a cool financial head when her twin brother, Roland, came to her six years ago and asked for her support.

Roland wanted to start a fashion house, and he wanted to use principal from the family trust to do it. Anyone else would have said no, but on this occasion Guipure let family feeling prevail.

Or did she? Seated in her office at the highly successful House of Sauveterre fashion label, Guipure insists it wasn't an emotional choice, but a careful decision based on the detailed plan her brother drew up. "We had a very clear idea of what we wanted Sauveterre to be right from the start," she says. "A family business. We wanted our customers to feel that we would welcome them at any and every stage of their lives, and we wanted our employees to know we would be as loyal to them as they were to us."

Such loyalty makes sense coming from two members of a family known for its conscience. Antoinette and Roland's grandfather, the art dealer Maximilien Sauveterre, is a quiet hero in France because of his fair dealings with Jewish customers during World War II. After his death his daughter, the twins' mother, Danielle, sold the art gallery and used the profits to found a nonprofit that supports numerous philanthropic organizations.

You could say, then, that House of Sauveterre—named in honor of their grandfather—is just following family tradition when it lavishes care on its customers and workers. At the same time, this strategy has been the recipe for a flourishing brand. The business that began with a seed investment of €1m five years ago is rumored to have earned around €2m in profits this year. It seems keeping it in the family has paid off handsomely for the Guipures.

Antoinette Guipure wears a sleeveless knit top, Sauveterre, £320, black silk trousers, Sauveterre £820, mock crocodile slingback brogues, Salvatore Ferragamo £1,450.

Coldwell Banker Richard Ellis, France, April 2008

Sales of Note

Sauveterre Couture, SARL, has purchased 21 Rue la Boétie for €3,990,000. The parcel (Parcelle 13—Feuille 000 BL 01—Commune: PARIS 08 [75]) was formerly owned by Malraux Financiel and rented as individual offices. Before that it was the art gallery and home of Maximilien Sauveterre (the well-known Second World War philanthropist). It will now be redeveloped as the House of Sauveterre headquarters.

quelles.nouvelles, September 4, 2014
www.quelles.com/latest/gui/2015104
Which fashion designer has been lacing his system with something stronger than silk thread? Out and about looking drowsy, with his sleeves rolled down in the middle of a Paris canicule, we hear that he's using more *poudre* than a model with a pimple.

The New York Times, March 7, 2015

Walking, Wounded
Paris—Last night Sauveterre's Roland Guipure sent down the runway his A/W 16 ready-to-wear fashions. It grieves me to report that not only was it not fashionable, but it was also anything but ready to wear.

Guipure is known for his almost-but-not-quite outré ruffles, his delicate folds, and his keen eye for the kinds of charming details that keep clothes fresh. But this show offered none of those. Instead, what Sauveterre showed was a series of dull looks in drab fabrics. Guipure's palette for this year seems to run the gamut from muddy green to mud-brown, while the dresses made repeated—one might say too much—use of wrist-length sleeves and exaggerated Peter Pan collars. The models appeared to take their cue from the clothes, their expressions so sullen that they looked like dissatisfied escapees from some school that required its pupils to wear camouflage.

A design house is entitled to try something entirely new. After all, only by such attempts do designers emerge from old forms and into new ones. Unfortunately, here Mr. Guipure seems to have dressed his models in the leftover cocoons.

The Fit, August 10, 2015

This morning the House of Sauveterre announced that its chief designer and Creative Director Roland Guipure has entered a rehabilitation facility. "I'm pleased that my brother has decided to confront his demons," Chief Financial Officer Antoinette Guipure said in a written statement. "Everyone in the House of Sauveterre family wishes him well and looks forward to the day he returns."

VOGUE.com, October 2015

RUNWAY
Spring/Summer 2016 Ready-to Wear—Sauveterre

When Sauveterre announced two months ago that Head Designer Roland Guipure would be entering rehabilitation for an addiction to heroin, no one knew quite what to expect for the future. As it turns out, the answer is "miracles."

When Guipure left for a facility in Greece after showing an Autumn/Winter collection that British *Vogue* labeled "the kind of clothes a depressed Goth would find too lifeless," it seemed his label had only two possible paths.

The house could enter hiatus until his return, or it could draft in a new designer. The first risked incurring heavy financial losses; the second risked losing continuity for a label so closely associated with its head designer.

In the end, Sauveterre made the only decision that seemed more perilous. They decided to use designs Guipure completed in his *désintox* for this season's collection.

I can't be the only critic who was concerned after the house announced this plan. But when I entered the Petit Palais, transformed into a stark black cube for the Sauveterre *défilé*, my worry was replaced by delight, courtesy of the series of exuberant designs that filed down the runway. After last season's muddy colors and heavy *tissus,* here was a return to the vivid jersey and bright silks of Sauveterre's earliest outings.

Guipure has always excelled at treading the thin line between bold and *outré,* and here he walked that tightrope successfully once again. These clothes cling to the body with a sinuosity that plays against the square white, almost puritan, collars. The shades are hot pinks, bright yellows, with occasional soft blues and greens to give the eye a rest. The wedding dress at show's end, long soft rectangles of painted habotai wafting down raw-edged from a loose duchesse bodice, was a masterpiece in the true Sauveterre mold: youthful but elegant, subtle but eye-catching. If this is what Guipure produces when he is half recovered, fashion eagerly looks forward to his full reemergence.

BuzzGoss, December 1, 2015
www.thebuzz.com//15121

He's baaack! The word on the catwalk is that Roland Guipure left rehab last week and is currently holed up in his *atelier.* A little bee tells us he's already started sketching for next year's collections. It's looking like a Merry Christmas for Maison Sauveterre!

Elle, December 2016
House of Sauveterre has announced that it will not be showing spring/summer 2017 haute couture. Creative Director Roland Guipure returned from an extended stay at a rehabilitation center earlier this month, and a press release from the company explains, "We're mindful that we don't want to overtax Roland during a delicate time. We're committed to continuing to produce the exciting and innovative prêt-à-porter we showed last October, so we've chosen to focus on that. Look for new Sauveterre haute couture in July 2017."

WWD, March 9, 2016
Sauveterre RTW Fall 2016

You would be forgiven for thinking that a designer emerging from recent personal troubles would offer a sober collection to mark the occasion. At Sauveterre, however, Roland Guipure went in the opposite direction, offering a burst of innovation to announce a comeback that most had been eagerly, if tensely, awaiting.

The invitation to Sauveterre's *defilé* announced the show as "A Garden of Possibility," and it says something that Guipure made this abstract phrase take vivid concrete form. Perhaps channeling Dior's postwar exuberance, his pieces offered flowers everywhere: in skirts artfully swirled, in high collars twisted into Guipure's beloved architectural shapes, in sleeves that blossomed at the shoulders. But perhaps hinting at his recent brush with drugs, these flowers were no delicate blooms, but rather fashioned from rough plaids, twists of dark tweed, and in the case of one memorable skirt, intricate purple leather panels made to imitate an upside-down rose.

It wasn't difficult to see the connection between this show and the looks the House of Sauveterre presented last season in a *defilé* made up of designs Guipure had completed while in rehab. There the sculpted collars framed the face; here they nearly swamped it. The princess lines that are an instinctive part of Guipure's repertoire had allowed the clothes to sinuously frame the body last season; this season they seemed to make the pieces cling to the models like spiderwebs threatening to overwhelm. Everywhere sleek exuberance was transmuted into darker, yet still arresting, echoes of the forms of a few months ago.

When Guipure emerged at the show's end, dressed all in white and hand in hand with his sister and business partner, it was hard not to think that a talent that had nearly shriveled was now well on its way to a rich reblooming.

The BoF: Business of Fashion, 24 March 2016

Deals

Tokyo, Japan,– CHIEKO Group S.p.A and the HOUSE OF SAUVETERRE today announced their intention to ink a new license agreement for the exclusive development, manufacture and distribution of a new perfume, *Lace, by Sauveterre*™. The objectives of the new license agreement are to build a successful scent product line linking Sauveterre's brand recognition with Chieko Group's manufacturing and production capabilities.

Sato Asuka, CEO at Chieko, stated that *"We are extremely pleased that this agreement is about to reach completion. Chieko is proud to partner with the House of Sauveterre in a relationship that we are sure will bring great mutual satisfaction."*

A life charted in media, Rachel thought. Rise, fall, and rise again, all of it watched, noted, and judged. Under this constant observation she'd probably have turned to drugs too. It seemed like the only way to get some peace.

She leafed back through the printouts. She saw Magda's point. Guipure's life after rehab seemed charmed: professional acclaim, a chunk of money, all topped off with a celebration of his very existence at the trendiest club in town. She could see him being convinced enough of his own invincibility to take just one hit. She drummed her fingers on the table and bit her lip. Maybe she *was* wrong.

She took a deep breath and started to say so, but Magda preempted her. "Now you see. He had a licensing deal in *Japan*; he was going to make a fortune! And all the reviews of his last show are like that one from *WWD*. Every single one is a rave. For God's sake, the critics even loved the clothes he designed while he was in rehab! Plus, no one in any of these articles has a bad word to say about him. I don't see a hint here of jealous rivals or disgruntled employees . . ." She corrected herself: "In fact, the reverse, according to the article in the *Times*." She took a breath. "On the other hand, he's at a lavish party at a trendy club, surrounded by friends from the fashion world—not exactly known for just saying no—and probably suck-ups eager to offer him things to make him happy. It sounds like the backdrop for a cut-and-dried celebrity over-dose. Even in the bicep."

This was no more than Rachel herself had been going to say, but she didn't respond. She was staring at the cover of *Oops!* "No, it isn't," she said.

"Oh my God! You just want to win. That's all this is about. Who would want to m—"

"I don't know," Rachel cut in. "And I don't know why. But let me ask *you* a question." She picked up the magazine, flipped to the article about Guipure, and read aloud. "The left sleeve of his three-hundred-euro Armani shirt was dotted with blood where he'd stuck the needle in his bicep." She flipped it closed and pointed to the glossy cover, where Guipure was pinning pleats on a bored-looking mannequin, his left hand working busily. "How does a left-handed man inject heroin into his own left bicep?"

Chapter Four

～

Of course it wasn't as easy as that. Guipure might have been ambidextrous, Magda pointed out. Even if he wasn't, injecting oneself didn't require much in the way of fine motor skills; he could have done it with his nondominant hand. Or, in a pinch, he could have injected his left arm with his left hand—she folded her arm in half and demonstrated, jabbing uncomfortably but still accurately into her bicep. He could even have had someone else inject him. He was a famous man in a profession known for its hangers-on: someone at the party would no doubt have been delighted to help him out, and then could have vanished when things went wrong.

"In that case, why didn't they use a vein?" Rachel widened her eyes and spread her hands.

"I don't know." Magda's voice was a shrug. "But I don't have to know. If a junkie is found dead of an overdose with an injection mark on his arm, the simplest answer is that he did it himself, with his dominant hand, his subordinate hand, or whatever hand he could manage it with. And how often have you said, 'Occam's Razor' to me and insisted that the simplest answer is most likely to be the right one?"

Many times, Rachel acknowledged. But this time was different. This time there was something . . .

Her dissatisfaction must have shown on her face because Magda said, "What's going on here? I understand that this is like Edgar's murder, when no one but you believed it *was* murder. But there you had evidence that suggested he hadn't just died accidentally, and here you have none. And you don't know Roland Guipure, so it can't be that. Your only connection to him is fifteen minutes spent staring at a dress he made. So why does it matter if he was murdered?"

Because I know, Rachel wanted to shout. But it would have gained her nothing. Although Magda had plenty of time for sudden convictions and illuminations (which she put under the heading of *inspiration*), she'd never shared Rachel's faith in the validity of feelings, her belief that sometimes instinct is telling you a truth that will only be proved later.

Still, Rachel gave it a try. "I know." Her voice sounded weak, even to her. "I just know."

Magda shook her head. "Well, I don't." She crossed her arms mutinously.

Rachel was silent for a long time. Then she said, "Remember that time when you said you could pierce my ears with an ice cube and a needle, and I let you?"

A reluctant nod.

"And remember that time when you insisted that you'd seen Alain Delon go into the supermarket across the street, and we ended up following that man who was *not* Alain Delon all around the store?"

"You thought he was Alain Delon too," Magda said sulkily.

"I did not. But I said I did because I knew you loved Alain Delon. Just like I still know Alain Delon's birthday and the names of all his children. I learned them because it was important to you."

Magda bit her lip, but she didn't say anything. Rachel leaned across the table and looked at her so intently that she actually felt her eyes hurt. "Give me two weeks. Give me two weeks because the ice cube did *not* numb the pain, and the holes in my ears are lopsided, and Alain Delon's birthday is—"

"The eighth of November. Fine." Magda inhaled through her nose. "Two weeks. I'm with you for two weeks. But after that, if there's nothing, you'll give up?" Rachel nodded. "Okay. But what I said still applies. You don't know Roland Guipure. Or any of his friends or family. So I don't know how you're going to be able to find anything out." She gave a little shake of her head. "This isn't like our last case, where you found the body, or even like Edgar Bowen's murder, where you already knew the victim and his family. You don't know any of these people, and they don't know you. Our lives and the life of the alleged victim don't intersect anywhere."

Now that was a good point. And a fair one. Or—wait. Magda's mention of Edgar Bowen reminded Rachel that she did have one possible source for inside information on Roland Guipure, a source that she'd used when Edgar died. Her friend Kiki Villeneuve knew everyone in the Paris *haute bourgeoisie*, that world of old families whose names and connections stretched back for centuries. Hadn't one of the articles she'd just seen mentioned something about Guipure's grandfather being a war hero?

She flicked back once again. There it was: "a quiet hero in France because of his fair dealings with Jewish customers during World War II." Okay, not really the same thing—what exactly was a "quiet hero"?—but if Maximilien Sauveterre had enough money that his grandchildren only needed to cash in *some* of it in order to start a multimillion dollar business, it was just possible that he had entered Kiki's world at some point, in some way.

Besides, she concluded, she had nowhere else to start. And if she wanted to prove to her best friend that her instincts were sound, she had to begin somewhere.

Chapter Five

Kiki Villeneuve was Rachel's oldest Parisian friend. In her late sixties now, she had first met Rachel twenty years before, when she had been the hostess of a cocktail party and Rachel had been one of the catering staff. Madame Villeneuve, as Rachel had thought of her that evening, had been as warm and welcoming to the servers as she had been to her own guests, and somehow—the exact steps were now lost to Rachel's memory—they had struck up a friendship. Through Rachel's first years in Paris, the eighteen years of her marriage to Alan, her change from a stumbling foreigner to an established Parisian resident, plump Kiki had been a loving source of support and extremely enjoyable gossip. Kiki liked, she once told Rachel, to think of herself as Rachel's mother in France. And although Rachel adored her own confident, briskly capable American mother, she acknowledged that Kiki's soft hugs, her fascination with the minutiae of Rachel's life, and her absolute conviction that Rachel would succeed at whatever she tried filled some unspoken need in her. *After all*, she thought as she sank into one of the overstuffed sofas in Kiki's *salon*, *who doesn't need a second family sometimes, to fill the gaps left by the first?*

No sooner had Kiki poured their tea and put the plate of cookies in a prominent position, than she pointed to a copy of *Le Figaro* on her coffee table, folded back so the headline of Roland Guipure's obituary showed.

"You know about this, I suppose?" Rachel nodded. "All week I've been picking it up and rereading it. It's terrible when a young person dies."

Rachel hesitated, but then said gently. "Forty is hardly young."

"It's young to die." Kiki sighed. Late afternoon sunshine streamed through the windows, turning her pale yellow walls gold. She shook her head. "I danced with his grandfather once, and now the boy is dead. It's too fast."

"So you knew the family?" Rachel tucked her stocking feet under her on the sofa.

"Well, I met the grandparents a few times. Maximilien and Marthe Sauveterre. But I didn't really *know* them. They were closer to my mother's generation."

"And how did she know them?"

"Through her family. They moved in the same circles."

"In Moncontour?" This was Kiki's childhood hometown, not known for producing notable families.

"No, no, here. Remember, I told you that after my father died we moved back to Paris to be near my mother's family. When they heard she had a daughter of marriageable age, they decided to do their duty by me and introduce me into society. The summer I was twenty I went to all the debutante *bals* and teas. Parents were the chaperones, so my mother also attended, and so did the Sauveterres because their daughter was making her debut." She took a thoughtful bite of her cookie. "Geneviève Sauveterre. I lent her my lipstick once. Anyway, my mother introduced me to Maximilien and Marthe Sauveterre, and at one *bal* Monsieur Sauveterre asked me to dance."

"What was he like?"

"He was in his seventies then, so to me he was just old. But still *galant*." Kiki cocked her head to one side. "I think my *maman* would have been delighted to be seduced by him, but he was famous for his devotion to his wife. They were married for more than forty years, and my mother said that in all that time she didn't hear about more than one or two little affairs." She snorted a little laugh. "I remember my grandmother was horrified that their daughter was a debutante. She was a terrible snob, my grandmother; she never got over the fact that her father was the grandson of a *chevalier*. She used to say Maximilien Sauveterre's grandfather had been a *commerçant*, and nothing he did in the war could change that."

A bell chimed in the back of Rachel's mind. Here was a chance for clarification. "Yes, I remember the obituary called him a 'quiet hero.' What *did* he do in the war?"

Kiki leaned forward and lowered her voice, as if about to share a secret in a crowded room. "He bought art from Jews."

Rachel was confused, and she must have looked it, because Kiki held up a hand. "It might be easier to start further back. *Alors*. Maximilien Sauveterre's grandfather owned an art supply store in Besançon in the 1800s—this is what my grandmother couldn't forgive. This man's son, Monsieur Sauveterre's father, apparently had a very good eye, and he turned the business into a gallery and moved it to Paris. When he died,

Monsieur Sauveterre took over. It wasn't a very grand place—Rosenfeld had a much grander one only a few doors down—but it was solid, and it had a good reputation. And during the *drôle de guerre*, the phony war, and then after the Germans arrived in 1940, many Jews were looking for reputable dealers who would buy their valuables. They wanted to pay for emigration or to be able to live once they emigrated. Many dealers took advantage—"

"—And bought at knock-down prices." Throughout her childhood, Rachel's mother and grandmother had told her stories about what had happened to their European relatives during the war: Great-Aunt Sara who had sold her silver cutlery to buy her way out of Austria before it was too late; second Cousin Hans who had refused to sell the collection of Steuben glass he prized and hadn't made it out at all.

"I'm sorry. I forgot. Of course you know all this." Kiki looked abashed. She sipped from her cup, then picked up her thread. "But Maximilien Sauveterre *didn't* buy at such prices. He paid fair market value all through the German occupation. And then he held on to the paintings until the war's end so he could sell them back at the same price when the owners returned. Only . . ." she trailed off awkwardly, but Rachel understood. Only the owners never returned.

"But that's a good thing, surely. So why didn't the paper just say it directly?"

Kiki sighed. "Because here in France the past is always complicated. After the war, I remember my mother saying everyone looked out of the corner of his eye, waiting to see what his neighbor would admit before he said anything himself. There were tribunals, purges. If people thought you had collaborated with the Nazis, you could be killed. So of course everyone said they had been saints. When I was growing up, that was the story: every Frenchman a resister, every farmer a *maquisard*. Of course this is a lie, but we all have to live together, and the lie makes it easier. You agree to believe it, and that allows you to forget that your neighbor might have been a black marketeer, or the man whose liquor you're drinking might have bought the Chagall on his wall for a fraction of its real worth. And if you single out Maximilien Sauveterre, if you say, 'He was much admired because he didn't cheat Jews in World War II,' you crack the lie open because you are also silently saying, 'which many others did.' But if your newspaper says, 'He was a much admired art dealer,' those in the know will understand what you mean, and those reading it because it's part of someone else's obituary will pass over it. You've acknowledged his actions without opening old wounds."

What a complex dance! "But if everyone keeps quiet, how did everyone come to know?"

Kiki shrugged. "They just did. It was whispered."

"By Sauveterre?"

"*Ouf*, if he'd been that vulgar he would never have been forgiven! But there were ways. After a while he began to sell the paintings on: perhaps he had to mention what he'd done when explaining their provenance. Or perhaps he left the receipts where a tax inspector might see them when he came to look at the accounts, so the tax collector could whisper that he'd seen actual evidence of Sauveterre's largesse. But certainly my mother said that after the war, the gallery quickly became very successful. When the Rothschilds' collection was returned to them from Germany, they sold it through Sauveterre, and that was in 1947. By the time I met him, he was *the* art dealer one wanted to work with. *Everyone* went to him. My cousin Amandine used him to sell her little Magritte in the sixties; she didn't even consider going to anyone else."

"So what happened that made the business close?"

"He died." Kiki said this with typical French frankness. "And the daughter that Geneviève mentioned had no interest in art. She was involved with horses somehow, I think. At least, I remember hearing when she married Pierre Guipure that they'd met in a riding stable. In any case, shortly before her twins—Roland and Antoinette, that is—were born, she sold the gallery and the building it was in and invested the money from the sale in a family trust."

"This is the trust that Guipure and Antoinette used to start Sauveterre?"

Kiki nodded. "That's why they named it Sauveterre. To honor their grandfather." Her eyes slid away for a moment, lost in some memory Rachel couldn't see. Then she gave herself a little shake. "But enough of the past! Tell me how you are here in the present. Are you still studying to be a *grande investigatrice*?"

Rachel smiled. "Yes. But it turns out to be much more complicated than I thought." She explained the long road to private investigator certification, the required online courses in investigational ethics, management of an agency, and introduction to testimonials. Kiki looked so disappointed that she added, "But I did buy a set of lockpicks, and now I can pick a lock like a professional. I've managed to unlock all the doors in our *appartement*, then lock them back up again."

"But you must show me! I will lock all my wardrobe doors, and you can open them for me."

Rachel laughed. "That's very kind, thank you. But I don't want to risk leaving you with permanently locked wardrobes if I fail."

Kiki puffed out her cheeks and exhaled, the French expression for extravagant disbelief. "You would unlock them all in a few seconds! And if you didn't, I wouldn't mind. They might be better locked."

Rache smiled, basking in this unconditional support. Seeing her pleasure, Kiki gave her a soft pat on the cheek. "You know, *cherie*, I'm happy to help you in any way I can."

Chapter Six

Rachel knew that when you extol the virtues of a city you love, you are supposed to mention aspects like its arresting monuments, its lush and well-groomed parks, its pleasing scents, and the beautiful way the light falls through the air. You are not supposed to wax lyrical about its public transportation system. But the fact was that although she did love all those other facets of Paris, she also deeply loved its métro. In Paris you were never more than a few steps away from a métro station, and on an unexpectedly chilly afternoon in late April that was nothing to dismiss lightly. The métro cars were warm and dry, and their doors had little handles that a rider flipped up and over in order to open them, an old-fashioned touch that never ceased to charm. As her train moved from the Saint-Paul station to Concorde; as she then walked the reassuringly identical white-brick passages of the Concorde station to change to a different line; and as she settled into her seat heading toward Notre-Dame-des-Champs and resumed her meditations, she was thankful for the métro all the while.

How did people do it? she wondered as she looked out the window of her carriage into the darkness of the tunnel. How did they manage to reconcile great moral complexity and ordinary life? In her own life, the worst thing that had happened was temporary poverty, the greatest moral conundrum the question of whether to keep the two hundred dollars she'd once found in an empty washing machine. What must it be like when the stakes were infinitely higher, when good and evil weren't abstractions, but close at hand?

She tried to imagine Kiki's experience, standing in a room with someone you knew had saved lives—a neighbor or someone you met at a party—someone who had made genuine moral decisions at a time when such decisions were dangerous. Or, less pleasant to imagine, standing in that same room with someone you suspected, or even knew, had done the opposite. If Kiki was right, in 1960s Paris there had been plenty of former profiteers and collaborators seated around dinner tables and taking up space at cocktail parties. How could you make idle chitchat with someone who you knew had benefitted from the Nazi occupation? Better for the soul, surely, to call people out and punish them accordingly.

But for what? she asked herself as she walked through the tunnels of Concorde station. Justice? As her shoes slapped against the black-painted cement, she thought of the ever more ancient Nazis still being unmasked, the old men being wheeled into courtrooms to face trial. As the accused aged—these days well into their nineties, and the witnesses not far behind—she had to admit to herself, with a certain amount of shame, that she didn't see the point. What justice could be achieved by putting in jail for the few years left to him someone who had enjoyed seven decades of freedom and pleasure in the interim?

What real justice had ever been achieved by jailing any Nazi, or even by executing one? What *could* balance the scale with the deaths of millions of people who were just as dead whether or not their murderers were alive? And since the scales could never be balanced, maybe the French choice of discretion and deliberate ignorance was a better way to move through life.

By this time, she was coming up from the Notre-Dame-des-Champs station. She stopped at the corner boulangerie to pick up some bread—only stale baguettes were left, but what could she expect if she bought at four in the afternoon?—and on a last-second whim, decided to get a bag of meringues too. She smiled apologetically at the woman behind the counter, who had to ring her up a second time. Then she gathered her bread, her meringues, and her shoulder bag and stepped out from the warm yeasty air into the chill of the late afternoon.

Thus burdened, she nonetheless managed to press the entry code on the panel next to her building's door, push the door open with her shoulder, and step over the raised threshold into the inner courtyard. The mail had arrived, and she put down the shopping to collect it. Amid the pizza delivery flyers and bills in their blue metal mailbox, she saw a heavy cream envelope addressed to "Mr. and Mrs. Alan Field" in elaborately elegant calligraphy. She slit it open. An invitation to one of the many galas the financial community organized in support of various charities. These arrived on a regular basis—early in their marriage, Rachel had even served on the organizing committee for such a gala. As she remembered it, this mostly involved sitting around dining tables in gracious homes, discussing card stock weight and gift bags and who would be likely to buy the biggest table (and thus be named honoree, because in the strange world of charity galas, you paid to be honored). It was boring, but it was what you did if you were a young banker's wife, trying to fit in.

And then, her drying bread on the shelf in front of her and her mail in hand, she was struck by a realization. *She* was a banker's wife. And banker's wives organized charity galas. If a banker's wife wanted to meet with Antoinette Guipure to discuss making her brother a posthumous honoree at a gala, Antoinette Guipure would have no way of knowing that she'd stopped serving on organizing committees years before. And if a banker's wife was honoring someone at a gala, it only made sense that she would need to gather a great deal of information about his life, his habits, his friends and colleagues in order to do the job well. Kiki was an old friend of the Sauveterre family—she had known Antoinette Guipure's grandparents; she had lent her mother a lipstick. Old family friends could pave the way to meetings. And Kiki had said she was happy to help in any way she could.

* * *

"And she agreed to this?" On Rachel's computer screen later that night, Alan's face raised its eyebrows in disbelief.

"Yes." In fact, Kiki had been delighted to do it. So *mysterieux*, so *rusé*—a little like a spy, eh? Infinitely more exciting than offering up her locks as sacrifices to Rachel's picking skills. She would call Antoinette Guipure that very afternoon to offer her condolences and suggest a lovely way to memorialize her brother. Just an old family friend offering a thought.

When she told Alan this, he was skeptical. "It doesn't sound like Kiki's an old family friend. Maybe a passing acquaintance, two generations gone."

"Oh, you know how those old money people are. They meet someone once, and as long as they're the right class, they're intimate friends for life." She waved a dismissive hand.

But Alan went on. "I can't see Antoinette Guipure falling for this. She graduated at the top of her class from Stanford School of Business, and she moved that company from start-up to profit in less than five years. She's got a reputation as one of the most brilliant minds in major finance."

"She doesn't need to be stupid to entertain a suggestion from a family friend!" Rachel felt herself flushing. She said sulkily, "I thought it was a pretty good way to do some subtle investigating."

Alan raised his eyebrows, but he didn't respond. Instead, he said nothing for a long moment, then took a deep breath and began again. "A friend of my parents also just died."

"Oh, I'm sorry. You should have told me sooner."

"It's okay—I didn't know him. I wouldn't even mention it except that his wife told my mother he died on a business trip to Paris, of all places. Just keeled over in his hotel room, apparently."

"My God. Where?"

"Some hotel in the eighth."

"Sauveterre's headquarters is in the eighth!"

He gave a little sigh at the failure of his attempt to change the subject, then looked up into the camera. "You're not going to like me saying this, sweet, but I don't think you'll find anything out at this meeting. It's too soon. Not even two weeks after his death. They're still going to be in shock. I've seen it in business after a CEO has died. People won't be ready to talk. They'll be busy trying to distract themselves, focusing on practicalities. You should go later. It's going to be a wasted opportunity."

"You may think that." Rachel's voice was cold. "I guess we'll just have to wait and see."

Chapter Seven

～

On the métro to the Sauveterre headquarters, Magda narrowed her eyes as Rachel explained the story they would use. "What's the point of honoring a dead man? I thought you told me that honorees were selected on the basis of how much money they're willing to donate to the gala's chosen charity. Surely if you're dead, that amount is zero?"

Rachel shook her head. "That's how it used to work before the recession. Now galas pick their honorees on the basis of who will draw the largest number of people. The idea is that a lot of people paying a thousand euros a plate works out to more than any single person would give. So strictly speaking, it doesn't matter if an honoree is dead, provided his friends and relatives are willing to pay to listen to people say nice things about him."

Magda made a face. "I wouldn't put it that way to Antoinette Guipure."

"As if I would!" Did neither her husband nor her best friend have any faith in her? Maybe she *should* make Kiki her accomplice. But Rachel decided to be accommodating rather than outraged. "I'll tell you what." She turned in her seat. "Ask me some questions you think might come up, and I'll practice my answers."

Magda seemed delighted to comply. By the time the train reached their stop, Rachel had been so thoroughly questioned that this imaginary charity gala was as real to her as any she'd actually helped to organize. As they walked up the stairs of the Miromesnil station, her head was a whirl of napkin colors, potential head counts, and the size of Roland Guipure's name on the imaginary invitations.

As they stepped outside the station, though, all this was swept out of her thoughts. The Rue la Boétie was a view of Paris in all its complex glory. A long, straight vista bounded on either side by sandstone buildings with iron balconies all set at the same height. Its architecture drew the eye calmly but inexorably toward a little knot of trees at its distant end. At ground level, the buildings on the street were crowded with shopfronts and awnings—red and gold for a Chinese restaurant, orange for the café across the street from the station, garish black and yellow for a video store having a closing-down sale—but above them the facades rose in smooth blank stories, a collection of grandes dames ignoring puppies frisking around their feet.

They crossed and walked to number 21. A beggar sat against a pole across from the entrance; Rachel gave him a couple of euros before turning to look at what she was, literally, getting into.

This building had no obvious shopfront, but rather a glass door covered by an elaborate art deco metal grille painted a glossy white. A window to the right of the door offered a view into the Sauveterre boutique. The interior appeared to have been bleached. The furniture and carpet, the clothing on display, even the hanging racks, were all the color of freshly fallen snow. For a moment all this white seemed to turn the window opaque, and she saw herself reflected back. One only ever looks better or worse reflected in a window, and to her own eyes Rachel didn't look better. The pallid background turned her brown hair mousy and her skin pasty; her black turtleneck, made stark and hard in contrast to the surrounding paleness, washed her out even further. Meanwhile Magda, a head taller behind her, was somehow set off to advantage. Her dark skin was radiant against the uniform white, her black and caramel-colored curls enhanced by the red scarf she'd wrapped around the collar of her coat.

"You look great," Magda said. She smiled at her in the glass. "Let's go in."

The foyer was the same color as the metal grille and the store. The spotless pallor of its walls and marble floor was interrupted only by the entrance to the store on the right and a white marble staircase rising to the upper stories on the left. The wooden banister of this staircase had been painted white as well, so recently or so repeatedly that it looked as if it had never been defiled by the touch of a human hand.

Heels clicked on the stairs and a pair of white stilettos appeared, shortly followed by the rest of a young woman wearing a white sheath and holding a white clipboard. Her skin was pale—*Perhaps it's a job requirement,* Rachel thought—but her hair was bright copper, pulled back into a bun at the base of her neck. Her lips, painted the tomato red of every fashionable Parisian woman, opened. "Madame Field?"

Who was Madame Field? Then Rachel understood. Kiki had given Antoinette Guipure her married name, the better to mark her out as a banker's wife. For this meeting, then, she was Mrs. Rachel Field, wife of Alan Field, VP of international banking at CorBank. She recovered herself. "Yes. And this is Madame Stevens, my co-coordinator."

"I'm Gabrielle Aubert, Antoinette Guipure's assistant. Follow me, please. Antoinette's been slightly delayed—it's confused here at the moment, as I'm sure you understand—and she asked me to make you comfortable. As soon as she's done, she'll be free to talk to you about the—the . . ." She frowned at her clipboard.

"The Franco-American Heritage Society Benefit," Rachel supplied.

"Yes, the Franco-American Heritage Society Benefit. Antoinette was delighted at the idea of honoring her brother, and she's eager to hear more about what that involves."

They had passed the first landing. As they continued upward through an expanse of unadorned white walls and blond wood floors, Gabrielle's voice became increasingly mechanical, the sound of a tour guide giving an overfamiliar speech. "This building housed the gallery and home of Roland and Antoinette Guipure's *grandpère*, the art dealer Maximilien Sauveterre, from 1936 until his death in the seventies. The Sauveterre label is named in honor of Monsieur Sauveterre, who is known for his decision to pay a fair price for all art he bought during World War II, no matter who the seller." Thinking of Kiki, Rachel noticed this careful circumlocution and grinned to herself. "Once Maison Sauveterre began to do well," the girl continued, "Antoinette bought it back. She and Monsieur Guipure liked the idea of deepening the family connection. Since the purchase, it's been renovated into a complete work-life space. The top two floors are Monsieur Guipure's studio and *appartement*, and, as you've seen, the ground floor houses the label's boutique. In between are a couture salon and our storage; the ateliers for beading, embroidery, pleating; and of course the sewing rooms. Although you can't tell from outside," she said with automated delight, "this building extends for a full city block! Our third floor, where I'm taking you now, houses the label's business offices, while the basement holds the archives of both the label and the former gallery. Monsieur Guipure and Antoinette like the sense of continuity the blended archive provides." She stopped abruptly, her expression stricken. "Liked. I should say Roland *liked* the sense of continuity." Her face twitched, then smoothed to neutrality once more. "And here we are!" she said brightly as they came to the third-floor landing.

She turned right and led them to a set of double doors, gesturing to a framed document on the wall next to them. "Here is one of the receipts for a painting Maximilien Sauveterre purchased during the war. Naturally, these are very fragile, and we keep the rest in our archive, but Antoinette likes to keep one here as a reminder of the company's heritage." She gave a practiced smile. "As I said, she and Monsieur Guipure are proud of the family connection."

Rachel squinted at the receipt, which had an elaborate art nouveau letterhead identifying it as having come from Galeries Sauveterre, 21 Rue la Boétie, Paris, with some indecipherable cursive writing underneath and, at the bottom, a sweeping *145.000.* She made a noise of appreciation.

Gabriele opened the double doors, ushering them across a small white-carpeted room where a young woman in a white dress and wearing a white headset sat behind a white desk that held a white multiline phone. They emerged into a larger white room with a slightly larger white desk, on which sat a smaller white phone next to a white computer monitor and keyboard.

No sooner had they entered than the phone gave a chirrup.

Gabrielle moved to answer it. "Excuse me."

Rachel looked around as they waited. This room featured at least some color, even if it was of the most washed-out kind. The walls were dotted with gray and white photos of tailoring details—a box pleat in extreme close-up, a hugely magnified buttonhole, a hem photographed from the inside to show its neat stitching. From the addition of this decoration and the two white velvet chairs, placed on either side of a small white table on the left-hand wall, she concluded that it was the general reception room, where visitors were stashed before being admitted to whatever inner sanctum lay on the other side of the door in the far wall.

As if to prove her right, Gabrielle hung up the telephone and gestured to toward the chairs. "Please sit down. I'll ask the receptionist to bring you a coffee."

But as she took a step toward the outer office, the phone chirruped again and then, once she'd put down her receiver, again. Each time, Gabrielle's end of the conversation was monosyllabic and accompanied by careful note-taking. At the end of the second one, she smiled apologetically at them. "As I said, things are—"

Once again the phone rang, but this time a buzz instead of a chirrup. Her smile froze. "Excuse me." She picked up the receiver, listened for a moment, then put it back and rose. "Antoinette is ready for you."

Rachel and Magda followed her through the door. They found themselves in yet another white room, but here the frigid decor was slightly relieved by a fire that burned in the fireplace behind the desk at the room's far end. The illusion of warmth fostered by flames casting orange and yellow shadows onto the white brick, however, stood no chance against the countless floral arrangements of white or pastel roses, lilies, and orchids in baskets, wreaths, sheaves, and angular modernist groupings that seemed to cover every available surface. Sympathy arrangements, Rachel thought. Sympathy was always pale.

"Madame Villeneuve's friend," Gabrielle announced.

Standing behind the desk, next to a dark-haired man with whom she was conferring in murmurs, was a woman wearing all black: a black cashmere cardigan over a black blouse and black velvet trousers. The top of her head was also black, smooth dark hair neatly parted in the middle and falling down her back. She looked up from whatever she and the man were examining, and Rachel recognized her from the photographs. Now, though, her face was tired, her wide-spaced eyes deeper set than they had appeared in the pictures, and with an almost pearly sheen to them. Then she came out from behind the desk, and Rachel saw that her eyes seemed deep-set because they were swollen, their sheen the remainder of recent tears.

"Antoinette Guipure." Her voice was low. "And this is Keteb Lellouch, our head pattern cutter." She half turned and gestured at the man behind her, who gave a small smile of acknowledgment. In contrast to Toinette, he was dressed in white from head to foot, and against the color, his skin, a few shades lighter than Magda's, glowed like polished wood. His face was a curious mixture, the precision of its high cheekbones and long, narrow nose contrasted by a full-lipped mouth, but all these features were hidden by his dark hair as he bowed his head back over whatever he and Antoinette had been examining.

Having emerged from behind the desk, Antoinette held out her hand and gave an attempt at a gracious smile. "Please forgive me. I thought I'd be free before this, but there are so many details that need to be dealt with . . . Gabrielle?"

The girl stepped forward.

"Keteb has some ideas about fabrics. He'll give you his notes, so we can work on pricing. And did Saint Roch call back? And could we please get someone from publicity to compile the addresses for the thank-you cards for all these flowers?"

Gabrielle unclipped some sheets from her clipboard. "Here's the list of addresses; they just finished it. I've put a draft of the announcement on top; I thought you'd like to check it for changes before I pass it back to publicity. And Saint Roch just called and said yes. They're getting back to me with a range of possible dates."

In her head Rachel heard Alan say, *They'll be busy trying to distract themselves by focusing on practicalities.* But she and Magda were here now, so she returned the smile the head pattern cutter gave as he slipped out of the room in a blur of white and resolved to push on. She didn't have much choice.

As Gabrielle turned to follow Lellouch, Antoinette added, "And bring some coffee, please."

Although there were chairs drawn up in front of the desk, she gestured toward two chairs and a sofa that stood near the window, with a small table in between. "Please. And again, please accept my apologies—I only have fifteen minutes before I need to meet with my head of embroidery. Things have been chaotic since . . . well, since."

"Please don't worry. We understand." Feeling a stab of pity, Rachel tried to change the subject. "Your interior decoration is beautiful. So calm."

"Thank you. It was my brother's idea. After he came back, he wanted it all white. The shop, the offices, his private spaces . . . He said it would create an atmosphere of serenity that would reduce temptation and stimulate his creativity. Something he learned at the Eirini Clinic. We redid the entire interior for him. They did it in two weeks—can you imagine?" She gave a little laugh at the memory, but then her lower lip began to tremble. "Although I suppose in the end it didn't make any difference, given what he did." The sheen in her eyes turned to water, but she blinked it back.

Given what he did. So Antoinette also believed Guipure had overdosed. Rachel felt a twinge of doubt about her own conclusion, mingled with a strong dose of shame that she was the cause of Antoinette's unshed tears. She made to stand up. "We should—"

"No, no." Antoinette held up a hand; only its slight tremor revealed any emotion. "We haven't spoken at all about your gala. I was so pleased to hear from Madame de Villeneuve. A phone call from an old family friend is always a pleasure, but when she told me that you wanted to honor my brother, it was more than a pleasure. I was truly touched. Now"—at last she managed a smile, or at least a rictus in the shape of a smile— "what do you have in mind?"

Rachel attempted to rise to Antoinette's level of control. At the moment it might seem as if she was poking at a bereaved woman's pain but, she reminded herself, she was trying to do good here. It would all feel different if she unmasked a murderer. She gritted her teeth and continued. "Well, we see the gala more as a celebration than a memoriam. We thought we would ask committee members to loan us examples of your brother's pieces—several of our members are dedicated haute couture collectors—or we might have life-size images of his best-known designs. Perhaps hold a silent auction of some of his sketches, if you're willing." Antoinette certainly looked willing. Now for the step that would get them what they wanted: the names of others they could talk to about the details of Guipure's life. "And we thought a collection of testimonials from those who knew him printed as a program . . .?"

Antoinette nodded. "Yes, yes that sounds very good. Some of our employees, perhaps. They knew him quite well."

"And some friends?" Magda prodded gently. "Someone who knew him as a person?"

A frown replaced the eagerness. "Well . . . there's me, of course. And Keteb, whom you just met. He's been with us since the beginning. And Gabrielle, perhaps."

Rachel marveled at the difference between the public's impression of celebrity and its reality. Had Roland Guipure, the darling of French fashion, had no friends? Could his social circle really have been limited to his sister, his employees, and his sister's assistant?

She jumped as Antoinette's phone buzzed. "I have Gédéon Naquet," said Gabrielle's voice.

"Oh, not *again*!" The final word was nearly a yell. "Tell him I'll call him back." She closed her eyes for a moment, then turned back to Rachel and Magda. "I'm sorry. I didn't mean to . . . He was Rolé's biographer, and now he keeps calling, and I just *can't*." She moved forward in her chair. "I think I may have given you a wrong impression. I don't mean my brother didn't have friends. He had many friends before his problems. But over the last year, he lost them. They were replaced by . . . well, by the kind of friends a rich addict has. Enablers." She looked to one side, then back. "False friends, Rolé told me they called them at Eirini. 'Fire your false friends' was one of their phrases. After you left Eirini, you were sup-posed to get rid of such people, cut them out of your life. He did that—and God knows it was hard—but once he'd done it, he didn't really have anyone left. And he hadn't had time to restart his old friendships yet." She paused, a frown crinkling her forehead. "No, that's not right. To be honest, he didn't really seem to want friends. He said he was striving for serenity by concentrating on his comeback. 'Striving for seren-ity'—that's another Eirini phrase. As far as I could see, he was content to work on the collection and focus on that and the licensing deal." Her voice became tight. "Although it seems I saw less than I thought."

The buzz of the intercom cut across the silence. "Antoi-nette," said Gabrielle's voice.

Antoinette sighed. "I'm sorry. I asked Gabrielle to let me know when our time was up. I hope you'll forgive me. I don't think I've been much help to you."

"Oh no, you should forgive us!" Rachel said at the same time as Magda said, "No, it's our fault."

"We should go." She picked up her bag.

Magda stood up. "We'll make another appointment."

Antoinette started to apologize once more, then gave up. "Yes. Yes, you're right. Later would be better. Perhaps after the memorial service." She had started to walk them to the door, but now she paused. "In fact, why don't you come to the memo-rial service? It would be a good way to meet people who knew Rolé before, people who could be helpful for your program. I'll have Gabrielle contact you when arrangements have been finalized."

A memorial service! Now that was a potential mine of information. Rachel nodded. "Thank you."

"De rien." Antoinette opened the door. "Gabrielle!"

Her assistant stood at the desk, a tray holding a white cof-fee service on the desk in front of her. She had obviously stopped on the way in to answer the incessantly ringing phone.

"Gabrielle, please take Madame Field's information so that we can send her an invitation to the memorial. And you might as well take that coffee into your meeting with Keteb now." She nodded at Rachel and Magda. "I look forward to seeing you there."

She retreated into her office and closed the door firmly behind her.

Chapter Eight

～

Neither woman spoke until the white metal door to number 21 closed behind them. They shouldn't have come. This was now so obvious that Rachel wondered why she'd ever thought the visit was a good idea. Had she really believed that this devastated woman would somehow be willing to open up her brother's life to them? Or that two complete strangers walking into a company for the first time would find its secrets so easily laid bare?

"That poor woman. What was I thinking, trying to squeeze information out of her?" She shook her head. "Alan was right."

Magda had the good manners not to respond to any of this. Instead, she pointed to a bistro across the street. "Come on. We never did get coffee."

The restaurant had the scent that seemed common to every Paris café in mid-afternoon: mingled strands of yeasty bread, gently stirred sauces, and the faint earthiness of poured red wine. They sat down at a table near the door, next to the broad front window. Once seated, Rachel slipped out of her coat, leaving it flopping inside out over the chair back; Magda, always tidy, arranged hers cape-style before sitting down.

"Un café, s'il vous plaît," she said to the waiter. "And a hot chocolate for my friend."

Rachel nodded her thanks and added, "With cream."

But all the whipped cream in Paris wasn't going to cheer her up, especially once Magda echoed her own earlier thoughts: "'Given what he did.' It sounds like even Guipure's sister thinks he overdosed."

"'Just because she thinks it, that doesn't make it true.' But Rachel's protest was feeble. If it looked like an overdose, and the most logical explanation was that it was an overdose, and even Guipure's own twin thought it was an overdose . . . maybe Magda was right, and the question of the dominant hand was irrelevant.

She looked across the table. "I'm sorry I dragged you into a pointless errand. And a painful one. A pointless and painful errand."

"It's okay." Magda emptied a packet of white sugar into her coffee. "I mean, it was awful, but we needed to go. Otherwise, we never would have known for sure that it wasn't murder."

Oh, how grateful Rachel was for that "we"! Magda had every right to be smug, even superior, but to choose solidarity instead was an act of immense support. Rachel took a deep breath to thank her.

She found herself cut off by a sharp double chime from Magda's phone. After a moment's digging, she extracted it from her bag. "I set it to alerts for Guipure's name," she explained.

"What is it? Some real charity ball organizers announcing a gala in his honor? Harrod's bought up the whole *prêt-à-porter* collection?" She smiled as if those ideas didn't actually sting.

But Magda wasn't looking at her. Instead, she was staring at her *portable*'s screen.

"What? What is it? Is something wrong with your mother?" They were at an age when such possibilities loomed closer.

Magda shook her head. She turned the *portable* so Rachel could see the headline on its screen:

Police treating Roland Guipure's death as suspicious.

"What?" Rachel restrained herself from grabbing the phone. So she had been right! "Do they say why?"

Magda's thumb flicked the screen. "It just says 'in light of further evidence.'" She looked up, catching her bottom lip with her upper teeth. "But you could call and ask."

"What? No, no."

"Why not?" Magda eyes widened. "Go on. Call Boussicault. Don't you want to know how they arrived at their conclusion?"

Dammit, she did. What had made the police agree with her?

"He'll never tell me." It was true that twice now Capitaine Boussicault of the Paris police had listened to her when no one else took her seriously, and twice now he'd helped when no one else would. But he'd also gotten into a good deal of trouble the last time, when he allowed her to go undercover to help him with an investigation. Two weeks' suspension without pay had made it plain what his superiors thought of the use of civilians in police work, and only the fact that they'd solved two murders and the theft of a series of national treasures had prevented a worse punishment. After all that, Rachel wasn't sure he'd be all that pleased to hear from her, never mind spilling details of another murder.

But Magda was right: she did want to know what the further evidence was, and Boussicault was her only possible source of information. She took her phone out of her bag, tapped through to her contacts, and hit the button next to his name before she could stop herself by thinking it through.

He picked up on the fourth ring. "Ah, Rachel! You're calling about the Guipure murder."

For a moment, she was struck dumb. Then she asked, "How did you know?"

Boussicault laughed. "The police alert the media that they are treating Monsieur Guipure's death as a murder, and half an hour later you call me? It doesn't take a great detective to make the connection. I know your . . . interests. And I would imagine Madame Stevens is next to, or at least somewhere near you."

Was it good or bad to be so well known by someone who was not quite a friend? Rachel decided it was best to just get to the point. "Yes, she is. And we were wondering, would you be willing to tell us anything about the murder?" A passing waiter jerked his head in her direction. She lowered her voice. "About what's happened to make you think it's a murder? I mean, nothing that would . . . cause difficulties, but . . ."

As her voice trailed off, she heard him rattle some papers on the other end of the line. "I can tell you what I would tell any reporter who happened to call me looking for information on the subject, and for both our sakes, I'm happy to tell you it's not much. Guipure was killed in the third arrondissement and lives in the eighth, neither of which are in my jurisdiction, so I know only what is in the daily informational report."

He paused in a way that suggested he was waiting for agreement, so Rachel agreed. "I'm fine with that."

"D'acc." More paper rattling, although Rachel suspected it was just for show. How long could the daily report be? "When Monsieur Guipure was found, the immediate assumption was that he'd died of a self-administered overdose into his left arm. Some doubt was thrown on this when one of the scene of the crime officers pointed out that callouses and relative hand size suggested Guipure was left-handed, but given that it's not impossible for someone to inject the dominant arm with the dominant hand, no conclusion was drawn until we had the autopsy findings."

"And what did that show?"

Boussicault cleared his throat. "It showed that Guipure had fifty milligrams of heroin in his system, which is twenty grams more than a lethal dose for a man of his size and weight."

Rachel heard her chair squeak as she sat back. Of course she had thought she was right, and once Magda had shown her the headline, she was certain, but it was still nice to be able to think, *I knew it!* She gave in to a moment's enjoyment.

"Rachel? Did you hear me?"

"Yes, yes." She glanced across the table at Magda as she repeated, "Fifty milligrams." Then, making eye contact, she added, "almost twice the lethal dose."

"Twenty milligrams more than a lethal dose. If you want to be a detective, you need to be precise."

If only you knew, Rachel thought. *Never mind wanting to be a detective; it looks like I'm about to be one. Again.* But aloud she said only, "Good point. Twenty milligrams."

But Boussicault must have caught something in her voice, and his tone became grave. "Licensure is a long process, Rachel. Don't confuse two instances of good luck with practical capability. The police will handle this case."

Rachel felt the resentment that had mingled with her fondness for Boussicault before. Every time she started to think of him as a mentor, perhaps even as a colleague, he had a way of making it seem that detection was just her hobby, and one she only succeeded in by luck, at that. "Don't worry," she said stiffly. She broke the connection. Yet again, she and Magda would have to prove themselves to the police.

They ordered a second round. Rachel asked for double cream.

"Twice the lethal dose!" Magda whistled. "All right, I take it back: it was murder." She bit her lip. "Now the question is, where do we start?" She nodded toward the building across the street. "It's pretty clear they're not going to be much help."

"Maybe with the rehab place?" It was the first thing that popped into Rachel's head. "People reveal all sorts of secrets in rehab. And even if he didn't, I bet they're a breeding ground for resentments and feuds."

Magda shook her head. "Doctor–patient privilege. Unless it's some sort of nonlicensed venture." She fished her *portable* out of her bag. "But the background information is as good a place to start as any." As the waiter put her coffee down, she started typing. After a few seconds, she read out, "'The Eirini Clinic is a seaside facility in Aspous, Greece. It is a health-driven well-being organization that practices opioid, alcohol, and sex addiction rehabilitation for adults and young adults. Each client lives alone and receives one-on-one treatment through a collection of approaches tailored to fit their specific needs.' Okay. Apparently its treatment philosophy is twelve step, and holistic with a spiritual emphasis. That explains the 'striving for serenity.' And it costs fifty thousand euros a month."

"Jesus!"

"They stay in individual cottages. So much for contacting fellow patients." She stabbed her phone screen a few more times. "Apparently that's not unusual. Here's The Cottage, in England, one patient at a time and fifteen thousand pounds a week. Some place in South Africa will give you a private executive villa, whatever that is, for seventeen thousand dollars a week. Fifty thousand euros seems cheap compared to that."

But Rachel had moved on from the residence arrangements at luxury rehabs. "What about the false friends Antoinette mentioned? Resentful ex-leeches might be very eager to tell tales."

Again Magda shook her head. "I don't see how we could track any of them down. Antoinette couldn't even name any real friends, never mind false ones. I know she tried to rationalize it, but—is that really what it's like to be famous?"

"I thought exactly the same thing. But then I thought, Is it a world where people even have real friends?"

Magda shook her head. "Not judging by what I read."

Rachel sipped her hot chocolate and thought for a long while.

"They might not have friends," she began slowly, "but they almost certainly have something even more useful to us than friends." She sped up as the thought took clearer form. "People who watch you like a hawk and pay attention to every move you make. People who will try to anticipate your moves and second-guess everything you think. People who would store up every little thing they heard about you and pore over it in case it might be useful in the future." Seeing the confusion on Magda's face she broke into a grin. "Rivals."

Chapter Nine

The Sauveterre fashion brand was both popular and successful, but it wasn't one of the towering eminences of the fashion world, a Dior or a Chanel with decades of money and cachet supporting it. This was fortunate for her and Magda, Rachel reflected. They could never have talked their way into a meeting at a top-tier fashion house. But as two gala organizers who'd recently had a meeting with Antoinette Guipure, they could bluff their way into a meeting with a designer on the second or third rung of fashion's ladder, one who hoped to overtake Guipure. Because of this, the next Monday morning found them on their way to the thirteenth arrondissement to meet Cecile Phan, whose label had just been invited to join the *Chambre Syndicale du Prêt-à-Porter*, shortly after showing its fourth autumn/winter haute couture show the previous year. Phan, her assistant had confirmed over the phone, would be delighted to meet with two members of a charity organization seeking remembrances of Roland Guipure for their gala's program.

Rachel had never been to the thirteenth, and as they came out of Olympiades métro, she made a mental note not to come again. The arrondissements of Paris were arranged like a snail;

the thirteenth was on the outermost spiral, the circle of relatively new districts, and it looked like a suburb trying to disguise itself as a city. Although the boulevard they walked down was as wide and tree lined as those in the inner spirals, it was almost deserted, the storefronts glass rectangles filled with fluorescent light pastily illuminating unremarkable interiors. On either side, concrete-fronted boxes with flat, contemporary exteriors outnumbered the gracious facades and zinc roofs of more traditional buildings. Cecile Phan Couture took up the bottom two floors of just such a building, a bland high rise entered via smoked-glass double doors.

Inside, though, everything was different.

If Sauveterre's headquarters were a glacier, these were a sunset. The offices had deep orange walls lit by standing lamps and wall sconces that made them glow. The reception area was filled with low dark-wood benches scattered with cushions in marine blue and moss green, one wall bearing a huge brush and ink painting of a group of elaborately dressed figures journeying through red-blossomed trees toward a mountain peak in the far distance, all drawn on a square of parchment that had aged to a soft sepia. Everywhere was warmth and comfort; even the young receptionist wore a dress patterned with blooming golden peonies.

Amid all these lush tones, Cecile Phan was displayed like a small jewel. She sat across from them in her office, on a yellow silk chair, her tiny feet—what were they, a size four or a three and a half?—resting on a stool in front of her. She wore a vivid crimson top cut in the style of a Mao jacket, paired with wide black trousers bearing Chinese characters embroidered in the same shade of red. Her bangs were cut straight across her forehead, and beneath them her features were as small and delicate as the feet on the stool. When the receptionist showed them in, she stood up and offered each of them in turn her hand, fingers impossibly long and palm impossibly narrow. Then she settled back into her chair, listening silently as they explained once again who they supposedly were and what they supposedly wanted.

Now Phan clasped her slender hands in her lap as she spoke. "Roland was an inspiration to me, an absolute inspiration. When I was in design school, he was a legend. We even learned about the House of Sauveterre in our lectures. And to all of us who were so busy learning how to cut correctly, how to position ourselves in the history of fashion, how to take the steps that would allow us to reach our full potential, he was a kind of wish fulfilment: a designer who'd had no training, served no apprenticeships, not really given any thought to brand promotion or significance, but nonetheless managed to become a star. We all hoped to imitate him when our time came."

Rachel had never heard a better series of left-handed compliments. Guipure had been old enough to be a legend. He had been untrained and thoughtless, a freak of nature who—unlike Cecile Phan—hadn't put in the hard work that meant he'd earned his success.

"That's terrific." She nodded earnestly. "It gives a real sense of his value to other designers. And as for his place in the larger world of design, you say he featured in some of your lectures? Could you say more about that?" *And perhaps offer some inside information even an old family friend wouldn't know in the process?*

"He was a case study in our module on the business of fashion. Most fashion houses take years to make a profit, and these days that profit really comes from licensing, like my own deal with Porthault to produce a line of linens. But Sauveterre was successful almost immediately. It was held up for us as an example of"—she put a hand to her chin—"oh, what did they call it? Consolidation by commitment, that's it. They weren't a public company, and in some ways they seemed more like a family than a business. The sister ran the financial side, Roland did the design, and the employees were very loyal." She said this last phrase ruefully. "It's generally known that you can't poach talent from Sauveterre, and you can never, *never* get any of their employees to give you inside information." She flushed slightly. "That does happen, people trying to get other people to spill in-house secrets. Anyway, the idea was that this structure produced Sauveterre's success. It was an example of achievement based on a conviction that the House was a community, not just a business. A very Eastern concept, actually. One I've tried to put into practice myself."

"And what about Guipure himself," Magda broke in, leaning forward, "did you ever meet him? Perhaps you have a more personal impression we could feature?"

"Yes. I met him when I was just starting out. He came to my graduation show."

"When was that?"

"Seven years ago. That was before all the—" Phan gestured toward her forearm, her expression changing to something between distaste and contempt.

"What was he like?"

"Absolutely charming!" Her face smoothed out. "He shook my hand, told me he loved my work . . . I think I might have a photo somewhere, if you'd like it. It meant so much to be acknowledged by a couturier of his generation."

"Any encounters more recently? In the last month or so?" Perhaps realizing that she was sounding less like a charity ball organizer than a detective, Magda added quickly, "Just if you happened to run into him."

"I don't think anyone ran into him. As I understood it, he was working so hard on his autumn/winter prêt-à-porter that he'd hardly come out of his *atelier* for months. And since the shows we've all been resting. If you can call it that. More like a week's breathing space before I need to start all over again for haute couture."

And with that, she looked at her gold sliver of a watch, swung her feet off the ottoman, and stood up. "I'm sorry. I have a meeting with some potential investors. But please feel free to use what I said earlier, that he was an inspiration. An *inspiration*." The little hand quickly clasped Rachel's, then Magda's, then reached out and pressed a button on the desk. "Jeanne will show you out."

They stood in awkward silence, waiting for the assistant to appear.

"Your offices are beautifully decorated," Rachel said finally. "They feel so warm."

"Exotic." It was said mildly, but it was still a reproof. "My aesthetic is exotic." A young woman appeared in the doorway. "Ah, here's Jeanne. Jeanne, could you show Madame . . . ah . . . these ladies out?"

* * *

Although they left the building by a different door, the street they found themselves on was just as stark and anonymous as the one they'd walked down earlier. Here, though, the fronts were all given over to Asian restaurants: Chinese, Vietnamese, Korean barbecue. On the other side of the street Rachel saw a sign for *Shanghai Prêt-à-Porter* poking out above the pavement, and as they walked they passed a travel agency offering cheap fares to and from Japan. She began to understand why someone whose aesthetic was exotic might choose to have their offices in this area.

"I'm starving." Magda stopped in front of an open door under a huge neon sign that said "I ♥ Pho." "How about here?"

The restaurant was furnished with rickety rectangular tables and even more rickety chairs, and although the menu was in both French and Vietnamese, Rachel had the sense that it was more at home in the latter. But the waitress was welcoming and helpful, and when their pho arrived in huge steaming bowls, it was so delicious that neither spoke until they were well embarked on it.

"Well, that was a waste of time," Magda said at last. "We could've learned as much from a couple of hours on Google."

"I don't know . . ." Rachel considered. "I thought there were a couple of things." She put down her spoon and held up an index finger. "One, she said that designers' real profits come from licensing deals. And we know that Sauveterre had just signed a licensing deal with . . . who was it?"

Magda swallowed. "Chieko. A Japanese company."

"Right. I bet a licensing agreement could founder if the designer was doing something that could potentially damage his reputation. The fact that Guipure wasn't taking heroin anymore doesn't mean he didn't have other vices that might put the deal in jeopardy, and if he did, someone who stood to benefit from the licensing would have had reason to kill him." She put up a second finger. "Second, she said Sauveterre was more like a family than a company."

"Well, at least to some degree they *are* a family. Antoinette and Guipure are."

"And families don't always like each other. They carry grudges; they blow tiny slights out of proportion; they get jealous and feel hard done by. And I don't mean just Antoinette and Roland. Anyone near enough the top to feel personally connected to them might have a reason to be angry at Guipure."

"Or just the reverse." Magda paused to dig a noodle from the bottom of her bowl. "Families can also be very loyal. They stick by each other. It could be that Sauveterre was that kind of family."

"Fair enough." Rachel wiped her lips with her paper napkin. "It's true it isn't much to go on, but at least it's something to *build* on. We can try other designers who might know more. I was thinking maybe Damien Punet at Atelier de Grace?"

Magda's mouth was too full for her to respond. She held up a finger, then swallowed and said, "Gédéon Naquet."

"Naquet? I've never heard of him. What's his label?"

"No label. He's not a designer. He's the biographer. Don't you remember? The first time Gabrielle buzzed Antoinette, she said he was on the phone. God knows why a fashion designer has a biographer, but it seems like a better bet than another designer. After all, it would be his job to know about Guipure. We should talk to him first."

"Yes, but as a wise woman once said, what pretext do we have? There's no reason for two gala organizers looking for quotes from friends to want to talk to a biographer. Or for him to want to talk to them."

"What pretext, what pretext?" Magda drummed her fingers on the table and stared out the window. A bus stopped in front of the glass, a giant iPhone on its side, and next to the phone, huge pink letters that promised, *"Une cinéma dans votre poche!"*

Rachel translated the phrase silently: "a cinema in your pocket." Letting her eyes lose focus, she thought for a second, then answered her own question. "We'll say we're making a film."

Magda looked dubious.

"I'm serious. Everyone's an amateur filmmaker these days. All those Netflix documentaries? We'll say we're making a documentary about Roland Guipure—we'll say we're in the early stages, so we don't have to answer any awkward questions. And we want to talk to him because we've heard he's the foremost authority on Guipure."

Magda shook her head. "He'll never buy it."

Ten hours later, Alan echoed her. "He'll never buy it," he said from Rachel's computer screen.

She gave him the same reply that she'd given Magda. "Trust me, he won't even stop to question it. The prospect of fame is the author's catnip." For the second time that day, she was pleased with herself. Oscar Wilde couldn't have put it better.

Chapter Ten

The next morning Amazon.fr revealed to Rachel and Magda that Gédéon Naquet had written three books, all of them biographies: one of Francois Mitterand's long-term mistress Anne Pingeot in 2000, one of Monica Bellucci in 2010, and one of French music icon Johnny Halliday in 2014. The Gibert Joseph bookstore on the Boulevard Saint Michel was only a short distance from Rachel's apartment, and according to its website it had a copy of *Blond Tiger: The Life of Johnny Halliday* in store. They decided to walk down.

"We're looking for the name of his editor." Rachel dodged a tourist who was standing at the intersection of the Boulevard and the Place de la Sorbonne, checking a map. "There are no agents here, so it's the editor who's the author contact." Twenty years as a poet might not have given her much, she reflected, but at least it had given her a thorough a knowledge of the French book trade.

As they passed the Pret à Manger on the Place de la Sorbonne, a young man stepped out in front of them, carrying a croissant in one hand and a cup of coffee in the other. A messenger bag was slung over his navy peacoat, the strap pushing up the back of his collar where it crossed from his left shoulder to his right hip. A student on his way to a seminar, Rachel guessed. The coat and bag were virtually their uniform. As if to prove her right, he turned sharply toward the Rue de la Sorbonne and the university, the warm, nutty scent of his drink trailing faintly behind him. Rachel sniffed appreciatively: although she hated the taste of coffee, its smell was divine.

She could make out the royal-blue awning and bright yellow lettering of Gibert Joseph just ahead, and as she opened the door, the interior heat hit her in a wave. Was it her imagination, or did she feel the cold more than she used to? Was she getting old? She thought of asking Magda for reassurance, but she was ninety percent sure she would just answer, "You say that every year."

"I feel like I get colder these days. I must be getting old."

"Oh please." Magda rolled her eyes. "You've said that every year for the last five years."

Rachel tucked her chin into her scarf and smiled.

The dust jacket of *Blond Tiger* informed them that Gédéon Naquet was a graduate of the Paris Institute of Political Sciences School of Journalism, and he had published articles in numerous well-respected newspapers and magazines. The black-and-white author photo showed a man in his late thirties, a lock of his dark hair flopping over his forehead and his arms crossed on the table in front of him so that his pale hands contrasted sharply with his dark turtleneck. Rachel, whose own author photo was more than fifteen years old, knew better than to believe the picture still represented its subject, but she wasn't there to reflect on authorial vanity. Flipping to the

Remerciements section at the back of the book, she found what they needed in the second paragraph: "and thanks to my tireless editor, Pierre Joralet."

Pierre Joralet, a commissioning editor at Publications Apropos, was delighted to hear that two aspiring filmmakers wanted to interview one of his authors. No, he was sure Monsieur Naquet would have no objection, neither to being involved with the project nor to being interviewed at an early stage. If they could give him a contact number, he would have Naquet call them.

* * *

At Les Deux Magots, where Simone de Beauvoir and Jean Paul Sartre had debated philosophy in front of the long mirrors and Albert Camus, hunched into his overcoat, had worked on his essays at one of the little tables outside, Gédéon Naquet had set up a makeshift writing station next to a front window. There was no mistaking who he was. His hair was thinner, but it was still carefully disarranged, and although he had changed his turtleneck for a shirt with the top two buttons undone, it was still black. Add in the crumpled napkins and empty espresso cups strewn across the table in front of him, and the pack of cigarettes and slim gold lighter next to his right hand (a decade after Paris had introduced a smoking ban in restaurants), and he was the very picture of A Writer at Work.

Les magots—the two porcelain Chinese mandarins that gave the restaurant its name—stared down from their perches near the ceiling as Naquet rose to shake Rachel and Magda's hands. A server soon appeared to take their orders. The *magot* in the red hat looked surprised at Rachel's request for a hot chocolate; the *magot* in the green hat serenely approved when Magda asked for coffee. Neither seemed surprised when Naquet simply said, "I'll have my usual."

"They know me," he explained as the waitress retreated. "I use this as my office. It's cheaper than renting space, and I don't have to make my own coffee." He leaned back against the red banquette, stretching out his arms as if he owned the air. "Perhaps you could film me here. You know, show me while I work, to set the scene."

"Sure, when the time comes that sounds great." Magda took out her *portable* and laid it on the table between them, setting it to record. "This is just a preliminary interview, though. We're still trying to gather funding."

"In fact"—Rachel leaned in confidingly—"we're hoping that our interview with you will lure investors. Show them that we have cooperation from reputable sources."

Naquet preened a little, brushing back his artful hair. "Whatever I can do to help."

"Well," Magda said, smiling, "why don't you tell us how you first started working on the biography? What made you pick Guipure?"

"It was right after his 'Opéra' collection in 2013. I'd just submitted *Le Tigre Blond*"—he held up a hand—"although I'm not assuming you've read any of my little books."

Magda smiled, "As it happens, I've just finished *Le Tigre Blond*."

Naquet bridled again, although Rachel thought he'd be a lot less pleased if he knew "finished" meant "read the acknowledgments and closed the book cover." Still, he didn't, and she admitted to herself that it had been wise to let Magda handle this interview. Her friend had a skill for believable lying that Rachel could only admire and envy.

"There was a lot of positive press on the Opéra collection," Naquet was saying. "People were suggesting that Roland was at the height of his powers, and I suddenly thought he'd make a terrific subject. So I pitched it to Joralet, he contacted Sauveterre, and Antoinette loved it." He sped up. "We negotiated, signed the contract, and I began work in January of 2014."

The waiter arrived with their drinks. Naquet's usual turned out to be espresso in a cup barely bigger than a shot glass, accompanied by a spoon tiny enough to match the one Mediouri had used the week before at the *pressing*. Rachel's hot chocolate was served "à l'ancienne," thick as pudding and with a small pitcher of warm cream on the side, to use to thin the chocolate. She poured a little into her cup and began stirring.

As Naquet reached for the container of sugar packets and selected a long straw of brown sugar, Magda asked, "And what was your impression of Guipure when you met him?"

"To the extent *that* I met him." Naquet said sardonically. He tore open the packet and emptied it into the black liquid. "We started our first interview late because he was taking a nap, and no one wanted to wake him up. And when I showed up for our second interview—an interview scheduled well in advance– he was napping *again*. No apology to me, just 'Monsieur Guipure will be late.'" He took a swallow from the little cup. "That's when I decided I'd start by doing background research. They let me use their archive." Another swallow. "Do you know about the archive? They're very proud of it, and justly so. It's like a Bibliothèque Nationale of Sauveterre. Nineteenth-century advertisements for the original Sauveterre et Fils art supplies store in Bezance, the grandfather's bills of sale from during the war, the contract from when he first bought the house, the contract from when they rebought it . . ."

He was a talker, Rachel saw. But Magda expertly headed off his flow and steered it where she needed it. She had evidently decided that if Naquet couldn't offer them any information on Roland, perhaps he could help identify possible suspects.

"We'll absolutely make use of the archive when the time comes," she said smoothly. "But for now . . . The people around Guipure, what were they like?" A little smile. "I'd really like to exploit your observational expertise, to get some background." A little smile.

Who could resist such flattery? Not Gédéon Naquet. He gazed into the middle distance for a moment, then said, "When I went there first, the impression that I had was of a group of people all focused on the same goal. And that goal was Guipure."

Magda nodded thoughtfully, then asked, "How do you mean?"

He folded his arms on the table. "When you've spent as much time in the celebrity world as I have, you see that there's a structure to it. And Sauveterre as I saw it fit that structure perfectly. There was a creative, and there was the practical army that protected him." He cocked his head to one side, plainly pleased with this image. "Everyone in the place worked to make Roland's life as easy as possible. His assistant could have been a nightclub bouncer: one minute past your allotted appointment time, and Dolly Fauré made sure you were out. His sister took care of all the financial issues, so he didn't have to worry his creative mind with any of that. Their head pattern cutter was in and out of his office every two minutes with suggestions about fabric, about cutting angles, about buttons or trimmings. Even that little redhead who worked for his sister would pop up to ask if he needed her to order his lunch or bring in some delivery."

Magda began to ask another question, but Rachel cut in. Something was scratching at her. She couldn't quite put her finger on it, but she came up with something else. "You keep saying things were a certain way when you first saw Sauveterre, or when you were first there. Were they different when you went back?"

Magda looked slightly put out that she hadn't made this analysis; Naquet gave a little smile, as if he'd been deliberately hinting and was glad someone had picked up on it. "They were worse." He stopped smiling. "Much worse." Then he stopped. "But this can't be the kind of thing you want for your investors."

"Yes, it is," the women said together.

"It gives the project shape," Magda added reassuringly. "Tell us as much as you can."

Naquet thought for another second. "Look, there's no good way to say it: he was high out of his mind, and no one seemed to be in control of him." He raised a hand, palm out.

"Correction. He'd acquired this"—he pursed and thinned his lips at the same time, producing an expression of dislike that was nearly disgust—"this young man, and *he* was very much in control. When I arrived to try to interview Guipure, he came up, stuck out his hand, and offered himself as an interview subject. Said he was Cyrille Thieriot, Roland's *partenaire à vie*." Again the expression. "Whereas in fact he was a leech. You spend enough time around celebrities and you recognize the type. The whole time I was trying to do the interview—I say *trying*, because I'd ask a question, and Roland would start to answer it, maybe get three or four words out, then lose his train of thought and nod off—the whole time this kid sat in a chair nearby, playing on his phone. Sometimes he'd interrupt to show Roland something he wanted him to buy, or sometimes when Roland dozed off, he'd take the cigarette out of his hand if it looked like it might burn him. And every time one of the *croquis* would fall on the floor, he would pick it up—"

"Sorry," Magda interrupted. *"Croquis?"*

"Sketches, design sketches. That's what they're called in fashion, *croquis*. Roland drew them all the time. It was his thing, apparently. I read a couple of articles in which he said that if he made *croquis* when his mind was elsewhere, his unconscious produced amazing designs. He was still doing it, only now it was like the talking, but on paper. He'd fade off in the middle of one, then wake up and forget he'd started that one, start a new one, then forget that one too. There were all these half-finished sketches all over the floor. And the boy just took them and—" He wiggled his fingers to indicate disappearance.

"Then about half an hour in, Roland started to wake up. He became very jumpy." Naquet darted his eyes around exaggeratedly, miming nervousness. "The kid suddenly asked him if he wanted lunch, asked him for some money, then went off and came back a little while later with a paper bag, saying it was the delivery. Roland looked a lot more cheerful, so I figured—" He spread his hands, and looked at them. Rachel understood: he figured it had been a drug delivery. "I didn't want to get involved with any of that, so I ended the interview."

Magda tapped the nail of a forefinger on her saucer, making a light chinking noise as she frowned. "And where was the practical army during this?"

Naquet shrugged. "The sister's assistant and the *chef modéliste* were nowhere to be seen. The dragon Fauré was still guarding the outer office, and she obviously hated Thieriot. She did everything but spit on him. But she couldn't kick him out or bar the door to him, could she? That's problem when the boss is a *drogué*." He raised his eyebrows. "He's the boss. If everyone depends on you for their check, who's going to stand up to you?"

"What about his sister?" Magda asked.

"What about her?"

"Well, she was also the boss. The CFO. She didn't depend on Guipure for her check, and surely she cared about him. She didn't do anything?"

He held up his hands. "I don't know what went on when I wasn't there. But I do know that when I saw him, he was in terrible condition, and I also know he only did the *désintox* after the reviews turned bad. You do the math."

"What do you mean?"

Naquet's sigh said that Magda was unutterably naïve. "Remember John Galliano, yelling at those women in that bar? He did exactly the same thing the year before, but he was making big money for Dior then, so they hushed it up. Then someone recorded him doing it on their phone and put it online, and he was *out*. Coincidentally, his most recent collection for Dior hadn't done so well. As long as he was an anti-Semitic drunk who could make money for them, they would cover for him. As soon as he could affect the bottom line, off he went to *désintox*. That's what I mean."

"And what about after the *désintox*? Were calm and happiness restored when he could make money again?"

He drank the final mouthful from his little cup. "I couldn't say. I didn't see him after he came back."

"What?" Magda raised her eyebrows. Rachel shared her surprise. Antoinette's description of Naquet as "Rolé's biographer" had led her to assume his work was ongoing. To learn now that he hadn't been in contact with Guipure during the period they cared about! She felt a snap of annoyance.

Whatever Magda felt, she hid it well. "I'm sorry." She frowned. "We were under the impression that you were Guipure's current biographer."

Naquet shifted in his seat. "Well, yes and no. That is, I was, and I'm hoping I will be again." He scratched at an imaginary stain on the tabletop with his thumbnail, then looked up reluctantly. "After that interview, I telephoned to discuss—well, really to discuss how I should handle Roland. Antoinette's assistant told me that Antoinette would get back to me. Then a week or so later, I read on *The Fit* that Roland was going into *désintox*." He looked affronted. "That was the first I'd heard of it. The next day I received a letter from Antoinette saying that in light of developments Sauveterre had decided to shelve the biography, and here was a fat check for my troubles."

"Did you cash it?"

Magda's voice was neutral, but the implication was clear: cashing the check indicated abandoning the project.

"Of course I cashed it," Naquet snapped. "I need to eat. But I also—" He inhaled, then sighed the air out. "Look, when I began my career, I was a serious writer. My work on Anne Pingeot, that was a study of a complex woman who had made complex decisions. When Roland came out of rehab, I saw a genuinely intellectually engaging story. What's it like to rebuild yourself from your lowest ebb? I thought maybe I could pursue that with him."

"And?" Magda's voice was like a needle.

He looked up. "And nothing. I telephoned a few times, suggesting we collaborate, but I never heard back. I thought maybe he was busy with the upcoming show. Then I got the alert that—" He shrugged, raising a hand and letting it fall. "Of course, *now* the time is really ripe for a study like that. A respectful summation of Roland's life. And who better to get it out quickly than someone who already has substantial material? But Antoinette won't take my calls."

There was a moment's silence, sorrowful on his part and thoughtful on the women's. Then Magda cleared her throat. "I'm sorry to hear that. I do think, though, that our film will allow you to engage with that story. It might even reignite her interest." Naquet perked up a little. "And I hate to ask you for even more than you've given, but could you possibly point us to anyone else we could interview? You've been very helpful, but the more fully rounded our pitch is, the more likely we are to get funding."

Naquet squinted slightly, considering. "Well, no one at the company itself. But I did keep the number Thieriot gave me, if you want to try that. If his behavior with me is anything to judge by, you'd have no trouble getting an interview." He picked up his phone and stabbed at the screen a few times. Magda's *portable* chimed. "There it is. Now," he said, his voice turning crisp, "when do you think you'll know about funding?"

"A couple of months," Magda said vaguely.

"Great, great." He craned his neck, looking for the waiter. It was plain that now that he was no longer their focus and he'd found out what he wanted to know, he had lost interest. "Well, let me know as soon as you hear anything. I'm thinking of moving into television, and some footage would really help my showreel." He spotted a server and raised his hand for another espresso. Their time was up.

* * *

"Not at all helpful in some ways, but very helpful in others," Magda said once they were outside. She turned and began walking up the Boulevard Saint Germain toward the Rue de Bac métro station.

"God, didn't his description of Guipure before he went to rehab break your heart?" Rachel finished buttoning her jacket as they passed the Café de Flore. "How could people so protective of him let him get into that state?"

"He told us." Magda stopped at a pedestrian crossing and waited for the light to change. "It sounds like they were so used to catering to him that they didn't notice there was a problem until it was too late. And this Thieriot guy was obviously well dug in by that time"—she made air quotes—"'helping him out.' That's someone we really need to talk to."

"A false friend," Rachel said distractedly. She was noticing how many boutiques there were as they walked up the boulevard. Hermès on the corner as they crossed, Louis Vuitton back next to Les Deux Magots, and now Ralph Lauren, Sonia Rykiel, and something called Bruno Cucinelli that looked as if it could give those two a run for their money. Literally. She hadn't been in this area for a long time; had it always been like this? She started counting: boutique, café, boutique, boutique, boutique, café, boutique. Was this all Paris was now, a place for eating and buying, consuming in one way or another? She thought of Baron Haussman, building this street and the boulevards surrounding it by tearing down the homes of the poor; then her mind conjured up 21 Rue la Boétie, once the site of Maximilien Sauveterre's efforts to save Jewish lives and now a production line for expensive clothing that no one actually needed.

She sighed.

"What are you thinking?" Magda was digging in her shoulder bag.

"Just . . . existential thoughts."

"Oh, right." But she didn't seem interested in following up. Instead, she pulled out her phone.

"What are you doing?"

Magda put the phone to her ear. "Trying the number he gave me for Cyrille Thieriot."

"You don't want to regroup before—"

But Magda waved a silencing hand. *"Allo?"* Thieriot had answered the call.

Chapter Eleven

～

Cyrille Thieriot, who was delighted to give an interview for a film about his former lover, lived in the tiniest and most crowded *appartement* Rachel had ever seen. Perhaps ten meters square, it nonetheless managed to contain a bed, a table holding a huge television set, a kitchenette with a two-ring electric stovetop, a cube refrigerator, a bar sink and miniscule countertop, and a wardrobe made up of a complex series of drawers and doors. On the left-hand side of the room was a narrow door that Rachel assumed led to the bathroom; the remainder of the wall was covered with photographs of people smiling, laughing, or putting their tongues out in a variety of public areas, their youthful arms around each other's skinny waists. The right-hand wall was a collage of pictures of Roland Guipure, in different clothing and different rooms, sometimes with ordinary people and sometimes with celebrities Rachel recognized, but always in the company of the same young man, the one Rachel had seen with him in Magda's printed photos.

Against this background of memories sat the real-life version of that young man. Thieriot's eyes were outlined in orange shadow that stretched from the inner edge of each socket to the outer edge of each temple, his lashes were heavily mascaraed in purple, and for his lips he had chosen a bright matte fuchsia. Dressed in tight black jeans and a black turtleneck, he was skinny as a twig. He looked like an exotic hothouse flower brought to life.

"We were in love!" he was saying. He was a maker of exclamations and a stressor of significant words. "We were *devoted*. And then *it all changed*."

It was quite an introduction. For a moment the women were stunned into silence.

Then Magda cleared her throat. "I'm sorry." That seemed to be the safest response. "Would you like to start at the beginning and tell us how you met?" She discreetly tapped the "record" button on her *portable* where it lay between her and Rachel on Thieriot's peacock-blue bedspread.

"In a *resto*." He smiled as he remembered. "It was *very* romantic. I was a *garçon de table* at Bespoke. The place was so popular that it was impossible to get a reservation with us, but *he* managed it. He came in with a group. He sat at someone else's table, but he noticed *me*. The next day he telephoned the restaurant and asked to speak to me. One date, and we both knew." He lifted his arm and showed them an R tattooed on the inside of his wrist. "I had this done after our first month together. We were *that sure*."

"And this was before he started using heroin?"

Thieriot looked as if he would very much like to deny that Roland Guipure had ever used heroin—it was clearly too unsentimental for the story he wanted to tell. But he must have known that he couldn't get away with that, so he shook his head and said reluctantly, "He'd been using for a while by then. But only recreationally. He told me he started when he and some friends were vacationing in Goa. They took it to loosen up, the way you do when you're on holiday. And then he just didn't stop. But it wasn't a big deal. He never took very much. And I could see why he *needed* it."

Rachel's ears pricked up. Were they going to get a useful revelation at last? "Oh? Why?"

"Because he never had any chance to relax! When he and I first met, he did nothing but work on the clothes. Day and night! And even when he had a moment to spend with me, his harpy sister and that *salope* of a personal assistant were always interrupting, with something for him to *approve* or something for him to *sign*. He never had a moment's peace."

"And you think the heroin was an escape from that?" Magda sounded unconvinced.

"Obviously." Thieriot's tone said only a fool would believe otherwise.

"And that's why you bought it for him?"

"I didn't—"

"Gédéon Naquet told us that when interviewed, Monsieur Guipure said he saw you buy drugs for him." Magda's matter-of-fact tone managed to suggest that there was no point in denying it; she wasn't accusing him, just stating a fact.

Thieriot looked as if he had a few choice words he'd like to share about Naquet, but he rose above it. "Well, yes, I did do that. But it was part of a *plan*."

Magda raised her eyebrows and waited. Thieriot squirmed a little in his chair.

"You see, once we began spending all our time together, Rollie asked me to handle the . . . the acquisition. I saw that if I did that, I could control his intake. Rollie would give me the money, of course, but I made all the other arrangements, and *because* I did that, I could cut down the amount he took. I thought that if I did that and helped him to relax more, then I could *wean* him off."

"But his addiction grew worse."

"Yes, because no one was interested in *helping* me! They preferred him as he was. It made it easier for them to squeeze every drop out of him. Whereas I—I gave him *fun*! We went to Le Piaf, Chez Raspoutine"—Rachel recognized the names of two of Paris's most exclusive nightclubs—"we went shopping. Which," he added huffily, "*was* a kind of work, because he was looking at the work of other designers. And I *directly* helped with *his* work too. Those mirror dresses from spring/summer 2014? He got the idea for them from an after-hours drag club I took him to. But of course my ideas about how to save him never had a chance. Who was going to listen to a little waiter? That Dolly Fauré, his PA, *said* to me, right to my *face*, that Rollie didn't need nightclubs, he needed *désintox*." He leaned forward and locked eyes with Rachel. "You know, there's a long history of opiates being an asset to the creative process. Verlaine, Baudelaire, that fat English poet who wrote about the Chinese king."

Rachel considered him. This was not a Gédéon Naquet who wanted a moment's silence for his loss. This man wanted someone to echo his drama. That would be empathy, to him. She made her voice breathless. "And then what happened?"

"What happened?" He cast one elegant hand into the air. "What always happens when many line up against one. They waited until after that terrible collection in 2015"—he leaned forward confidingly—"which wouldn't have been so terrible if Rollie had been given more time to be open to *inspiration* and *relaxation*. And then they ganged up on him and convinced him to go off to that Greek island place."

"They?"

"His sister, that head pattern cutter Lellouch, and Dolly Fauré. She's the one that told me about it. Antoinette took him off on a plane, *and I never saw him again.*"

Rachel gasped, and made her eyes round for good measure. "But surely he contacted you at some point to break things off?"

"Never!" Thieriot shook his head. "Not before he went, not after he came back. Although *I* tried to contact *him*. I texted. I telephoned. I knew he'd want to hear from me. I *knew.*" He touched his chest lightly with a fist. "But I never heard anything. I didn't even know he had died until I read it on *Quelles Nouvelles*! I had to take the day off work."

"Where is work?" Magda took over the questions once again. "Still at Bespoke?"

He shook his head. "Rollie liked to have me near him all the time, so I stopped working while we were together. I had to find a new job after—after—" He turned his head in profile and covered his mouth. Only the city noises wafting through the window from the busy Rue Vieille du Temple below prevented the scene from being a silent tableau of grief.

"I'm so sorry." Rachel shook her head. "After all you were to each other, and all you did for him, to be dropped like that." She gave him a second to feel secure before she added, "But of course you had the *croquis* to remember him by."

Thieriot's hand dropped. He turned back to them. "What *croquis?*"

Rachel widened her eyes again. "Monsieur Naquet mentioned that you had a habit of collecting sketches Roland made and discarded. He seemed to think you'd kept them."

Thieriot's eyes darted around the room for a split second. If it hadn't occurred to him before that such an action could be seen as theft, it was certainly occurring to him at that moment. He said truculently, "Rollie was always sketching designs, and if he didn't like one, he would just *push* it away. But *I* thought perhaps they would be useful for future collections. So, yes, I held onto some."

Rachel forgot for a moment that she was supposed to be film director and became pure detective. "Did he sign them?" She didn't know much about the value of such things, but signed sketches by an established designer might well be a considerable asset for a man whose tastes seemed pitched higher than a closet-sized studio in a 1980s breeze-block building.

"Maybe. I don't know. Probably." He recovered his equilibrium. "Why?"

"They'd make such a good visual for the film," Magda supplied smoothly, knocking Rachel's knee warningly with her own. "You know, a panning shot across them with a little subtitle saying, 'Signed sketches by Guipure, from the private collection of Cyrille Thieriot.'"

"Oh. Yes, yes, he certainly signed some of them."

"Well, we'd love to use them. And of course it would add to their value. Not that you necessarily care about that, but Naquet seemed to think you had saved them because they might be valuable, so . . ."

"He thought that, did he!" Thieriot snorted. "Well, *he* would know about people trying to make money off Rollie. You know what he did before he pitched his book to Sauveterre? He wrote trashy celebrity biographies—the kind that you make by quoting other people because the *real* subject won't speak to you. Rollie was the first significant figure who'd ever actually *agreed* to talk to him, and he couldn't believe his luck. He saw a ticket up." He shook his head at the shamelessness of the world.

"Well, it doesn't seem to have worked out very well. Sauveterre halted the biography when Guipure went into the *désintox.*"

Thieriot snorted again. "That doesn't have to stop him. If Sauveterre won't talk to him he can just make the book unauthorized and put in anything he wants. He'll make a *fortune.* People might have liked the story of a genius who became an addict but managed to pull himself back up, but the unauthorized biography of a junkie designer who ended up dead outside a nightclub? *That* book will sell *millions.*" He looked up at the ceiling, and his voice wobbled. "If Rollie had only stayed with me, none of this would have happened!"

The women knew a good exit line when they heard one.

*　*　*

Outside, a thin drizzle had begun to fall. The paving stones had lost their mica glitter, the cream-colored building facades had turned a wet yellow, and even the linden tree next to Thieriot's building looked as if it would rather be indoors. Snapping open the umbrella she extracted from her bag, Magda turned right onto the Rue des Francs Bourgeois. Rachel gazed longingly at a window that said "Palais des Thés" as they passed it, but Magda was walking at a speed that made it plain they wouldn't be stopping.

"He's one to talk about people exploiting Guipure." Her heels banged on the gray pavement. "With that wall of photos and that version of their relationship. And all that stuff about trying to wean Guipure off drugs by encouraging him to relax!"

"I don't know." Rachel waited for a car to pass before she crossed the street. "I think he believes his own rationalization. People don't like to admit their ulterior motives, especially to themselves. And I think it's possible he loved Guipure, even if what that really means is that he loved the fact that Guipure was giving him the life he wanted. Just the way Guipure seems to have used him partially as a . . . a drug courier."

Magda's face showed what she thought of that reading, but she shrugged. "Well, it doesn't really make any difference. Whatever motivated either of them, he's our number-one suspect, as far as I'm concerned."

Rachel stopped. "How do you figure?"

Magda turned around and held out her unencumbered hand. She began putting up fingers, one per point. "If he actually loved Guipure, then suddenly being ghosted might well have been too much to take. People kill for love all the time.

And if he was trying to leech off Guipure, he must have thought he'd hit the jackpot. A rich, famous designer. Then to have that snatched away from him? Being dumped without so much as a thank you? I could see him killing Guipure over that. And once Guipure was dead, Thieriot could sell those sketches for a tidy sum, even if he's pretending he didn't take that into account. That was the first thing I thought when Naquet said he picked up the drawings."

"Oh, Naquet." Rachel rolled her eyes. "Talk about pretending! If Thieriot's right, all that about wanting to write a legitimate book was just lies. I can see him being angry enough to kill Guipure if he'd invested a year's work and suddenly had nothing to show for it but a check for a few hundred euros. Particularly if offing him would make it possible to write a bestselling book."

Magda made a disbelieving face. "That seems pretty ruthless."

"You don't know authors," said Rachel.

"Except that Guipure wasn't responding to him, so how could Naquet get into his birthday party to kill him?"

"How could Thieriot?"

"Fair question." They had reached the Centre Pompidou, with its exoskeleton of metal pipes and rivets, and its white ducts looming up from the ground like the periscopes of some lost submarine. "I'd like to find out more about Cyrille Thieriot. I don't like to take people's word for things, even details about themselves. *Especially* details about themselves."

Plus, Rachel thought, *you don't like him.* But all she said was, "And I'd like to try to track down this Dolly Fauré."

"The assistant? Yeah, I noticed they both mentioned her too."

"And both obviously dislike her, which makes me think she'd be an excellent source of information. About them, at least."

Magda laughed. "Okay, then. Let's get started." And down they went into the métro, the umbrella leaving a trail of drips behind them.

Chapter Twelve

Unfortunately, the first thing Rachel did when she arrived home was fall asleep. She meant only to rest for a moment on the sofa before making a cup of tea and bringing over her laptop to look up Dolly Fauré, but the grayness outside, the warmth inside, and her own damp and chilly feet conspired against her.

When she woke, it was dark out and too late to call anyone before dinner. So she heated up some leftovers and ate them while reading the *Memoirs* of the great nineteenth-century French detective Eugène Vidocq. She had downloaded it onto her Kindle in the hope that it might offer her some tips, but Vidocq's swashbuckling tales of the Paris underworld and the maneuvers and disguises he used to catch his criminal prey were enjoyable in their own right.

Just as she was finishing his story of capturing a forger who had pretended to be a clergyman and so swindled a small French town for years, her computer made the clanging chime that announced a Skype call.

"Hello, love," she said when Alan's face appeared on the screen. "I'm so glad to see you. Remember how I told you that we were going to meet with Guipure's biographer? Well—"

He cut her off. "My mother wants me to ask you something."

He sounded like a ten-year-old sent on a reluctant errand. He looked so much like one, too, that Rachel couldn't help but smile. "Okay."

"Remember her friend? Whose husband died in Paris?"

Rachel nodded, but as he opened his mouth to continue, a voice murmured off screen. He leaned out of camera range. "No. No, I'm handling it. I *will*. Fine, fine." His face loomed back. "She wants to ask you herself." Now he sounded like a petulant fifteen-year-old.

Before she could say anything, the head and shoulders of Alan's mother appeared next to him. Jean was one of those who seemed to move through life untouched by spills, perspiration, or the creases and snagged threads that afflicted common mortals, and sure enough, on the screen her silver pageboy was straight and smooth, her pink lipstick as fresh if it had been applied just a moment before.

"Hello, darling. How's the poetry?"

So Alan hadn't told his parents about her plan to change jobs. Rachel took her cue from him. "Oh, you know. Coming along."

"Good, good. Listen, I wonder if you could do something for me. Well, really for a friend of mine, Ellen Ochs. Al told you about her husband."

"Yes, he did, and I was so sorry to hear it. What can I do for you?"

"Well, it's a bit complicated, so I apologize in advance for asking. She got an e-mail from the French police this morning, and they need her to come collect Jack's belongings—you know, what was in the hotel room. For ten days they won't tell us anything, and now they say she has to come collect his things by Monday or they'll get rid of them!"

From behind his mother's shoulder, Alan raised his eyebrows at Rachel. Such behavior was typical of French bureaucracy. Some functionary had probably been told to deal with a backlog and had done so by sending out an e-mail that shifted the burden onto the general public.

Alan's voice broke into her thoughts. "My mother wondered if you'd be willing to pick up his stuff."

"Of course I would." Rachel began a comforting smile, but a new thought turned it into a frown. "But will I be allowed to? Don't I need some sort of connection to the deceased? And some sort of document to prove it?" French bureaucracy was also very keen on documentation, in her experience the more complicated the better.

But Alan had looked into that, and the answer was surprisingly straightforward. He could e-mail Rachel a scanned copy of a letter signed by Mrs. Ochs, stating that she deputed Rachel Levis to pick up her husband's belongings from the police commissariat in the eighth arrondissement. Rachel could take this and some identification to the relevant police commissariat, which would have received a scan of the same letter. The police would then allow her to make the collection.

"Theoretically," Rachel said darkly. But she promised to go as soon as the e-mail arrived, and Jean promised Mrs. Ochs would send it that night.

Awake, fed, and sitting at her computer, she decided to end the evening doing what she'd meant to do at the beginning. The first internet hit for "Dolly Fauré" was an e-mail address at

Sauveterre, but the message Rachel sent bounced back immediately. Fortunately, whitepages.fr showed only four Faurés in Paris, and only one D. Fauré. After five rings, a woman's recorded voice explained to Rachel that she couldn't make it to the phone, but she would respond to Rachel's message as soon as she could.

Her name, phone number, and reason for calling clearly enunciated into Madame Fauré's voice mail, Rachel closed the computer and picked up Vidocq once more. *The night before our intended departure, I met in the dusk of the evening a woman of Brussels, named Eliza, with whom I had been on intimate terms.* She settled back into the sofa.

*　　＊　　＊　　＊*

On Monday morning she woke to an e-mail from Alan with the promised letter attached. As she was printing it and struggling to extract her passport from the back of a desk drawer to use as identification, the phone rang. It was Dolly Fauré.

Madame Fauré had seen that the police were treating her former boss's death as murder, but she was confused about where Rachel fit in. Was she a reporter? "Because I have nothing to say to the press." Not a reporter? Was she with the police? "I should tell you that one of your colleagues already called to arrange an appointment for later this week." At last Rachel, reaching for an explanation and steeled by the memory of Matthieu Mediouri's easy acceptance at the *pressing*, said, "I'm a private detective. I'm investigating the murder of Monsieur Guipure."

Madame Fauré's tone changed from forbidding to intrigued. She wasn't sure how much help she could be, but she was willing to meet. There was an excellent café a few blocks from where she lived in the ninth arrondissement, Le Grand Comptoir d'Anvers. Could Rachel meet her there at two o'clock this afternoon?

That left Rachel with the rest of the morning to fulfill her promise to Jean. Folding the printout into an envelope and stuffing her passport into her bag along with it, she took the métro to the Commissariat Rue du Faubourg-St. Honoré.

The eighth was home to some of the city's most beautiful buildings: the church of the Madeleine with its classical friezes above Corinthian columns, the domed extravagance of the Église Saint-Augustin, even the fantastical exterior of the Pagoda Paris on the Rue de Courcelles. Unfortunately, the Paris Prefecture de Police had decided to ignore all this and place the Commissariat Rue du Faubourg-St. Honoré inside a modernist box of stained beige concrete and exposed gray girders, an excrescence that emerged from the side of a bland nineteenth-century building made beautiful by contrast.

Inside it was better. The box proved to be merely the security entrance, and once Rachel put her bag through X-ray and explained her errand, she was pointed in the direction of an airy two-story foyer with what appeared to be a giant mobile made out of hundreds of paper cranes suspended from its ceiling. A staircase curved downward on the left side of the space, extending from a mezzanine of offices above. Crossing to the reception desk, she held out her letter. "I'm here to pick up the belongings of Monsieur Jack Ochs? Monsieur Ochs's wife sent a letter here by e-mail earlier to say I would be acting as her proxy."

The *gardien* behind the desk looked up from her computer. She took the envelope reluctantly, read the letter, and then said, "Your ID?"

Rachel handed over her passport. The *gardien* looked at the photo page, then at her, then at the letter, then back to the photo and from the photo to her. At last she said grudgingly, "I will need to consult my *chef* regarding our policy on this." She disappeared into a back room.

That was the French bureaucracy Rachel had come to expect. The woman could be gone for hours. She picked up a pamphlet that promised to help her recognize telephone scammers and began to read.

"Rachel?"

She turned around. Capitaine Boussicault stood at the bottom of the stairs.

"I thought it was you!" He crossed the lobby and kissed her on both cheeks. *"Ça va?"*

She nodded. *"Oui, ça va."*

"What are you doing here? Looking for clues in the case of Roland Guipure?"

Rachel felt herself grow cold, then hot. How did he know they had decided to investigate Guipoure's death? Then she saw his smile and realized he was teasing.

She laughed in a way she hoped sounded amused, not relieved. "I might ask the same of you. You're far off your patch! what brings *you* here?"

He shrugged. "Just a meeting. Some inter-arrondissement liaison. And, really, what brings you here?"

Rachel explained about her errand for Jean.

The captain started slightly. "Ochs? Jack Ochs? The tourist in the hotel room?"

"Yes." Rachel didn't see what was so surprising about a tourist dying in his hotel room. It must happen all the time.

"Let me take you for a drink," the captain said. But just then the *gardien* reemerged, pulling a roller bag with one hand and holding a folder in the other. She stood the first beside the counter and held out the second. "You'll need to fill these out before we can release the effects to you."

"I'll wait outside," Boussicault said.

For the next twenty minutes Rachel filled in blanks and signed her name on one form after another, had a photocopy taken of her passport photo that she then signed, had it countersigned by the *gardien*, and finally received the salmon-colored copy of an elaborate receipt informing her that the Paris Prefecture of Police, as represented by the Commissariat at 210 Rue du Faubourg-St. Honoré, had consigned the effects of Monsieur Jack Ochs into her possession. When at last she emerged from the building clutching this in one hand and pulling the roller bag behind her, Boussicault stood waiting on the pavement, slightly out of breath.

"I found a good place a few streets away. May I?"

He took the handle of the roller bag and led her briskly down the fan-shaped cobbles to a side street, across a grand avenue, then finally around a corner, stopping outside a restaurant surrounded by tubs of tall bamboo trees. The interior was a landscape of starched tablecloths and deep velvet chairs, and as he led her to a table in the back, Rachel began to feel guilty that she hadn't been frank with him about the fact that she was investigating the Guipure murder. He obviously thought well of her if he was bringing her here.

They made halting small talk until the waiter arrived with their pastis. Only once he had retreated out of earshot did Guipure lean forward, his ribs almost touching the table, and say, "Do you know that Monsieur Ochs was killed during a robbery?"

"What? No." How had Alan neglected to tell her that?

"Sss, sss." He put out his hand, palm down, and wiggled his fingers, indicating that she should lower her voice.

The restaurant was very dark, and as she leaned forward she felt like a character in a spy movie. She murmured, "Do they know what happened?"

"No. The room was ransacked and his wallet was taken, but there were no fingerprints, and the gun wasn't left behind. He was staying at the Holiday Inn Elysées, and the thinking at the moment is that the thieves just walked in and tried random rooms until they got lucky. It's a common method. Hotel staff think they're guests; the thieves tell the real guests they're maintenance or housekeeping so they let them in, and once they're done, they walk right out again."

"Well, if you've seen it before, you must have investigated it before too. Are there any suspects? Or informants who can help?" She thought of Mediouri.

He shook his head. "Normally I'd say yes, but—" He looked around the nearly empty café and lowered his voice even further. "The *prefecture* has just received a credible accusation of corruption against the *commissaire* here. That's what my meeting was about. I'm part of a task force that deals with these accusations."

"Oh." Rachel didn't see the connection. "What does that have to do with the investigation into Ochs's death?"

"Theoretically nothing, but in fact it could make quite a difference." He made a face. "The situation is messy. The commissaire has been very careful to make his officers like and trust him over the years, partly by letting them get away with not doing their jobs. Now he's just been suspended and a replacement put in his place. So now the commissariat is filled with a bunch of lazy resentful men with even less motivation to work than usual." He puffed out his cheeks and exhaled sharply. "We're trying to have the most important cases transferred out, but a tourist shot in the course of a hotel robbery comes fairly low down on the list, I'm sorry to say. So do Mrs. Ochs a kindness and tell her that the investigation of her husband's murder may proceed very slowly." He took a sip from his glass. "But don't tell her I told you that. In fact, don't tell anyone."

The waiter appeared at his elbow, and he straightened and smiled at him. *"L'addition, s'il vous plaît."* Once the man had slipped back into the shadows, he leaned in again. "This is not for public consumption."

"No, no, of course not." Rachel shook her head as if she understood why, and as Boussicault reached to take the bill from the waiter, he added, "Now you know why I brought you here. I didn't want to be overheard, and no policeman can afford to drink in a place like this."

* * *

"You don't want us to investigate Ochs's murder, do you?"

Rachel couldn't tell if Magda was excited or alarmed by the idea, but she said into the phone, "God, no. I just thought it was interesting to have a glimpse into the inner workings of the police. Corruption, lying, currying favor . . . you get a whole different view of things from someone on the inside."

"What are you going to tell Mrs. Ochs to explain why her husband's investigation is taking so long?"

Rachel inhaled through her teeth and sighed the air back out. "I'm thinking I won't tell her anything." When Magda stayed silent, she said quickly, "After all, Jean didn't tell me that Ochs had been murdered, which means that either she or Mrs. Ochs didn't think I should know. So I'm just going to pretend I don't. In fact, I think I'm just going to Skype Alan to let him know I picked up the suitcase." She looked at her watch; it would be six AM in Miami. "Or rather, I'll do that after I come back from meeting Madame Fauré."

After she hung up, Rachel looked at Jack Ochs's suitcase, where it stood in her foyer. What were the rules of etiquette regarding handling the belongings of a dead man you'd never met, which you'd collected on behalf of a wife you'd also never met? Should she open the suitcase so she could tell Alan what was inside and he could tell Ellen Ochs? She wasn't sure she was up to that. She might have recently told two people that she was a private detective, but she wasn't yet enough of one to feel that she could look coolly on the clothes of a dead man. And it felt shabby somehow, the idea of peering at someone's clothes without their permission. She crossed the room and rolled the case under the hall table, where it fit neatly. She'd ask Jean later how to send it back to Mrs. Ochs.

Chapter Thirteen

Rachel wasn't a fan of the northern part of the ninth arrondisse-ment. She had no particular interest in sex shops or strip clubs, and although she knew the Moulin Rouge, the chief tourist attraction of the area, which had been a bohemian centerpiece in its time, on her one trip to see it she'd found its peeling red paint and unmoving neon windmill dispiriting rather than erotic.

But Paris has a way of being many things within a small space. Le Grand Comptoir d'Anvers, only one street over from the bleached pavements and shabby deep discount clothing stores of the ninth, looked out on one side to a lush green park, and on the other faced an upmarket children's clothing bou-tique with nothing in its window priced under a hundred euros. It might have been in not just another city, but another world.

As if to make up for the previous day's rain, the sky had been brightly sunny all day, and when Rachel turned into the restaurant at two o'clock, the abrupt change from the bright outdoors to the dim interior blinded her. As she stood blinking to adjust her eyes, the outline of a woman appeared.

"Madame Levis, I'm Dolly Fauré."

Influenced by Naquet's and Thieriot's descriptions, Rachel had expected a stern matron in at least her late sixties, but the Madame Fauré who came gradually into focus was smiling warmly and only about ten years older than Rachel herself. Rachel recognized the brown silk shirt she wore as part of Sauveterre's winter 2012 collection; she had paired it with faded jeans and burgundy ballerina flats the same color as her lipstick. With her brown hair pulled into a loose bun at the base of her neck and her face free of makeup, she looked relaxed and completely without guile. But her blue eyes flashed over Rachel from head to foot, assessing her in one quick glance.

"A pleasure to meet you." Her voice was warm, her hand cool and firm.

"Madame Fauré. Good to meet you too."

"I found us a table." She nodded to her left, and Rachel saw a coat and burgundy leather bag resting on the top of a table tucked just behind the door. "And please, call me Dolly."

Once Rachel had settled, they ordered two glasses of red wine.

"You have an unusual name," she said when the waiter had gone.

Dolly looked rueful. "My parents were both music lovers, and they knew the composer Gabriel Fauré composed a piano duet called the *Dolly Suite*. When they had a daughter, the temptation was too much to resist. I comfort myself with the knowledge that at least I have it better than my brother. Him they named Giacomo Puccini Fauré."

When Rachel finished laughing, Dolly sat back in her chair and folded her arms. The small talk was plainly over. "So. I made a *recherche google*, and I found only your poetry collections. I recognized you from your author photo. But your detective business doesn't seem to have an online presence yet." She raised her eyebrows.

Rachel began to see why Naquet and Thieriot, each a bluffer in his own way, had disliked her. Her tone said she that would take no nonsense and that she could spot nonsense a mile away. So Rachel told her the truth. She explained about the previous two cases she and Magda had worked on, the decision to try to become private investigators and the long road involved, her initial suspicions about Guipure's death, the awkward visit to Sauveterre, and the interviews with Naquet and Thieriot. She didn't know how she managed to reduce it to a short speech, but by the time their wine arrived, Dolly was all caught up.

"So, in a way, you're racing the police," she said after she'd taken her first sip. "Well, it sounds like you were ahead of them when you talked to Naquet and Cyrille, and now you're ahead of them when it comes to talking to me. They've arranged to speak to me tomorrow." She tapped her nails against the stem of her glass. "I always like to back a front runner. And I read some of your poems and liked them, which inclines me to like you too. Why don't you ask your questions, and I'll tell you what I can."

No one had ever used literary taste as a reason to cooperate with Rachel before, but she wasn't going to question it, especially since it was in her favor. "Well, to start with, what was it like working at Sauveterre? It would help to know who might have had a grudge against Guipure or a reason to hate him."

The other woman looked amused. "In fashion, no one needs a reason to hate anyone. It's a very small world full of people with very big egos, which is a recipe for resentment and cruelty." She shook her head. "But I never saw any of that at Maison Sauveterre. In fact, I don't think Monsieur Guipure had any ego at all outside the clothes."

"How do you mean?"

Dolly took another sip, letting it rest in her mouth before she swallowed and spoke. "I've worked in design houses my whole career, and he was the most focused creative director I ever saw. When he was working on a collection, there was nothing else for him. Then, once that was done, he would rest for perhaps two weeks, and it was on to the next production. There are people, you know, who have determination like a laser. They must make what they see in their head a reality. He was one of those. I always thought that was the attraction of the heroin: it helped him not to focus."

Rachel had been thinking something similar since she and Magda had heard Thieriot describe Roland's addiction. Perfectionism could be as much a matter of habit as anything else, and she'd been wondering if heroin had been Guipure's way of forcing himself to break that habit—only, of course, to find it replaced by a much more pernicious one.

"Do you think he worked so hard because he was a genius," she asked now, "or did he need to work that hard to produce something that looked like genius?"

Dolly considered. "Everyone at the company certainly thought he was a genius. And the *maison* was structured to cater to his creative work. The business side, for example, was almost completely separated from the creative. Antoinette would communicate through her assistant, and sometimes come for meetings about matters that required both of them, but there were no casual encounters, no melding of the two sides, at least during work hours. Antoinette and Gabrielle dealt with everything practical and left Monsieur Guipure to create."

This description fit with what Naquet had said. "Like an absent-minded professor." Rachel smiled at the image.

But Dolly's face was grave. "Or a prince in a tower, walled off from the outside world. I'm not sure such separation was ideal for either side. I confess, when I read that the police were treating his death as murder, I was surprised. If you'd asked me to predict which one of them would've been murdered, I'd have said Antoinette. She was the one who risked more."

Rachel was taken aback. "How so?"

"Oh . . ." Dolly leaned her head on the wall behind her, so that her hair made the blackboard say the restaurant offered "whiskies and c ails" and turned her cheek to touch the window's long curtain for a moment. Then she sat up again. "Although they both had very clear ideas about how things should be done, Roland could do those things alone or with a very small group of people who were totally loyal. Whereas Antoinette had to work with suppliers and bankers, deal with all the legal issues. Which is where people make enemies."

Something in Rachel's face must have asked for more, because she expanded. "Look at Maison Sauveterre's headquarters. Both of them dreamed of owning that building again—they'd spent time in it as children; it was a symbol of their family for them. You know about their grandfather's dealings during the war, of course." Rachel nodded. "So they both also understood that it would be wonderful for business to be based in the same building where their grandfather had actually *bought* the Jewish art." Rachel thought of the framed receipt on the wall of the landing outside the business offices. "But Antoinette handled the actual purchase of the building. She arranged the mortgage, the surveys, the negotiating. She had to deal with the other potential buyers; she oversaw the renovations . . . Such things require hardness, build resentments. I know she found that difficult sometimes—I heard them argue about it once or twice."

Again Rachel's ears pricked up. "Did they argue a lot?"

"They were business partners and brother and sister. What do you think?" Rachel acknowledged the point. "But nothing out of the ordinary, I would say. She was angry at him sometimes, but she loved him."

It seemed to Rachel that love didn't stop you from murdering someone. If anything, it was often a motivating factor. She kept that thought to herself, though.

"I went with her to identify his body," Dolly said abruptly. "Their parents are dead; there are no other siblings—I think she asked me to come because she thought that after her, I was closest to him." She closed her eyes. "It was terrible. I'll never forget the noise she made. She cried like an animal, for hours. It was only after I finally persuaded her to take a sleeping pill that I was able to slip out."

"Did you hear from her afterward?"

"Not until the Monday. She came in as usual. She said there was just too much to do for her to stay home. But she looked like a ghost."

What must it be like to go to a police station and identify your dead twin? Rachel, an only child, found she could not imagine it—she didn't even know how to start imagining it. Instead, she focused on trying to examine logically what she'd just heard.

Two equally driven people—Antoinette had come to work two *days* after her brother's death—leading a company that prided itself on loyalty and dedication. One of these people, by Dolly's description, might invite resentment and anger (she thought of Naquet's face when he described Antoinette's lack of communication with him and the brisk severance letter that followed it) and thus might make a plausible victim. But the actual victim seemed only to have inspired protectiveness, at least in those who were close to him before his death—well, protectiveness and exploitation. And, she reminded herself, he had recently been bringing money and critical praise to his company.

She exhaled, an irritated little puff. The case would make a lot more sense if Antoinette *had* been the victim. But fine: if asking about Guipure wasn't turning up anything useful, maybe she should try the two suspects.

"May I ask you some questions about Gédéon Naquet and Cyrille Thieriot?" Dolly nodded. "Thanks. Let's start with Thieriot. What were your impressions of him?"

Dolly thought for a minute. "If you work in fashion for even a short time, you come to recognize Cyrille's type. He was a person who was exceptional at nothing except overvaluing himself." She shrugged. "He thought he deserved the best, but really he was just a leech."

Another echo of Naquet. But Rachel didn't say anything, and Dolly continued. "And when he met Monsieur Guipure, he found an ideal person to leech off. Monsieur Guipure already . . . wasn't well, and Thieriot took advantage of that. He was always persuading Monsieur Guipure to take him out, and always to places where they could spend a lot of money and be seen together. He said Monsieur Guipure worked too hard, but his answer to that always involved buying things, or staying in expensive places, or giving parties where all his so-called friends could see how well he'd done for himself." She kissed her teeth. "And he was absolutely responsible for the growth of Monsieur Guipure's habit. Within two or three months after they met, Monsieur Guipure was a hardcore addict."

"He told us he had a plan to get Guipure off heroin."

She scoffed. "If that plan involved buying it for him in large quantities, sure." Then she closed her eyes, pulled in a long breath and exhaled it. "No, let me try to be fair. When it came to the heroin, Monsieur Guipure was using Thieriot too. He knew that having him make the buys meant less likelihood of being caught, and made it harder for anyone to realize how much he was taking. But if buying is easier, you buy more. And there was no reason for Thieriot to try to stop him because being the middleman meant that he could skim money off the top, and it made Monsieur Guipure more dependent on him."

"He claims that buying was an easy way to control the amount he was taking."

"Lies." Dolly's voice was clear and firm. "He bought him heroin because it was to his advantage." Again she sighed, then passed a hand over her forehead and tucked a loose strand of hair behind an ear. "I'm making him sound like some sort of Machiavelli, and he's not. He isn't intelligent enough. But he knew which side of his bread had the jam. He knew that a clean Monsieur Guipure would need him less." She met Rachel's eyes. "As proved to be the case."

Rachel nodded. "As proved to be the case. But can you tell me what happened between them when Guipure came back from Eirini? He told us a story of undying love and a conspiracy to keep them apart, but I have my doubts."

"Very wise. However—" Dolly looked uncomfortable. "I said Monsieur Guipure didn't have many dealings with the outside world, and he didn't. But because of that, he didn't have very much experience with problems either. Antoinette took care of all his problems for him, so he didn't really know how to deal with the ones he couldn't avoid."

Rachel raised her eyebrows. "Like ending relationships?"

Dolly nodded. "Like ending relationships. For him the solution that removed a problem most quickly and completely was the right one. And after he came back from Eirini, the quickest and most complete solution to the problem of Thieriot was simply to cut him off. He told me to delete any messages from him—I sorted Monsieur Guipure's e-mails—and not to put through any calls from him."

"Thieriot said he contacted your office several times trying to reach Roland after that. Is that true?" Dolly nodded again. "And how did he seem?"

"Like a tramp locked out of his usual hostel." After a second, she elaborated. "First he telephoned the office over and over, insisting there must be some mistake. Then he sent an e-mail to me and Antoinette, in which he accused the two of us of working to keep him and Monsieur Guipure apart. The whole time he was also calling and texting Monsieur Guipure's old *portable*—I know because I had it in my desk, waiting to be recycled. Finally he telephoned the office again and pleaded with me to let him speak to Roland just once, just for one moment. He was sure if Roland heard his voice, he'd want to see him. But Monsieur Guipure insisted that he didn't want to hear from him at all, under any circumstances, ever."

"And Thieriot gave up?"

"Eventually." She looked unhappy. "But I can't lie: I thought Monsieur Guipure behaved badly. I didn't like Thieriot, but he had made Monsieur Guipure happy, at least for a while. He deserved better than the treatment he got. But I always thought . . . you know, he found one meal ticket, and he's still young. He could find another."

Rachel looked out of the restaurant's long window. The leaves on the trees in the square were dark against the sunshine, and as she watched a tiny boy in an impeccably cut miniature corduroy blazer and little dark trousers guided a scooter along the white pavement. She thought of Cyrille spending the next few years of his life looking for men who might keep him, then all the time after that when he would be too old to be kept. Still, his future was her concern only insofar as it might involve a jail cell. She drew herself back into the restaurant and to the matter at hand.

"And what about Naquet? What was your impression of him?"

"Oh, him." Dolly rolled her eyes. "He was just a mosquito. He was Antoinette's idea. His publisher approached us about his biography, and Antoinette thought if we timed it right, it could coincide with the announcement of the licensing agreement. Of course, it would be a rush job, but it would be in every store window right after we announced."

"But Naquet started in 2014. The licensing agreement didn't happen until this March."

She frowned. "Oh. Yes. Yes, that's right. I was confused. Probably because the biography was called off at the same time that the original agreement stalled. Now I remember: Gabrielle told me he'd been sent a check to compensate him for his time."

"According to him, he's thinking of getting the book restarted, only in a more serious vein. A 'respectful summation,' he called it."

"Oh, he did, did he?" Dolly laughed. "You know, I vetted him when his publisher approached us. His editor at his previous publishing house told me that as soon as it was clear the Ann Pingeot biography wasn't going to get noticed, Naquet approached him about writing a celebrity biography. Not a particular celebrity. He had a list of possible subjects, and he told the editor he could have a biography of any one of them ready in six months. The editor just needed to tell him which he thought would sell the most." She gave a thin smile. "He doesn't want to be a serious author; he wants to be a rich author."

Rachel smiled. "Thieriot said something similar."

"*Ah, bon?* Maybe he's smarter than I gave him credit for. Or maybe like recognizes like."

It was Rachel's turn to laugh. "If you don't mind my asking, Dolly, what happened between you and Sauveterre? Until

Naquet and Thieriot mentioned you I had no idea Guipure had *had* an assistant. But it sounds as if you worked for him for years. What made you leave?"

"Oh, they fired me." She waved away Rachel's surprise. "It's standard practice. They'll appoint a new creative director at some point, and he'll bring in his own assistant. And in the meantime, I was given a healthy *indemnité de licenciement*. I have no complaints."

* * *

"So he and Antoinette argued." Over the telephone line, Magda's tone was speculative.

"But it sounds as if they were reasonable arguments. Plus, to put it at its most brutal, wasn't Antoinette better off with him alive? There's no business without him."

"Well,' Magda said practically, "Dolly did say they would hire a new creative director."

"Yeah, but how long is that search going to take? And given that Guipure was so closely associated with Sauveterre, how wise would it be to get rid of him unless Antoinette absolutely had to? They created a season's looks out of designs he made while he was in rehab, for God's sake—that gives you an idea of how dependent they were on him. So Antoinette's hardly going to off him out of irritation over unfair division of duties."

"I'm not saying it was that simple."

"I know you're not. To be honest I wondered the same thing until . . . you should have heard her describe Antoinette's reaction to seeing his body." She repeated what Dolly had said.

"A good actress could fake that."

"Again I'd agree with you if not for the crying. You can't fake tears without people noticing, and you can't conjure them out of nowhere."

Magda's silence indicated that she wanted to argue but couldn't. Rachel generously changed the subject. "How are things going in the Cyrille search?"

It turned out that Magda had overestimated her skills— "although only a little." She had found a number of Cyrille Thieriots online, but without their Cyrille Thieriot's birth date or identification number, she had been unable to determine which of them was him, never mind anything beyond that. Amazon had just delivered a book she thought would help, though. "So call me again tomorrow afternoon. I should have more for us by then."

Chapter Fourteen

At eleven the next morning, Magda texted her.

Meet me at Temple station.

Outside the Temple mètro station the news kiosk showed Rachel that the gossip magazines had moved on from Roland Guipure. Some reality star was engaged; some footballer was divorcing. The bright sunshine almost balanced out the chilly air, and passing pedestrians had opened their coats and let their scarves trail unwound from their lapels. Only a few elderly men and women kept their overcoats closed to the neck and bundled themselves up—they had been around long enough to know that Paris weather will fool you if you give it a chance.

For some reason Magda had decided that a skinny wooden bench set close to the curb was the perfect venue for their meeting. Whether this was because the only obvious choice of restaurant was an establishment called O'Tacos or because she was tired of hunching indoors to talk about murder, Rachel neither knew nor cared. It was pleasant to be able to sit outside in the sun and not talk in low murmurs, even if it did mean an occasional noseful of diesel fumes.

Magda pulled out her neatly labeled folder once again. She waited for a passerby to move on before she spoke.

"So I hacked into the employment records at Bespoke, the restaurant where Thieriot used to work."

"You *what*? How?"

"Oh, well . . ." Her tone was casual, but a tiny smile twitched at her lips. "Once I read the book it wasn't really very hard. It said that if you can get into a restaurant's reservation system, you can get into everything else. So I made a reservation and then just followed the book's instructions. And that's how I found Thieriot's tax number, and that's how I was able to track his employment history, and that's how I found out that Cyrille Thieriot works at the *LaLa Lounge*."

"You're *kidding.*"

"I am not. I thought it was odd when I asked him where he worked and he just said, 'I've gone back to the hospitality industry.' Now we see why."

"And was he working the night of Guipure's party?"

Now the twitching became a full-blown smile. Magda pulled a printed screenshot out of the folder and handed it to Rachel. It was the schedule for the week of April 11, and on Thursday the fourteenth, the day of Guipure's party, Thieriot's name appeared with some others in the rectangle for each hour between 20:00 and 23:00, and then through 03:00 the next day.

"This," Magda continued after a pause, "is why we're meeting here. We're going to see who's available to talk to at the LaLa Lounge."

Like most people who live in a large city, Rachel knew every street and alleyway of the part in which she lived, but had only a hazy outline of most of the rest. "Where is it?"

The Rue Nôtre Dame de Nazareth angled off the Rue du Temple. There was a branch of the CIC bank at the top of the street and a discreet synagogue midway down, but otherwise it was crowded with the mixture of boutiques, cafés, and store-fronts with "To rent" signs that seemed to characterize every side street in Paris. The LaLa Lounge was at the end of the first block, next to a nail bar and across from a shop selling counter-feit designer clothing—which had a version of one of Sauvet-erre's dresses in its window, Rachel noticed.

"I know the papers said it's a known drug area, but it doesn't seem like the kind of place where someone would overdose, does it? The street's not very wide, there really isn't anywhere to hide, and now that people have to come outside to smoke, you'd think someone would have noticed him."

The entrance to the club, however, was certainly designed to be unnoticed. It was a black recess in a black wall with no sign or number to identify it, the only indication of its exis-tence a copy of its liquor license propped in an otherwise blacked-out window. *Complete discretion guarantees complete exclusivity,* Rachel thought.

She mounted the three steps to the door. There was no buzzer, so she knocked. Then she pounded. Then, while she rubbed the side of her hand, Magda pounded. At last there came the sound of locks turning, and the door opened just wide enough to reveal a man standing on the other side. He had the stocky build of a boxer gone to seed, and, under narrowed eyes, his cheeks and chin were pricked all over with black and gray stubble. He was chewing what appeared to be a mouthful of egg salad.

"Go away," he said.

"I'm sorry to disturb you, but we're—"

"I don't care who you are. Go away."

"If we could just—"

"No." He swallowed. The hand that held the black metal door ajar tightened. "The police have already been here, which means you're either press or just death gawkers, and I've had enough of both. So get going."

The door swung closed, but before it could shut Magda stuck her foot in it. "We're not press, and we're not gawkers. We're detectives, and we want to talk to you about one of your employees."

The man didn't open the door, but he peered around it. "Which one?"

"Cyrille Thieriot."

"Thieriot! That *emmerdeur*! What's he done now?"

Magda gave the classic detective's response. "What makes you think he's done anything?"

"Because he lives to make other people's lives difficult. As he demonstrated right before I fired his ass, which is why I did fire his ass."

"What did he do?"

"What am I, the front page of *Le Figaro*?" But he opened the door a little wider. "Look, I'm going to tell you this, and then I'm going shut the door and not open it again. Thieriot spent all his time here telling anyone who would listen that he used to be Roland Guipure's *compagnon*, so when Guipure's company rented this place for his party, I had a little fun by putting Thieriot down to work. I figured he was lying, and I wanted to see his reaction. Well, his reaction was to disappear during the party and not come back. I had to get behind the bar myself! And when I play the security footage afterward, what do I see but him following Guipure into the men's room and then come rushing out two minutes later, heading straight out the back door. Staff are not supposed to interact with customers, and they sure as hell aren't supposed to bring their personal dramas into my club. So when he showed up for his next shift, I gave him the boot, and I don't know or care anything else about him."

Then, true to his word, he pulled the door back to slam it. But Rachel put her hand on it.

"Wait. Please. Could you just tell me if you saw this man at the party?" She held up her *portable*, where she had used the search engine to find Naquet's author photo.

The man tried to close the door, but she braced her arm with all her weight. After a few seconds of unresolved back-and-forth exertion he gave up and leaned forward, squinting at the screen.

"Who the fuck is that?"

"He's a writer. I just . . . Imagine him older, and with less hair."

The man squinted harder, with his head slightly tilted. "Okay, maybe. I think so. I might've seen him a couple of times in the course of the night. I mean, he wasn't taking notes or anything, so I can't be sure it was him." He laughed uproariously.

"And did you see—" But in her excitement Rachel had relaxed her pressure on the door. He slammed it shut.

"What was that about?"

Rachel relayed what Dolly had told her about Naquet's book. "And I just thought, if Naquet was desperate to talk to Roland, he might try to sneak into a party where he knew Guipure would be."

Magda made a face. "Seems like a lot of work. All Thieriot had to do was follow him into the men's room. And then he rushed right out the door afterward."

"Thereby drawing attention to himself as all cunning murderers do?" Rachel shook her head. "He showed up for his next shift, which doesn't really indicate guilt."

"Or it indicates that he's guilty but smart enough to cover it up."

Rachel thought of Dolly first saying Thieriot wasn't smart enough to be a Machiavelli and then saying he might be smarter than she thought. He might be. But even if he was, murder wasn't the most logical motivation for following an ex-lover into the bathroom. "He could've been trying to patch things up so he could get back on his gravy train."

"I could say the same of Naquet. And Thieriot was the go-between for Guipure and his dealer, so we know he knew where to get heroin."

"I think a celebrity biographer knows where to buy drugs."

"Ah, you *think*. But you don't know. But that's what it really comes down to, isn't it? Not who had the best motive or was in the best place, but who had the heroin. If we know that, we know our murderer."

Rachel looked down at the pavement, made up of the same gray stone rectangles that lined the Rue Vieille du Temple, the Place Saint German des Prés, the Rue St. Paul. In her mind's eye she saw a cup, filled with hot minty tea; a plate glass window that offered a full view out onto the street and in from it. She saw a business card that at that moment lay somewhere in her bag, its edges becoming increasingly frayed and its glossy black surface turning dull from scuffs and scratches. She took a deep breath, then sighed it out. "Matthieu Mediouri can help us with that."

Chapter Fifteen

Once he was done laughing with surprise and exclaiming in disbelief, Mediouri said yes, he could find out what they wanted to know. But it wouldn't be quick. He would need to contact some former friends, and those friends might need to contact some people themselves. The process couldn't be rushed, and he couldn't promise a result. Rachel should wait for him to contact her.

"Don't tell Alan," she said to Magda the next day.

"So far there's nothing to tell."

Two weeks earlier, it had been cold enough to wear a winter coat; four days earlier, spring had been near enough for that coat to be worn open; today, on the morning of the second of May, it was warm enough for a man to sit outside in only his blazer and smoke a cigarette. Rachel knew this was the case because that was precisely what Gédéon Naquet was doing when she and Magda arrived at Les Deux Magots. He sat beneath the restaurant's green and white awning at a table near the door, his chair angled so that he could keep an eye on the computer Rachel could see through the window behind him.

"We want to catch him off guard," she had said when Magda suggested they contact Naquet to arrange a second meeting, so she was gratified by his start of surprise when he realized who was standing in front of him. But he recovered quickly, half rising with a smile and inviting them to join him.

"Monsieur Naquet." Rachel scraped her chair as she sat down. "We're here because we spoke to the owner of the LaLa Lounge." Had it been the owner? Well, Naquet would never know if it had or hadn't been. "I showed him your author photo, and he told us that you were at Guipure's birthday party." She cut him off as he opened his mouth. "Not outside, but inside the club itself."

Naquet was a quick thinker. "What is a pair of filmmakers doing questioning the owner of the LaLa Lounge?"

But Magda was a quicker thinker. "It was the scene of Guipure's death. Of course we were going to go there as part of our research."

Outfoxed, Naquet put down his cigarette and crossed his arms. "Yes, I was at the party, but so what? Roland invited me. I forgot: he did call, after the collection showed. He suggested I come to the party."

Magda raised her eyebrows.

"He did," Naquet said sulkily. "He said we could talk there."

Magda folded her hands on the tabletop, leaning forward and looking him in the eye. Her lips made the shape of a smile. "Monsieur Naquet, let me explain. Rachel and I are trying to be filmmakers. We thought the story of Roland Guipure's life would make a wonderful documentary. Then the police said Roland had been murdered, and we thought the story of his life *and* death would make a wonderful documentary. But then we did some research, and in the course of that research we found out that you were at the party where Guipure was murdered, even though you told us you hadn't had any contact with anyone at Sauveterre since Guipure went into rehab. And now you are claiming, in a very unconvincing tone, that you forgot that Guipure *had* contacted you after all and invited you to that party—that you forgot you were there on the night of his death. I think you can see why we might feel that *your* story would make an even better documentary."

While she had been reading *Knight's Forensic Pathology* and taking Approach to Agency Marketing online, had Magda been taking Approach to Interview Techniques? Rachel felt her own throat go dry, and Naquet drew on his cigarette so hard that she expected to see it burn up to the filter. He stamped it out, then lit a new one with a shaking hand.

"I can see why you'd think that," he said at last, "but you'd be wrong. All right, Roland didn't contact me. But I meant what I said about thinking there was a great book in his recovery. And I thought—I thought if I could just talk to him, I could make him see it that way. But *Madame* Fauré would never put me through, and he never answered my e-mails. Then I read on *Quelles Nouvelles* that he was holding a big party for his fortieth at the LaLa Lounge the next night, and I—" A flush crept up his face. "I waited outside and asked someone going in if I could be her plus one. I—I gave her fifty euros to do it."

"And?"

Naquet snorted "And much good it did me. There must have been two hundred people in the place. The only time I even *saw*

Roland was once when I spotted him hugging his sister, and that wasn't until around two in the morning. Then he vanished again. I waited another hour, then went home. The next day I got an alert telling me he'd died outside the club." He pulled on the new cigarette and exhaled. "I suppose I must have walked by him on my way home and thought he was a *clochard*."

He said this not with pity or even disgust, but rather in the tone of a man trying to figure out how he might develop that detail into a marketable story. Rachel felt a strong desire to be out of his company.

Magda must have felt something similar, for they stood up at the same time.

*　*　*

"What do you make of his story?" The sun had begun to shine as they walked back down the Boulevard Saint Germain. Rachel noticed that the Deux Magot's curious little outdoor island—a covered dining area walled in by shrubbery and set in the middle of the Place Saint Germain des Prés—was entirely filled, and when she looked at her watch, she was surprised to see that it was lunchtime. The smell of butter from the crêpe kiosk a few meters away banished the memory of Naquet's cigarette smoke from her nostrils, and the attention she'd need to weave in and out of the hungry pedestrians hurrying to find a place to eat distracted her from the disgust she'd felt in his company. Still, she waited until they were close to the *Sèvres portique*, the extraordinary ceramic archway created to showcase the skills of the Sevres porcelain company for the 1900 World's Fair, before she replied. She had forgotten the *portique* in her gloomy assessment of the Boulevard Saint Germain after their first meeting with Naquet, and as they drew closer, its art nouveau beauty, combined with the green scent of the garden next to the Église Saint Germain, restored her to rationality before she replied.

"It could be true. He certainly seemed to legitimately believe that he could have convinced Guipure to work with him."

"And to be legitimately angry that he didn't get the chance to ask him."

"On the other hand, if you were a murderer, you'd probably work hard to be seen as legitimately something else."

By this time they had turned onto the Rue de Seine. Rachel paused in front of the glossy blue front of an antique bookshop, where the window displayed a medieval manuscript open to an illuminated picture of Romulus fighting Remus. The tips of their swords had been gilded, and behind them the hills of Rome were a wash of verdant green. Why did art always depict murder so elegantly? There was never any of the confusion or grotesqueness of the real-life act, just an obvious murderer tidily and simply killing an obvious victim.

"What are you thinking?"

"Oh, just aimless thoughts about death." She took Magda's arm and continued down to where the Rue de Seine became the Rue de Tournon. This turned right into the Rue de Vaugirard, which eventually led to Rachel's own street. At least geography offered direct routes to the goal.

Chapter Sixteen

The next few days passed slowly. Rachel scoured the newspapers and websites, but there were no mentions of breakthroughs in the Guipure investigation. She briefly reconsidered telephoning Capitaine Boussicault to see if she could worm anything out of him, but again decided against it. His final remark in the restaurant rankled. So she tried to occupy her mind by walking in the Jardin du Luxembourg. The benches started to fill with workers on their lunch breaks and young mothers taking a rest from guiding *poussettes*; the kissing couple that seemed to be required scenery in every Parisian park changed their winter coats for spring jackets, but to Rachel it all merely showed that the world was moving on from Guipure's murder. The food kiosks took down their shutters and began serving again, but she ate her favorite mango gelato wanly, thinking of Cyrille Thieriot, former waiter and possible murderer.

This was the problem with the reality of detecting, Rachel thought: it wasn't very speedy and it wasn't very cool. No teenager was going to mutter "Sick!" when you described how you'd found your murderer by using shoe leather and good old-fashioned interview techniques, or when you finished your story about contacting a former drug dealer for information by admitting that you had to wait by the phone for him to call you back. And while age forty-six might seem (to her) embarrassingly advanced in life still to be worrying about being cool, it was (also to her) not.

In a belated attempt to be at least a little more state of the art, on Wednesday night she set up her phone for news alerts. As her key words she selected *Roland Guipure, Sauveterre*, and—after some thought—*Gédéon Naquet* and *Cyrille Thieriot*. Let the pings ring out! Even if the only teenager around to be impressed was the one who still lived inside her.

It should have been cheering, then, that the next two days passed in a symphony of pings. But Rachel had reckoned without technology's lack of discernment. Her phone notified her that Sauveterre items would be included in the spring sales at all three of the most expensive department stores in Paris; it told her that Naquet's biography of Johnny Halliday was included in Amazon.fr's €1.99 Kindle book offer; it informed her that Manhattan's Fashion Institute of Technology would hold a retrospective exhibition of the designs of Roland Guipure. Her mood wasn't improved by the fact that, having managed to set the alerts up, she had forgotten how to turn them off.

Her only useful digital communication arrived by e-mail on the next Thursday afternoon: the announcement of Guipure's memorial service. To the extent that she had remembered Antoinette's promise, Rachel had been anticipating an actual invitation, something involving heavy cardstock and a thick black border, but she supposed the times were changing even for funerals. The e-mail simply said that the memorial service would be held in the Église Saint Roch at eleven am on Sunday, May 15, with a reception to follow at Restaurant Le Taillevent. Those needing further information or assistance should contact Gabrielle Aubert, whose contact information was at the bottom of the e-mail. Rachel forwarded the message to Magda.

On Friday afternoon, just as she reached the final chapter of Vidocq's memoirs, her phone pinged yet again. With a mixture of hope and anticipatory disappointment, she picked it up from the coffee table and woke the screen.

Sauveterre Names New Head

The fashion house Sauveterre announced today that Head Pattern Cutter Keteb Lellouch will succeed Roland Guipure as Creative Director. "Keteb has been with Sauveterre from the early years," said CEO Antoinette Guipure. "He's thus perfectly placed to continue our tradition of excellence and innovation grounded in love of the female form."

Sauveterre's licensing arrangement with Chieko, Ltd., of Japan, is unaffected by the new appointment.

Well, that was to be expected. He knew the business from the inside; he'd probably been trained in its ways by Guipure himself. And promoting from within would reduce the risks to the company. She thought of Dolly's remark about the egos and narcissism of fashion designers—Sauveterre would undoubtedly benefit from avoiding that not once but twice.

A quarter of an hour later the *portable* chimed again, this time not a ping, but an actual ring. It would be Magda, of course, calling to inform her of this latest development.

But she didn't recognize the number on the screen, and when she accepted the call, the voice that spoke was Dolly Fauré's.

"Rachel, I'm sorry if I surprised you. I retrieved your number from my landline, but I'm calling you from my *portable*. I don't know if you saw, but Sauveterre just announced that Keteb Lellouch will be their new creative director."

"Yes, I saw."

The line went quiet; then an inhalation rasped through. "Are you free to speak? Could we meet at the Starbucks near Le Grand Comptoir, on the Boulevard de Rochechouart?"

*   *   *

Rachel liked the Starbucks on the Boulevard de Rochechouart very much. All glass and warm lighting, it was a serene pause in the middle of a busy city intersection. But Dolly, shifting from foot to foot outside the entrance when she arrived, was clearly in no mood for calm. She suggested they get their order to take away.

Today Dolly was wearing a sanded black silk blouse over black silk jeans (both Sauveterre 2012, Rachel recognized) that covered the tops of a pair of shiny leather ankle boots. Rachel, who had dressed in a hurry after Dolly's phone call, chose not to compare their outfits, although, since she was wearing a white shirt with blue jeans, she would at least win on brightness. Dolly's only concession to color was her red lipstick, and Rachel wasn't surprised when she ordered a black coffee. She was surprised, though, when instead of turning back toward her home arrondissement, the ninth, Dolly led Rachel down the busy boulevard and deeper into the urban sprawl of the eighteenth.

Whereas turning off onto the Rue Lepic would have led them up into the maze of winding lanes and stucco houses for which Montmartre was known—and which seemed to Rachel an excellent background for a walking conversation—Dolly firmly led the way down the Boulevard Rochechouart until it turned into the more pleasant Boulevard de Clichy. Here, as if acknowledging the improved scenery, the sun suddenly came out. It glittered the droplets on the leaves of the trees that lined the boulevard's central island, and it brightened the colors on the restaurant awnings and the advertising kiosks. Rachel saw it turn into a silver blaze the steel sculpture of an apple that decorated the intersection of Clichy and the Rue Caulaincourt.

But before they reached the sculpture, Dolly took a sharp right and led Rachel up a completely anonymous street, the chief feature of which was a huge funeral parlor with racks of decorous bouquets and potted plants outside. As they reached the far end of this mournful superstore, Rachel understood both its size and its flowers: at the end of the road a pair of gates opened off two stone pillars, one of which bore a neat brass sign that read *Cimetière du Montmartre*.

The cemetery appeared to be deserted, and Rachel began to worry just a little. She tried to remember if Dolly had said anything that, coupled with Keteb Lellouch's promotion, could somehow be incriminating. Hadn't she once read a mystery in which the murderer left the body in a cemetery? If only Dolly would say something!

Then, as they passed into the first lane of graves, she did.

"I'm sorry. I haven't been honest with you."

Rachel relaxed. She didn't think someone who was going to leave you dead on a gravestone would start by apologizing.

"As I told you," Dolly continued, "I signed an *accord de non-divulgation* when I joined Sauveterre. It's standard. The *accord* remains binding even after severance. That, too, is standard. When we last spoke, I left out some information, information that the accord covered. But now, with this announcement about Keteb . . ."

She turned and began to walk down the cobbled path.

"I understand," Rachel said. She didn't, but she knew something big was coming. She hurried a little so she was at Dolly's side.

They walked silently, for a few more seconds, until Dolly said, "I'd like to tell you what I know, but the accord presents a problem. Of course, if what I tell you isn't important, then we can forget it, and it will be as if the *accord* were never broken. But," she said, speaking more slowly, and Rachel could tell she was choosing her words, "if it is important, you would need to promise me that you would find a way to use it without . . . without . . ."

Now she did understand. Dolly was trying to see if Rachel could say she found the information some other way. "Yes, I could," she said firmly. "And I would."

They took the sharp right turn that ended the path. Dolly stopped to look at Rachel, checking her face for a moment. Then she nodded. *"Bon."*

Dolly took a deep breath. Over her shoulder, Rachel could make out the grave of the Goncourt brothers, the nineteenth-century diarists who had recorded the secrets and scandals of literary Paris. In front of the tomb of these two relentless gossips, Dolly began her story.

"*Alors.* I'm sure you remember that Gédéon Naquet had a couple of initial meetings with Monsieur Guipure two years ago, before he started his background research?"

Rachel did.

"Well, what Naquet didn't know was that at that time Monsieur Guipure was already taking heroin. He'd been using it for about two years by then."

Rachel's heart jumped. That explained the three-month stay in rehab. For an addict of a year or so, it seemed excessive, a rich man's self-indulgence. But two years of heroin use that no one noticed suggested a maintenance addiction, and that could be very hard to kick.

"He was smoking it," Dolly said. "That's how he started. Antoinette caught him in the atelier one day—it must have been in 2013—and he told her it was just an occasional thing. Whether it was or not, it didn't seem to be damaging his health, or his design skills, so she let it go." Rachel just had time to remember Naquet's remark about addiction and the bottom line before Dolly went on, "She didn't know anything about addicts—none of us did—or else we would have known where things were heading." She looked chagrined. "Which is, of course, where they went. At some point Monsieur Guipure stopped smoking and started injecting, and then at another point he got Cyrille Thieriot to do his buying for him, and things were worse still. But he kept saying he was fine, it was all fine, until the January and March 2015 shows."

"Yes. I read the reviews."

"Then you know. And that's how Antoinette persuaded him to go into *désintox*, by reading him the reviews. But by that time, given the length of the addiction, the Eirini Clinic recommended a stay of at least a month."

She tried to take a drink, but it seemed there was nothing left in her cup. Popping the plastic top off, she flattened the cardboard container in her hand, then looked around for a trash bin. There was none, so she held the cup awkwardly in one hand, top in the other, as she continued.

"You must understand. A *defilé* isn't the work of a couple of weeks or even a couple of months. It was late July by the time he agreed to go, and Spring prêt-à-porter was in October. Monsieur Guipure should have been cutting the *toiles* and booking the venue, but he'd done nothing. *Nothing.* And we had sold scarcely anything from the March show, and buyers were reporting to us that what they had taken wasn't leaving the stores. We couldn't afford to go dark for six months with those terrible clothes as everyone's last memory of Sauveterre. I mean we literally couldn't afford it. A design house is a huge business; many people depend on Sauveterre for their jobs."

She paused, and the pause became a silence. Now they were coming to it, Rachel thought.

"In August, Antoinette called me in for a meeting. When I arrived, Gabrielle was there as well. Right at the start Antoinette reminded us that we'd signed *accords*. Then she said that Eirini was recommending that Monsieur Guipure stay for at least another month, and we knew what that meant for spring prêt-à-porter." The flattened cup bent a little as Dolly tightened her grip. "Except there was a solution. She'd found some sketches Monsieur Guipure had left behind, things he'd half finished, and she'd taken them to Keteb. She'd shown them to him, and he'd agreed to work with them for the October show. He would finish the designs, fit them on the *mannequins*, curate the *defilé* . . . everything. According to her it was the ideal solution. As *Chef Modéliste* Keteb knew Monsieur Guipure's preferences and trademarks. He could use the sketches to produce true Sauveterre pieces, and since the finished looks would be based on Monsieur Guipure's original ideas, it would be perfectly correct to call them Monsieur Guipure's work."

Rachel wasn't a lawyer, but she could recognize fraud. No wonder design houses had their employees sign nondisclosure agreements! But she couldn't see why Lellouch had agreed. If he wasn't allowed to claim the finished garments, what did he gain? She said as much.

Dolly nodded. "I wondered the same. So the next time I saw him alone, I brought it up." She bit her lip. "We were friends. Well, work friends. So I told him what I knew and asked him why he'd agreed."

"And what did he say?"

"He said Antoinette had told *him* that the last season had almost ruined the business, and that she was afraid that if she announced there would be no spring shows or that we would show designs that weren't Monsieur Guipure's, it would mean the end of Sauveterre. And then he told me not to say anything to anyone, but Antoinette had confided to him that she didn't think Monsieur Guipure would be coming back. Eirini already thought he needed to stay longer, and she was afraid that even if they could cure him, the heroin might have destroyed his talent. Or if it hadn't, he wouldn't be able to manage working in fashion anymore because of all the stress and temptation. Keteb said that she had promised him that if he did this, if he created the show, as soon as the *maison* was back on secure footing, she would name him creative director."

Rachel was shocked. Had she understood right? Never mind trashy biographies and pilfered sketches: this was a motive. This was an *Agatha Christie–sized* motive! To have been promised the top spot and then have it snatched away . . .

But maybe she was wrong. Maybe she had missed something. She swallowed to wet her dry throat and said, "But Guipure did come back. And then Keteb was just left empty-handed?"

"Well, he took that risk. But, yes." Dolly's tone grew speculative. "I never knew if Antoinette had expected that all along or if she made her promise in good faith. I do know that Keteb received a huge raise after Monsieur Guipure returned. And of course he'd signed an *accord de non-divulgation,* too, so what could he do?"

What could he do? What could he do? Rachel left the path and sat down heavily on the flat slab of a tomb, covering her mouth with her hand. She needed to talk to Magda.

"It's not uncommon," Dolly said, standing over her. "In every house at least some of what goes out under the label name is the work of other people. That's why there are titles like junior designer. I suppose Keteb was just doing a form of that."

Maybe. But labels were open about the fact that some of what they produced was designed by juniors. And a junior designer wasn't promised he'd be made Creative Director if he did a good job. Rachel swallowed again.

"And Gabrielle? Did she have anything to say about this plan? Or about what happened afterward?"

"She'd signed an agreement as well. And anyway, she was in love with Monsieur Guipure. She wasn't going to object to anything that preserved his reputation or helped him once he was back."

Gabrielle had been in love with Guipure? Rachel was beginning to feel it was all too much. "I'm sorry?"

"Oh, I thought you would know. Everybody knew. She thought he was the eighth wonder of the world. Before Thieriot arrived, she was the one at his beck and call. No matter how much she had to do for Antoinette, she would drop everything to get his lunch and pick up deliveries of samples he needed. And even after Thieriot came on the scene, she would look at Monsieur Guipure in meetings and—" Dolly winced. "It's hard seeing that much love on someone's face."

"Didn't she know he was gay?"

"Does it make a difference?" Dolly pulled a face. "When has rational knowledge ever controlled romantic yearning?"

Rachel had to agree. She added Gabrielle's feelings to the list of things to tell Magda.

Chapter Seventeen

~

They arranged to meet on the steps of the Opéra Garnier, midway between the cemetery and Magda's apartment. While Rachel waited for Magda to arrive, she scrolled through the alerts on her phone. She had once been told that Friday afternoon was the worst time to release news, since it virtually guaranteed that it would be ignored until Monday, but apparently fashion didn't pay attention to the rules: her screen was filled with headlines that varied in tone from serious to breezy, depending on the source.

Keteb Lellouch Made New Creative Director at Sauveterre, Formerly Head Pattern Cutter

Sauveterre Keeps It in the (Fashion) Family: HPC Is New CD

New Head Is Old Hand: Sauveterre Names Head Pattern Cutter Creative Director

In Keteb Lellouch, Sauveterre Makes Exotic but Familiar Choice

Ten Things You Didn't Know About Keteb Lellouch, Sauveterre's New Creative Director

Lellouch? All the Deets on Sauveterre's New CD

"Hey." Magda stood over her.

"Hey."

"Do you want to go somewhere? We could walk to the Starbucks on Boulevard des Capucines." She tilted her head in that direction.

Normally Rachel would have jumped at the chance to go to this gold-swagged, ceiling-muraled extravaganza, but her stomach was still full of the tea from half an hour before. "No, let's just stay here." She glanced around. "No one can hear."

"Okay." Magda sat down, putting her bag between her knees. "So, Lellouch. You said on the phone that Antoinette promised him the top job months ago?"

"Not exactly." Rachel repeated everything Dolly had told her.

When she finished, Magda said nothing for a moment. Then, "What a business!" She barked a laugh. "This one is bribed to stay quiet about doing the other's job, then the other comes back and takes the job this one was promised. Fashion is even worse than I thought."

"Well," Rachel qualified, "Lellouch was promised the job only if Guipure didn't come back."

"With the barely hidden subtext that he wouldn't."

"I know." She looked at Magda. "It's enough to drive someone to murder, don't you think?"

But Magda didn't seem to think so. Rather than answering, she stared out over the Avenue de l'Opéra as if trying to see the Louvre at the other end. At last she said, "Four months is a long time to wait to kill someone. Guipure came back in December, and he wasn't murdered until April."

Rachel considered. "Maybe it took that long for the resentment to build. It took some time for him to stop seeing Guipure's return as just a disappointment and to start seeing it as a roadblock that needed to be overcome. And to make a plan to overcome it. That's the definition of premeditation, right?"

"Yes. But that outline also suggests that all it took was this one disappointment to turn a loyal employee into a rage-fueled murderer—Naquet said he was protective, right? And Dolly makes it sound as if he agreed to do what Antoinette asked, at least partially out of devotion to the company."

"Well, it was quite a disappointment!"

"Or, in the world of fashion, garden-variety treachery. And Dolly did say he got a big raise after Guipure's return. Not a bonus: a raise. That's long-lasting compensation."

Rachel set her jaw. She'd actually done a decent bit of real detecting, meeting a connection, extracting information. She'd spent the métro ride over imagining Magda's face when she heard the whole story, her excitement matching Rachel's own. And now . . . "Why are you trying to take my suspect away from me?"

"I'm not! It's just . . ." Magda opened up a little space between them so she could get to her bag, then reached in and took out her neatly labeled folder. "Before I left the apartment I looked him up on LinkedIn."

"LinkedIn?" This never would have occurred to Rachel.

"Sure, it's a professional networking site, and he's a professional, right? I mean, I know fashion doesn't seem like a profession, but it is."

"And what did you find?"

Magda opened the folder. "He graduated from the Institut Français de la Mode in 1993 and started an apprenticeship at Dior the same year. He was at Dior until 1996, moving up the ranks. Then in 1997 he joined a company called AuSecours—I looked it up; it was a small label that folded about five years ago. He joined them as senior pattern cutter, and according to his profile, he did a little design work for them too. In 2005, the original creative director of AuSecours left, and so did Lellouch. He joined Sauveterre as head pattern cutter. And that's it until . . . well, until what happened today."

"And 'what happened today' is his possible motive."

"Yes, it could be. But his résumé shows that he's perfectly capable of leaving a job if he's unhappy. The creative director of AuSecours retires and Lellouch leaves. That can't be a coincidence, right?" Rachel nodded wary agreement. "Presumably he didn't like the new CD, or something like that. But he didn't kill anyone; he just found another job. Which he could've been doing this time, too, in the four months since Guipure came back." She closed the folder. "Did Dolly tell you *anything* else?"

"Nothing that's relevant to this."

"That means she told you something. What?"

Rachel repeated what Dolly had told her about Gabrielle's feelings for Guipure.

"Even though he was gay?"

She repeated what Dolly had said about that too.

"She's right there." For a moment Magda looked overwhelmed by the mystery of human feelings. Then she said, "Do you think Gabrielle's feelings for him are important?"

Rachel thought. "Love is one of the most common motives for murder, but it's usually murder of a rival or murder after you've been rejected . . ."

"And in this case, Gabrielle knew from the start that her feelings were unrequited, and Thieriot is still alive," Magda finished.

Rachel generally gave more weight to emotion than Magda did, but in this case her summary would have been just as brisk. Gabrielle hadn't been cheated of Sauveterre's top position; she hadn't been cut out of Guipure's life without a word of warning. "Unless she's in cahoots with Lellouch for some reason, I don't see it either. Although it does explain why she was always ordering Guipure's lunch and collecting his deliveries. Given that she was Antoinette's assistant."

"No one ever loved someone because they acted as their lackey," Magda said. Rachel thought how true that was, and how little difference it seemed to make to human behavior.

Still, it wasn't human behavior in general they were dealing with here; it was the specific behavior of a group of people about whom they persistently knew very little, no matter how hard they tried. This was the problem that had prompted her to take Matthieu Mediouri's card all those weeks ago. They had no real sources outside the usual ones. If what they wanted to know wasn't mentioned in the press (or in this case the gossip sites) or couldn't be found on the internet, their options were very limited. Would the private detective certification program offer a course on How to Build a Network of Snitches? She wished suddenly for a hundred more Mediouris, scattered around Paris, insiders in every area, waiting to whisper their truths to her.

Absent an army of mini-Mediouris, though, in the real world as it currently existed, what did she have to work with? She bit her thumbnail again. She sucked her cheeks in and gripped them lightly with her teeth. The sky began to darken. She squinted ahead of her at nothing. Then at last she said, "Maybe the way to move forward is to work not with what we know about this case *specifically*, but with what we know about crime *generally* that we might be able to apply to this case. After all"—she held out an explaining hand—"we do have some experience."

Magda looked confused. Rachel couldn't blame her. Her idea was one of those that strikes like a lightning bolt but only becomes clear slowly. She began trying to explain, as much for herself as for Magda.

"We can safely say that crimes arise from two kinds of motives, right? Recent and what we could call long-simmering." Magda considered briefly, then nodded. "Okay. And when it comes to Lellouch we know that there's something recent that *could* be a motive, but that also could not. Guipure's return took away his chance at the top job, but a large raise can go a long way to balance out a sense of injustice."

Magda still looked confused, but she also looked interested, and she nodded slowly. Rachel stopped for a second, trying to grasp her own line of thought as it whisked through her brain, then continued. "But we don't know if there's any *long-simmering* motive that might have influenced Lellouch as well. Maybe Guipure constantly belittled him, or maybe when he was high, he said Lellouch could have the creative director position, or . . . or maybe he asked Lellouch for pins in a way that drove him crazy." Magda gave her a look. "I know, but people have killed for less. And it seems to me that while we don't have sources to tell us anything more about recent events, at least until Mediouri calls us, we do have a source that could tell us more about the past and maybe about any long-simmering resentments."

Magda frowned. "But it sounds like Dolly told you everything she knew in the cemetery. And Kiki doesn't know anyone else connected with the Sauveterre label, does she?"

Rachel shook her head. "Not Dolly or Kiki. You're right: I don't think they'll be any help to us with this." She took a deep breath. "I was thinking of Cyrille."

"Cyrille?" Magda's voice bounced off the gold-tipped gates of the Palais Garnier. The allegorical statue representing Song looked shocked behind her. "Cyrille, as in our suspect Cyrille?"

"As in *one* of our suspects, Cyrille. And not even the best one now that we know about Lellouch."

"He has just as much motive as Lellouch, if not more—spurned love and the pretty penny he could make from selling those sketches once Guipure was dead!"

"We don't know how much he could make," Rachel said warningly.

"Well, we know he's the only person we *know* had contact with Guipure at the party. And who left the club at a run after he'd had contact!" Magda shook her head in disbelief. "What makes you think he'll be a reliable source for information about another suspect? Why wouldn't he just lie to steer us away from him?"

"He could," Rachel acknowledged. "But if we ask him about events that occurred before Guipure went into rehab, I don't think he'll have any reason to be worried enough to lie. Also," she said, making a rueful face, "he's not that bright. And he's a lousy liar. When he tried to fool us about his motivation for buying Guipure's heroin or why he was in a relationship with him, all he did was make it plain that he was trying to fool us. I'm pretty sure we'll see through him if he lies."

Magda thought. The sky grew darker still; Rachel sucked the insides of her cheeks.

At last Magda said reluctantly, "Okay. But can we please meet him somewhere outside that tiny apartment? Another visit there and I'm going to end up claustrophobic."

Rachel grinned. "As far as I'm concerned, we can meet him on a football field."

Chapter Eighteen

～

Thieriot was just as eager to meet with the film directors a second time. Ever since their first encounter, he'd been thinking of memories he'd forgotten to tell them, incidents he knew they'd be interested in. He was interviewing for jobs at the moment, but he happened to have the next morning free. In fact, no sooner had Rachel broached the possibility than he made a suggestion. How about the Bar du Marché des Blancs Manteaux, just a few doors down from his building? It served a very fine coffee.

"The Marais is odd," Magda said as they walked to the restaurant the next day.

"I thought it was your favorite part of the city."

"It is. But it's still odd. Look." She pointed at the rainbow-painted crosswalk beneath their feet, then across the road, at a shop sign in Hebrew. "Gay pride and strict Judaism don't seem like they'd naturally coexist. I mean it's not like the Old Testament approves of homosexuality."

"I think it had more to do with a gap than a link," Rachel said. She was slightly distracted by keeping an eye out for the restaurant. "After the war, the Marais wasn't a traditional

Jewish area anymore—there weren't any Jews in Paris to live here. And although some came back"—she nodded toward a bearded man in a long black coat, turning a corner ahead of them, his prayer curl tucked behind his ear as he talked on his *portable*—"there was space for other populations too. Anyway," she said briskly, "Judaism is as much a culture as it is a religion, so it's not monolithic. It depends on the Jew." She checked shopfronts as they passed and quoted idly, "'I am distressed for you, my brother Jonathan. Your love to me was wonderful, passing the love of women.' That's from the Old Testament. Ah, here we are."

She stopped in front of a red awning.

The mornings were still a little too cool for restaurants to fold back their doors and extend outward, so at nine thirty the pavement outside the Bar du Marché des Blancs Manteaux was bare. It shone where puddles left by the street sprayer had yet to evaporate, and tables and chairs were neatly piled in a corner in anticipation of warmer days. Inside, the place was nearly deserted. At a table deep in its dim recesses, a young woman sat reading a book and nursing a coffee, occasionally turning a page before returning her hand to the side of her warm cup. A bearded young man with a tattoo of a lizard on his left forearm stood behind the bar, wiping glasses. At a narrow table across from him, facing the framed mirror that hung opposite the bar, sat Thieriot.

Today he had given the outer corners of his eyes a double cat-eye flick in black, with the lids themselves painted gold and rimmed in orange-red. At the inner corners he had pasted silvery glitter, and his lips, surrounded by a light dusting of stubble, had been colored damson. His cheeks were rosy pink, and he'd drawn a mole high on one cheekbone. He looked as if he should have a spotlight shining down on him, and because this was Paris neither of the other people in the place gave him a second glance.

He stood and kissed Rachel and Magda as though they were old friends, twice on each cheek and then once more for good measure. He would *adore* another coffee, thank you—*"et aussi un pain au chocolat, s'il vous plait."* As they waited at the bar, in the mirror behind it they saw him examine his reflection and lean in to smooth an imperceptible flaw, but by the time they brought the drinks and the croissant back, he was sitting again, as still and perfect as Dorian Gray's portrait before the bad deeds began.

As Magda put her *portable* on the table between them and set it to record, Rachel considered Thieriot over the rim of her cup of hot chocolate. Something about him felt more tightly coiled than it had a week ago—not exactly nervous, but like a compressed spring waiting for the right moment to pop open. She decided to begin as calmly and neutrally as possible.

"Given Sauveterre's announcement on Friday," she said, "we're planning to extend the film to talk about Keteb Lellouch's appointment as creative director."

Thieriot bowed his head as if in a benediction. "He is a good choice. He will keep my Rollie's legacy alive."

So he had moved from connection with Guipure to ownership of him. Well, maybe they could turn that to their advantage.

"Cyrille," she said gently, "we know that nobody can take Roland's place." She couldn't bring herself to call Guipure "Rollie," but using his first name might foster the sense that this was a casual, open conversation among friends. She tried to make her voice soothing. "But we also know you knew Roland better than anyone. That's why we wanted to get your opinion on the choice of Keteb as his successor." She smiled at him. "What makes you feel it's a good choice? Were Roland and Keteb close?"

"Yes." His voice was firm. "Very."

This was a promising start. "Can you tell us more about that? You saw them together a lot?"

"Oh no." Thieriot shook his head. "Rollie and I liked to spend our time together alone. I told you. But I know they had an *understanding* between them."

An understanding? She tried not to get too hopeful. "What do you mean, an understanding? Had Roland told Keteb something about his plans for succession?" A nudge, but she couldn't help herself.

Cyrille looked puzzled. "No, nothing like that." Then his face smoothed. He widened his eyes and gazed at her earnestly. "They had an *artistic* understanding." He touched his chest lightly, as if showing where the connection resided. "I remember Rollie told me once that it was as if Keteb *shared* his imagination. He could just *describe* a garment, he said, and Keteb could cut it perfectly."

A psychic understanding? Rachel felt any excitement recede. Unless . . . "Did he say that to Keteb? Or when Keteb was around?"

Another shake of the head. "No, Rollie wasn't someone who felt he had to compliment people."

That opened up another possibility. "So would you say he was hard on Keteb?" Then, thinking that Thieriot might see this as a criticism, she added, "You know, some people use tough love to make others perform better. I hear that can be an effective management style."

Again the wide eyes. "Oh no! Rollie would never do that. In fact, he was always interested in the little ideas and designs Keteb brought him. His little imitations, Rollie called them." He smiled as if this insult was a prized witticism.

"I'm sorry"—Rachel took a split second to process what she'd heard—"Lellouch produced designs of his own?" A nod. "And he brought them to Roland?" Another nod. "Do you know why?"

Thieriot seemed astounded by her obtuseness. "For Rollie's approval, I imagine. He was *inspired* by Rollie. Of course, his ideas weren't very good," he said loftily, "but Rollie humored him. And he sometimes adapted a little detail or a touch—you know, he would put them on a piece and they would be *transformed* by the setting."

"And you don't think Keteb minded those adaptations?" Rachel's tone was gently thoughtful.

"Oh no! I think he was *grateful*."

And who would not be? was the implication. But Rachel knew how she would feel if she showed her work to someone else and they co-opted its details and touches. *Gratitude* was not the word she would use. She probed a little more. "Did he ever say so?"

Thieriot shook his head.

"Did he ever say *anything* to you about Roland? Or did Roland say anything else to you about him?" Hearing the edge of impatience in her voice and seeing Thieriot's look of surprise, she added hurriedly, "That's the kind of things an audience likes. A sense of relationship, maybe a hint that Roland *meant* Keteb to be his successor all along. Anything like that?" She opened her mouth, as if eager to marvel at what he might reveal.

But Cyrille held up a hand. "Wait." He sat up straight, and his voice became sharp. It was as if the spring inside him had suddenly been released. "Before I say anything more, we need to discuss my payment."

Rachel was taken aback. "Your payment?"

"Yes." Seeing her confusion, he clarified. "I've been talking to some friends, and they tell me that it's customary for filmmakers like you to give your participants a little acknowledgment, a little honorarium. So before I say any more, I'd like to be sure that I'm receiving one, and, if you can tell me, how soon I'll receive it."

She glanced across the table at Magda, but Magda was squinting at Thieriot as if trying to evaluate him.

"Cyrille," Rachel said, once again making her tone gentle, "we're not giving you any money." When he looked stricken, she searched for a plausible excuse. "If people are paid for appearing in a documentary, it compromises the integrity of the project. People will think you're just telling us what we want to hear."

"But—" A look of mingled disbelief and disappointment crossed his face, followed by what could best be described as worried calculation. He bit his plum-colored lip for a moment. Then he said, "All right. What about the *croquis*?"

Now she was completely confused. *"Excusez-moi?"*

"The *croquis* Rollie gave me. Last time, you said putting them in the film could add value to them. If you bought them from me, then you could have the benefit of that added value." His voice had turned wheedling.

"But we don't want the *croquis*."

"But you said they could be valuable! How could you not want something that could be valuable? And what's the point of owning something valuable if you can't sell it when you need it?"

Rachel felt that the conversation had spun off track somewhere. But Magda spoke for the first time since they'd sat down. "I thought you said you were interviewing for jobs."

"I am." Thieriot said, as if he and Magda were well embarked on a discussion about this. "I'm trying. But it's not easy, even in hospitality, even in Paris. You need a reference from your last job, and that *fils de pute* at the LaLa—"

He stopped abruptly. He folded his lips together between his teeth. His face wore the expression of a man who very much wished he could wind the clock back ten seconds.

But Magda's face wore a look of satisfaction. *I didn't even need to question him,* it said. "You worked at the LaLa Lounge." Under the table, her foot found Rachel's and tapped it lightly. She was taking over.

Thieriot closed his eyes, and for a moment there was only an elaborate painting of black, orange, and gold stripes. Then he opened them again.

"No, I don't work there." His voice was still sullen. A dull red flush began to work its way up his neck and face. "I didn't say I work there."

But Magda met hair splitting with hair splitting. "I said that you *worked* there, not that you work there now. Anyway, we already knew. We interviewed the owner, and he told us that you were working there on the night Roland Guipure died. And that he fired you for running out of the club in the middle of your shift on that same night. Why didn't you mention that to us?"

"Why didn't you mention that you already knew?"

It's like arguing with a five-year-old, Rachel thought. But Magda was up to the challenge.

"We hadn't mentioned it *yet*." Her voice was frosty. "The interview wasn't over."

Thieriot was no Naquet: it didn't occur to him to wonder why the owner of the LaLa Lounge had been talking to Rachel and Magda about his staff, or to try to bluff his way out of the situation. Instead, he asked a question that was also an admission.

"Why is it relevant where I worked?"

"Because we're making a film about Guipure's life. If you were at the club on the night of his party, you were a witness to his last night."

"You could have been the last person to see him alive!" Rachel pointed out. "Think of the impact *that* would have in the film."

Thieriot responded to this chance at significance as Rachel had hoped he would: he admitted everything.

"Yes, I was there. I did see him. I didn't want to tell you"—
his face turned sly for a moment, then wiped itself clean—
"because I thought he deserved privacy in his last hours. There
was no need to complicate his death with stories about our
personal business. But now I see . . . now that time has passed,
I can see the value of the full story. So, yes." He heaved a sigh.
"Yes, I saw him. We met privately. But only for a few moments.
I just wanted to tell him that I wished him well, and I wanted
to see his face one last time."

"Why one *last* time?"

Thieriot wrinkled his forehead. "Because our paths would
never have any reason to cross again." His confusion seemed
genuine.

"And what did he say?"

"He thanked me. And then he apologized for hurting me
and said he was grateful not to have to carry the burden of
my sorrow with him anymore. When I said our love could
endure even after everything that had happened, he told me
he would always remember our time together as precious."
He shook his head softly. "It was overpowering; I needed
space to process it."

*In other words, you asked to get back together, he gave you the
brush-off, and you didn't want anyone else to see your humiliation,* Rachel thought. Still, if Thieriot was telling the truth, it
had been smoothly done on Guipure's part. She didn't hear any
anger or resentment in his voice, and what he described fit the
time line outlined by the LaLa Lounge's owner.

But Magda needed more. "That was all? You didn't catch
up about the business or his plans? He didn't make any final

confidences that you've been saving up to earn a bigger payment?"

"A bigger payment?" This time Thieriot's wide eyes were not the result of a performance. His face was suddenly pale. "How did you find out? He promised me that no one would find out!"

The barman looked up from wiping the counter, mild interest creasing his face at Thieriot's raised voice. Thieriot clamped his mouth shut.

The three of them sat silent for a long minute, then Magda let out her breath. "Why don't we all have another drink?"

She waited until Thieriot had taken a couple of swallows of his black coffee before she said calmly, "I was talking about the payment you thought we would give you for information. But it sounds like someone has already been paying you for your knowledge. Why don't you tell us about *that*?" She smiled. "Since you're more than halfway there already."

Thieriot took another sip, plainly to buy time, but his face said he could think of no way out.

He blotted his lips with the paper napkin and sighed. "Rollie spoiled me. I know that. But once he was taken away, it was hard to go back to the way things were before. And, well, I have needs." He gestured at his face. "You think this is easy? It takes money to look like this. This eyeshadow is Tom Ford." He sighed again. "At first I thought I could be one of those influencers. But companies won't send you things for free unless you have a certain number of followers, and you can't get followers without stuff to show off. People aren't interesting on their own.

I got a job at the LaLa, but that wasn't enough for me to manage on by itself. So I thought about what I had to offer, and"—he leaned forward—"I had *information*." He plainly expected this to be a bombshell, and when neither of the women reacted, he looked a little crestfallen. He went on awkwardly, "So I—well, *Quelles Nouvelles* . . . he's a person. I mean there's a *person* running that site. And he doesn't—he can't collect all that information himself. He works off . . . tips." He said the word as if it tasted unpleasant in his mouth. "He pays for them."

Magda leaned forward too. She said softly but precisely, "You fed information to the man who writes *Quelles Nouvelles*?"

Thieriot looked around. The girl had left, and the man behind the bar had now gone outside and begun to unstack the tables and chairs. Thieriot said, "Well, *mostly* to him." He leaned back again, stretching out his legs. "I knew a lot. The story that Cecile Phan was going to go geisha goth with her autumn/winter haute couture in 2015? That was me! I heard from Rollie that Rihanna was going to walk the runway for Dior, and I passed that on to him. He knew before anyone else!"

Rachel didn't look at Magda, but she knew they were both thinking the same thing: Why were they talking to Thieriot when they could be talking to *Quelles Nouvelles*?

"Can you get in touch with him again? Ask him if he'd be willing to talk to us?" Almost too late, she remembered their cover story. "It would be great for the film."

*   *   *

They couldn't wait to reach the Hôtel de Ville métro station before talking. Instead, they walked the few hundred meters to the Rue de Rosiers and stood in the shadow of the Korcarz bakery awning, facing away from the Rue Vieille du Temple in case Thieriot should unexpectedly pass by and spot them as they debriefed in low, urgent whispers.

"He admitted he followed Guipure into the men's room," Magda began.

"'Met privately,'" Rachel's tone was wry. "He admitted they 'met privately.'"

"Whatever. He admitted they were alone together." She snorted. "Even if he did try to make up all that gag-worthy stuff Guipure supposedly said to him while they were in there."

Rachel laughed. "Oh, that I completely believed. It sounded exactly like something someone fresh out of a twelve-step program would say. They're supposed to make amends, remember?"

Through the window behind Magda, she saw a tiny elderly woman holding an even tinier bichon frisé and pointing a girl behind the counter toward an enormous éclair. While the girl transferred it to a box, the woman checked with the bichon to be sure it approved of the choice, then kissed it.

She returned to the conversation at hand. "He also made it clear Roland stole Lellouch's ideas. I can't imagine that went down well." She remembered the remark about Guipure not being the kind to compliment people. "And he sounds like a bastard. Especially to Lellouch."

"If being a bastard was enough to get you murdered, the halls of politics would be littered with corpses," Magda said.

"And if being in a bathroom with someone was enough to make you a murderer, so would women's rooms all over the world," Rachel snapped back.

This standoff was broken by the elderly woman coming out of the bakery. She clutched her purchase in one hand and the leash of the bichon in the other. The dog was rather portly, Rachel was unsurprised to notice, and as it trotted behind its mistress, it had eyes only for the cardboard box in her hand.

Rachel sighed. "Well, I think we can agree that the best thing we got from him was the phone number that will put us in touch with Mr. *Quelles Nouvelles*. He'll be much more useful than Cyrille."

This was the closest she would come to acknowledging that Thieriot had not been the source she had hoped for, and Magda took it in the spirit it was intended. "Let's go have a mid-morning falafel at that place down the street." She took Rachel's arm. "Hey, did you see that fat little dog that just went past?"

Chapter Nineteen

The phone number Thieriot handed over turned out to belong to a baritone voice that, although perfectly polite, was also perfectly clear about his requirements. He might perhaps be the person they wanted, but before he agreed to say any more than that, he would need to call Thieriot to confirm that they were who they said they were, and that it was indeed Thieriot who had passed on his number. He would then call them back using the number Thieriot gave him, to check that it matched the one they were calling from. They should wait for that call.

Ten minutes later Rachel's *portable* rang. The baritone voice was warmer now. He understood from Thieriot that Rachel and Magda wished to ask him some questions? He preferred not to speak on the phone. Would they please give him their full names and an e-mail address for one of them? He would send them further information later that evening.

At ten PM an e-mail arrived in Rachel's inbox: *2 PM tomorrow, Apartment 4, 20 Rue des Vinaigriers.*

* * *

The Rue des Vinaigriers was one of the long, thin lanes that branched off Paris's broad boulevards. Narrow, flat-sided chutes crammed with *tabacs*, bars, churches, small supermarkets, parking garages, hairdressers, dentists, and all the other miscellany that make up communities, these streets are tiny neighborhoods spiking out from the public-faced boulevards. Unlike most of them, however, the Rue des Vinaigriers did not stop dead at its bottom end, but rather curved around sharply to the right. Just before this curve was an old social club, one of those ancient establishments where the elderly men of Paris gather to drink and remember together. Next to its burgundy façade, the curve of the street was backed by a wall with a shallow set of concrete steps inset. Once climbed, they opened on the left to a building shaped like a triangle with one of its points sheared off and replaced by flat windows and a glass door at the raised ground level. This geometric curiosity was the top six floors of the same building that housed the social club. Climbing the stairs was like a living magic trick, Rachel thought, one structure magically transformed into another just by turning a corner. As she and Magda waited for someone in apartment four to answer their buzz on the intercom, she stared over her shoulder at a mural of a young girl in cutoff overalls, her hair an afro of multicolored paint splats that seemed too heavy for her stem-like neck to support. The girl's painted face was tired but accepting, a model of dutiful compliance.

The man who opened the door to the apartment was short and on the plump side, wearing jeans and a gray T-shirt that matched his beard. His feet were bare, his eyes were shrunken by the thick lenses of his glasses, and his hairline was not so much receding as simply giving up the fight. "Hippolyte Foucher," he said. *"Entrez, s'il vous plaît."* As he stood back to let them pass, he added, "I apologize for all the *mise en scène* earlier, but fashion gossip is like espionage: secretive, cutthroat, and much less suave than it looks. It's better to take precautions than to be unmasked."

He ushered them into the *séjour* and gestured for them to sit down on a worn brown velvet sofa. "I know what you're thinking: What is there to unmask? I don't have the looks for fashion, and I don't have the fashion sense for fashion." He laughed lightly. "In fact, I don't even have much interest in fashion. But five years ago my wife was diagnosed with cancer, and I needed to stay home to look after her. Our daughter was crazy about clothes, and when I started to make jokes about what I saw in her magazines, she told me I should do it online." He widened his eyes behind his glasses, to show how mystifying this was to him. "At first it was just 'Chanel's jackets look like someone lost a fight with a bolt of bouclé,' or 'Hedi Slimane is making suits for pipe cleaners'—that kind of thing. But people loved it. And they loved it even more when I started dropping in little speculations about the houses based on what I read. All of a sudden my traffic shot up, and places were begging to advertise on the site. You wouldn't believe how easy it is to monetize gossip." He rolled his eyes, then slapped his hands on his thighs. *"Un café?"*

While he was in the kitchen, Rachel looked around. The *séjour* had the same air as its owner: a little shabby, vaguely messy, but clearly long inhabited by an interesting person.

Across from the sofa was a matching armchair, the lower half of its brown velvet legs showing that it had made the acquaintance of some sharp-clawed cat; the oriental rug on the floor was threadbare in places, and at some point someone had spilled something red on it near the left-hand corner. The bookshelves were jammed with volumes put in both vertically and horizontally. They had overflowed onto the coffee table, where Rachel could see that a pile of them were titles about the Hapsburg empire.

"What did you do before *Quelles Nouvelles?*"

"I was a professor of Spanish history." Foucher put a tray filled with mugs and a sugar and creamer set on the table (Rachel moved the pile of books out of his way) and handed her a mug of tea. "It was surprisingly good preparation for the site. Being a historian is all about doing the research. If you do the research, you build a complete picture, and the more complete your picture, the more you can see where things fit and why they matter. Same with fashion, same with gossip."

Magda settled back into the sofa with her coffee. "If you aren't interested, why not wind up the site when your wife was healthy again? Or—I'm sorry—is your wife still—"

He waved a hand. "Completely recovered. And my daughter's studying engineering at *Université de Lorraine.* But the answer to your first question is, having put in all the work to become an expert, I didn't want to just give up. Especially given how much I make. And I must confess," he said, smiling, "I enjoy the tone. It's a good way to get out my frustrations and unkind thoughts." He took a sip from his own mug. "But tell me why you're here. All I know is that you are friends of Cyrille Thieriot, and there is some information I might be able to give you."

"Well, yes and no." On reflection, Rachel considered it unwise to lie to a gossip blogger. "Cyrille thinks we're aspiring documentary makers working on a project about Roland Guipure."

"And in fact you are . . .?" Foucher's tone was mild.

Rachel smiled. "In fact, we are detectives, trying to solve Guipure's murder, and we're hoping you might be able to give us information on Keteb Lellouch, who just took his place."

He looked at them for a long moment. "Are you working with the police?"

"No." Rachel said.

He was silent for another long moment. "I don't like the police," he said at last. "I was a student at the Sorbonne in 1968 when they charged us with batons." He put down his mug and braced his hands on his knees. "So. *Bon.* Keteb Lellouch. I'll give you what I can." He paused. "And I hope that if, at the end of your investigation, you have any interesting revelations to give, you will return the favor."

They nodded in unison, two marionettes on a single string.

Foucher dipped his head to acknowledge the bargain, then drummed his fingers against his lips. "He started at Dior, if I'm not mistaken. Then moved on to AuSecours. Nothing notable at Dior, but of course that was when Galliano was there, so you didn't really need any other gossip. Also, at that point he was nobody, really—he'd only graduated from the *Institut Français* the year before." He drummed his lips again. "But at AuSecours there *was* something . . . It was a young label, and then the original CD left and a new one came in, and there was something there . . ." He rose. *"Excusez-moi."*

For a few moments they heard doors opening and closing in the inner recesses of the apartment. Then he reappeared, clutching a stack of tomato-red plastic index card boxes. "My AuSecours tips." Rachel and Magda's faces must have revealed their confusion, because he elaborated. "When I decided to do gossip full time, I built contacts by waiting at the employee entrances of the big houses. I figured it's the people you don't notice who have most information. Seamstresses, *flou* girls, even cleaners—they are there, but in the background, so people forget about them when they speak. And they often aren't paid well. Ideal informants. But from these beginnings a network grew, and eventually I had too much information to hold in my head. *Et voilà—les cartes!* And because each tip helps to build a history, I save the cards. Now, if you give me a moment . . ." He popped the top of one box and began flicking, his fingers almost a blur. "1998: a foolish vendeuse sent one client's couture to another's house. 2003: someone is stealing. He looked up and smiled. "Someone is always stealing. 2005: the CD is thinking of leaving. Yes, I think we're close. Yes!" He pulled out a card and squinted at it. "Yes, here it is. In 2005, the founding creative director of AuSecours decided to retire, and the head pattern cutter—that was Lellouch— was considered his logical successor. But the outgoing CD decided not to appoint him because he was Moroccan. The CD was worried that the press would brand the house as 'ethnic.'" He checked the card again. "They went with Antoine Delario instead. And folded five years later, by the way."

Rachel suddenly remembered Cecile Phan's stiff correction when she'd complimented her office decor as warm: "My aesthetic is exotic." Now it made sense. If "ethnic" was going to be forced on you, it was easier to embrace it than to fight it—at least if you embraced it, you could label it "exotic" and gain some power by insisting on it.

She put her mug down and moved forward on the sofa. "So, let me see if I understand. In 2005, at the house he worked for before Sauveterre, Keteb Lellouch was on track for the top spot, but at the last minute they yanked the job away from him and gave it someone else?"

"Because they didn't want the house to be seen as niche. Yes, that's what happened." Foucher cocked his head. "It sounds as if this helps you?"

"It certainly does."

"And you, Madame," Foucher said, looking at Magda, "you don't look as pleased."

"No, no, I am." She smiled tightly. "It's just that . . . well, I was wondering if there was more, about Sauveterre more generally?" She looked at Rachel. "We should know if there's anything else there." And back toward Foucher. "If that would be all right with you?"

"It's not a problem at all." Then he gave a little frown. "But I don't remember that I have very much on Sauveterre. They're a tight house. Their employees are notoriously loyal."

Rachel remembered that Cecile Phan had said something similar. Still, you never knew . . ." We'd be very grateful if you could look," she said.

Once he was out of the room, she turned to Magda. "Lellouch has *experience*. He has *experience* being passed over for the top job! Can you imagine how angry he must have been when it happened again? Talk about long-simmering motives! Especially if Guipure was already borrowing from his designs!"

But Magda shifted uneasily on the sofa. "I don't know." She held up a delaying hand. "I don't mean 'no.' I just mean . . . I don't know. I meant what I just said. I agree that Lellouch had motive. And now that we know about his previous experience at AuSecours, I agree that his motive plus that previous experience might have made him angry enough to kill Guipure. But we don't really know anything about anyone else at Sauveterre. And I don't care *what* picture Thieriot painted of their final encounter, he's still the only one we know for certain was alone with Guipure before he died. So it's not so simple."

Foucher reappeared. This time he held three index card boxes, all dark green. He looked chagrined. "I did say there wasn't much."

He sat down and popped the top of the first box, flipping through the cards. "No, this is all Guipure's addiction." He put it to one side and opened the second. "No, this is all family history. You know the father was a stable hand?" They shook their heads. "Oh yes, that's why the family money was put in trust. Maximilien Sauveterre made so much after the war—he sold the Jewish paintings for the same price he bought them for, appropriate given the circumstances, but of course word of what he'd done in the war brought him more than enough business to make up for that. And then, after he died, the gallery and building went for a nice amount. But the family lawyers didn't want Pierre Guipure to be able to get his hands on it, so they lodged it in that trust." Foucher pursed his lips and raised an eyebrow. "Not that he ever wanted any of it, from what I've read. He adored Geneviève Sauveterre."

He closed the second box, put it on the table, and popped the top of the third. "Ah, *d'accord*, now here we are. In 2008, they are buying their *grandpère*'s building. 2012, Antoinette Guipure is dating the head of Banque de Paris—that didn't last long. In 2014, the CFO's assistant hates the CD's new boy-friend. In 2015, the new collection will be inspired by drag." He glanced up. "Those mirrored dresses were terrible. So kitsch." He looked back down at the card. "Ah, that bit of news came from . . . our mutual friend."

"Oh yes, Cyrille." Magda moved forward on the sofa. "What do you think of him?"

Foucher rolled his eyes. "He's a type." The he shook his head. "Of course, I shouldn't be so unkind—that type is my bread and butter. But"—he shook his head—"there was always so much drama with him! He would telephone me with these little *commérages* and act as if they were great scoops. And always he complained about the money." He drew back slightly, looking at Magda, the corners of his lips twitching. "Or did you mean, what do I think of him as a suspect?"

Magda nodded, and Foucher shook his head. "Cyrille Thieriot wouldn't kill Roland Guipure." He rolled his eyes. "First of all, he's too lazy to kill anyone. But even if he could rouse himself to it, he wouldn't have killed him when they were involved because it would have ended the lifestyle Guipure was supplying. And he wouldn't have done it after they broke up because he would've been focusing his energies on finding a new meal ticket. He'd have been much more likely to want to win Guipure back, for the same reason—it's money he's inter-ested in, not revenge for a love spurned."

Nice phrase, Rachel thought. Not that it was much help to them.

Magda said something similar once they were out on the street. They had left Foucher's company with as many cheek kisses as they had entered Thieriot's the previous day. He had tried to press on them some of the various pieces of clothing and accessories that had been sent to him by designers hoping for a favorable mention, but each woman had declined—Rachel dimly felt there might be an investigator's code of ethics, so she turned reluctantly away from a Sur Le Banc military-cut wool coat that she was certain would transform her into the person she'd always wanted to be. Now, as they strode empty-handed back up the Rue des Vinaigriers, Magda said grimly, "Mediouri better hurry up and call. Without him we're going nowhere."

* * *

Then, two days later, Mediouri did call. In the end, though, the conversation Rachel had waited for in agony took all of fifteen seconds.

"Madame, your dry cleaning is ready," Mediouri said. "Tomorrow is our late closing day, so you can come collect what you need at eight PM." Then he broke the connection.

Rachel stared at her phone's dark screen. "Sick!" she muttered.

Chapter Twenty

The back room of the *pressing* was very warm, and this, combined with the racks of plastic-shrouded clothes that lined its walls, gave it a claustrophobic feel, although not an entirely unpleasant one. A fluorescent strip light hummed overhead, thick air pressed against Rachel like soft cotton, and the room was full of the smell of hot fabric. In other circumstances she might have pulled one of the duvets out of its cellophane wrapper and used it to take a quick nap on the floor. The current circumstances and company, however, did not encourage sleep.

The man sitting at the white-painted wooden table in front of them looked so much like the stereotype of a drug lord that Rachel nearly laughed aloud. His bullet-shaped head was completely bald and appeared to sit directly on his stocky shoulders, his thin mouth a line drawn across its lower half. He wore a leather blazer over a black T-shirt, and the fattest, goldest, ugliest watch she had ever seen. No doubt it was worth thousands.

"A former associate," Mediouri said. It was obvious there would be no further introduction.

The man stared at them impassively. The silence lengthened and widened until Rachel realized Mediouri was waiting for her to introduce Magda.

"This is Magda."

"Ah, the second investigatrix! Pleased to meet you, pleased to meet you!" Mediouri pumped Magda's hand and gave his dentist-enhanced grin. It could have been an introduction at some pleasant social occasion if it hadn't been for the man behind them, whose expressionless face spoke of purposes that could never be pleasant. As Rachel watched, he lifted his thick hands from his lap and rested them softly on the tabletop, as if to put them in a better position to turn into fists.

Mediouri gestured, and the two women sat down across from the man. This time there was no offer of tea, no charming little spoon. Instead, Mediouri took a seat across from them, next to the man, and cleared his throat. "My friend didn't want to me to talk about this over the telephone—"

"No phones," the man agreed.

"—so I thought it would be simplest to meet here, where we don't have to worry."

The man dipped his head in a single nod. "No phones," he repeated. It took Rachel a second to realize this was not for emphasis; he meant that she and Magda should surrender their phones. They shared a quick look, then slid their *portables* to the center of the table. The man picked up each in turn, switched it off, and returned it to the same spot. The silence and his total lack of expression gave the task the feeling of a strange ritual.

When the man finished, Mediouri left a moment's pause before he said, "Someone did buy *l'heroïne* for Guipure during the time you asked about."

Rachel felt her excitement rising. Would it be Naquet or Lellouch? Lellouch now seemed the more plausible suspect, but Naquet was so unpleasant . . . She dug her fingernails into her palms. "Who was it?"

"She said her name was Gabrielle."

"Gabrielle?" She and Magda said it together.

"Are you sure?"

Mediouri nodded. "Yes. She picked up a delivery at the Sauveterre offices."

"*She* did. Not a man. Not a man named Lellouch or Keteb? Maybe at the same address?"

The leather-clad man opened his mouth and spoke. "On the second Monday in April, at night, I made a delivery to a woman in the foyer of 21 Rue la Boétie. I remember because it had been a long time since we had an order from that address, so I made the delivery myself." He shrugged. "It's always good to reconnect in person with a customer who's been away for a long time. A little *giton* used to handle everything, but this time the caller said the name was Gabrielle. She was waiting in the foyer when I arrived. I asked her name. I *always* ask the name. And she was"—he grunted appreciatively—"*bandante*. Red hair, white dress, high heels, legs that wrap around you twice."

Rachel hadn't noticed Gabrielle's legs, but the rest of the description was a perfect match. Pulling her lips between her teeth, she looked at Magda.

"I don't doubt you." Magda leaned forward, one hand slightly raised as if to calm the man's temper before it flared. "But in our business we need to be sure. You're certain you went to 21 Rue la Boétie, and you're certain the person waiting for you was a woman."

The man barked a laugh. "In my business you also need to be sure, and I am sure I delivered to a woman at 21 Rue la Boétie." He too leaned forward. "Red hair. White dress. High heels." He looked at Mediouri. *"Une moule serrée."*

A tight pussy. Rachel flinched; she saw Magda flush. But it wasn't a time for feminist objections. "And you didn't make any delivery to anyone else at the same address around the same time?" She clutched at a passing hope, "Or to the LaLa Lounge?"

He turned his bullet head so he was looking her full in the face. "I made one delivery, and no one else on my team made any other deliveries there that week or any other week." He sat back. "As for the LaLa Lounge, that's outside my area. Maybe you want to ask Matti to talk to some of the other service providers."

The overhead fluorescent light hummed softly, and somewhere nearby a machine clicked. Finally Rachel said, "How much did she buy, this red-haired girl?"

He held up three fingers.

How much was that? Was it enough to kill someone? Rachel saw how completely ill-equipped she was to move in this world.

The man scraped back his chair and stood up. There was no bell attached to the back door, so when it closed behind him, all that was left was a click and the five indentations Rachel

181

imagined she could see where his fingers had pushed into the tabletop.

"Is that fifty milligrams?" Her voice came out small.

Mediouri nodded. "More than that. Did you learn what you needed?"

"I guess so. I mean, yes. It wasn't what we expected."

She explained, and when she finished, he widened his eyes and made the hard little puffing noise that the French used to indicate surprise, exasperation, or a mixture of both. "This detection is hard work, *hein*? You answer a question, and that answer leads you to another question. I think I liked my side of the law better. The only question I ever answered was 'How much?' and all it led to was money in my hand."

Chapter Twenty-One

~

"He's actually kind of nice," Magda said as they came out into the Rue St. Paul. In half an hour the sun would set, and the air around them was a pale blue tinged with pink.

"I'm going to assume you don't mean Mediouri's associate."

They made their way down the street. At its bottom end it opened out into a small paved semicircle. If you turned left, this led you to the Pont de Sully; if you turned right, it led you to the Pont Marie, the Pont Louis Phillipe, and eventually to Notre Dame. The semicircle itself was outfitted with a single wooden bench overhung by a thin tree planted in a small square of grass. It was a curious respite, an urban area that faced the thick traffic of the Quai des Celestins but nonetheless felt like an oasis. In the cool pre-twilight, it seemed like the ideal place to rest.

One of the tree's leaves had fallen onto the bench. Rachel picked it up, rolling it between her fingers. She felt it soften against the pressure.

"There's a restaurant in there." She pointed the little cigar at the squat neoclassical building across the street, which looked like nothing so much as a derelict boathouse. "Around the back. It faces the river, and they put on events."

Magda didn't reply, but Rachel hadn't expected her to. She had just wanted something to fill the space, a moment of normality while they processed their astonishing news.

"This should be exciting, right?" She said at last. "It's the kind of development that breaks a case wide open. So why do I feel like someone's let all the air out of our tires?"

"Because *it doesn't make sense.*" Magda stressed the last four words as if the two of them had been discussing the topic for hours. "We had two suspects with strong motives and logical narratives of guilt, and now all of a sudden we've got someone with no discernible motive, committing a crime with no discernible reason or means behind it." Her voice rose in mystification. "Why would Gabrielle do it? *How* would she do it?"

"Yes, that's it. That's exactly it." For a second Rachel felt the satisfaction of being completely understood. Then almost immediately it struck her that maybe they'd both understood wrong. "Except . . . except she was in love with him. And people do kill for love."

"Except that we've been over that, right? People who kill for love usually do it because they've been rejected, or they kill a rival. And Thieriot is still alive and there was no need for rejection, because Gabrielle knew from the start that Guipure was gay."

There was another long silence, then Magda said, "Except what if it's more convoluted? What if Gabrielle both loves and hates Guipure? People are complicated. Let's say . . . let's say something happens that pushes her over the edge. Maybe she tells him she loves him, and he reminds her he's gay. A clear rejection that means she can't daydream anymore. She's humiliated, but she can't stop loving him, which makes her even more humiliated. And people hate people who've humiliated them." She glanced over; Rachel nodded. "So she makes the call and buys the heroin. She knows that if the police ask any questions, she can say she bought it at Roland's order. There'll be proof that he used someone to buy for him before. She'll probably get in trouble for the buying, but the police won't suspect her of anything more sinister." She grabbed Rachel's wrist, and her voice sped up. "Then she takes the heroin to the party. Or maybe she prepares the syringe beforehand and takes *it* to the party, however you do that. Then somehow she injects him. He feels faint, goes outside to clear his head; next thing you know, he's dead on the doorstep. And no one suspects anything because—hey!—he used to be a heroin addict."

Rachel waited to be sure she was finished, then gently detached her wrist. She shook her head. "No. It has too many holes." Magda looked affronted. "Think about it. We have to assume a rejection; we have to assume it's shatteringly humiliating. Then we have to assume that someone who's never bought heroin before calls up a dealer. How does she know his number? How does she know how to make the arrangements, what to ask for, how to get the delivery?"

Then she stopped. It was the word delivery that did it. "Except—oh my God!" She crushed the green cigar between her fingers.

"What?"

"Remember when we were talking to Naquet?" An eye roll and a nod. "He said that when he first went to see Guipure, when the protective army, or whatever it was, was around, Gabrielle would come in and ask if Guipure wanted lunch, and she would bring in deliveries." Magda frowned and looked upward, trying to remember, then nodded again. "And then he said that when he interviewed Guipure while *Cyrille* was there, at one point Guipure started to—well, come down, I guess, and Cyrille asked him if he wanted lunch. Oh, what did he say exactly?" She closed her eyes, then opened them. "Can you tell me?"

"What makes you think I know?"

Rachel smiled. "Because I know you. I know you've transcribed all your recordings and put the transcriptions all neatly in your folder. And you've got the folder with you right now."

For a second Magda looked as she would like to argue. Then she gave up, reached into her bag, and drew out the folder. She flipped through its contents until she found the right page. "'The kid suddenly asked if he wanted lunch,'" she read out. "'Asked him for some money, then went off and came back a while later, saying he had a delivery.'"

"That was Guipure's code!" Rachel gritted her teeth. How obvious it seemed once you knew. "Asking if he wanted lunch must have been asking if he wanted more heroin, and saying you had a delivery must have been telling him it had arrived. Otherwise, why would Gabrielle and Cyrille have used exactly the same wording? And we know from Dolly that Guipure had been using before Cyrille ever since he came on the scene. It stands to reason that he would have needed a courier then too. Who better than an employee who loves you so much that you can easily exploit her?" She grimaced. "Then imagine how that employee would feel if she found herself replaced. No more special relationship; no more hope that if she did his bidding long enough, he might suddenly realize how wrong he'd been . . ." She met Magda's eyes.

A pause. "Except . . ." Magda squinted. "Except again, that's a really good reason to kill Cyrille, not Guipure."

Damn. Damn, damn, damn. Rachel bit her thumbnail for a minute. Then in a flash she saw it. She reached out and grabbed Magda's wrist. "Except what about this?" She leaned forward. "Gabrielle and Lellouch work together. They're work friends, like Dolly said. Lellouch has a reason to want Guipure dead, and he knows what happened between Gabrielle and Guipure once Cyrille showed up. So he spends a few months working on her, seeming like he's commiserating but actually reminding her what Guipure did; suggesting how her life might better if she didn't have to be reminded of her humiliation every day when she comes into work." She waved a hand. "Something like that. Who knows what he actually said? But gradually he wins her over. He persuades her that working with him is to both their benefit. He gets her to buy the heroin, knowing she won't be under suspicion because she can always tell exactly the story you just suggested. She passes it to him and at the party he finds some way to inject Guipure. Maybe he does some sneaky maneuver at the bar when it's crowded and no one will notice. Anyway, he does it. And the rest happens just as you said."

Magda considered, then wrinkled her nose. "No." At Rachel's exhalation of annoyance, she said, "It's just as full of holes as mine. We have to assume that Lellouch and Gabrielle are close; we have to assume that he cooked up a nefarious plan. And then they have to collaborate . . . No," she said again, "we're both just making conjectures based on stuff we want to be true, or stuff that could be true, but we have no evidence."

Rachel bit her lip. She had thought Mediouri would sort everything out because he knew people on the inside, but it turned out it was the wrong kind of inside.

Magda stood up. "I'm going home to research Gabrielle. People aren't doing much for us at the moment, so let's see what the web can do." She nodded goodbye and turned crisply left toward Sully–Morland station.

Although surprised by the abruptness, Rachel didn't disagree with the determination, and she shared the frustration. How could it be that a month had passed and she was no closer to solving this murder? Neither of the other cases had taken so long. As she turned right and walked along the Seine toward Pont Marie station, the houses of the Île Saint-Louis across the Seine seemed to mock her. Given the smallness and insularity of the fashion world, their glittering lights seemed to say, shouldn't it be easy to track down a murderer in it?

Except, she pointed out to herself, the smallness and insularity were the very things that made finding the murderer so hard. As her shoes patted against the pavement and the water of the river slapped against itself, she relaxed into this explanation. The smallness of the fashion world, its feuds and infighting, meant a vast array of suspects to be sorted through.

Except, her conscience responded, she and Magda hadn't found any feuds and infighting; in fact, they'd found nothing dramatic enough to point clearly toward anyone. Except, she responded back, for Gabrielle, now. Except, another part of her pointed out, that there was no discernible reason for that efficient girl in that spotless dress to buy a class-one narcotic to kill someone she believed was, in Dolly's phrase, "the eighth wonder of the world." Except, she reminded herself, that they didn't have enough information to be sure of that.

She sighed aloud. "Except," she said. Except, except, except. She crossed the road toward the lighted métro sign.

Chapter
Twenty-Two

～

The next morning at eight AM Rachel's *portable* rang on her bedside table.

"I spend three hours last night trying hack Sauveterre's e-mail network," said Magda, "and another three hours this morning."

"And you're calling me now because you finally managed to do it."

"No. I'm calling you because I managed to hack into the Sauveterre calendar. And there I found out that Roland Guipure had a meeting scheduled with a Jack Ochs the week that he died. That's the name of your mother-in-law's friend's husband, right? Jack Ochs?"

Rachel threw back the covers and grabbed for her robe. "I'm coming over."

* * *

Very early in her relationship with Magda, Rachel had wondered how a person who took such intense pleasure in keeping her space immaculate could be friends with someone like her, for whom there was always something more important than cleaning. Very soon after that, she had decided to stop wondering and just enjoy it. So when Magda opened her door forty minutes later, Rachel took a moment to admire the room in front of her: the gleaming kitchen countertops, the dust mote–free air, the plump sofa cushions, with books neatly alphabetized by author on the bookshelves opposite them. Sniffing the air lightly scented with lemon furniture polish, she seated herself at the recently wiped kitchen table and let Magda explain what she had discovered.

"This is the central calendar." Magda wiggled the mouse so the cursor hovered over the grid on her screen. "It's a standard shared office calendar. My books say that usually you can get into company e-mail by going through the calendar, but in this case that didn't work. So I decided to have a look at the calendar itself instead." She circled the cursor around a green rectangle on the grid. "Each person's appointments are in a different color. Antoinette is green; Guipure is blue; Lellouch is orange, etcetera. Red is for absolutely vital meetings that both Guipure and Antoinette are expected to attend. Now look." She rested the cursor on Saturday, April 16. "There. At two PM."

The bar next to *14.00* was blue, and typed inside it was *RB—J Ochs (HIÉ)*.

"Now look at this." She scrolled up to mid-February and hovered over Friday the 12th. Next to *17.00*, a blue bar read *Télé—M. Jack Ochs*.

Magda anticipated Rachel's question. "Telephone. And *RB* is Rue la Boétie. Which means a Jack Ochs had a scheduled phone call with Guipure at five PM on March fifteenth, and he was scheduled to meet him in person at Sauveterre's headquarters on April sixteenth. Which means Guipure was killed two days before he was supposed to meet with the husband of your mother-in-law's friend, and her friend's husband was killed the day after Guipure."

Rachel stared at the screen. "Could it be some other Jack Ochs? There's more than one in the world."

"More than one who traveled to Paris that week and stayed at the Holiday Inn Elysées?" Magda scrolled back down to April 16 and rested the arrow on *HIÉ.* "I doubt it."

"But he was killed in a robbery! Boussicault said they'd seen those kinds of robberies before!"

"What about if it walks like a duck and talks like a duck, then it's a duck?" This was one of Magda's favorite expressions. "Did Boussicault say the thieves routinely *killed* anyone in those kinds of robberies? Because if not, I think we have to consider the question of what possible connection there could be between Roland Guipure and your Jack Ochs."

He's not my Jack Ochs, Rachel wanted to say. But before she could, Magda said, "You need to talk to Ochs's wife."

Rachel laughed in astonishment. "No. Absolutely not."

"Why not? She's the only one who can tell us what was going on, and your mother-in-law is her best friend."

"*A* friend. She's *a* friend. And Mrs. Ochs has only been a widow for three weeks. She doesn't even have her husband's body yet." With a twinge Rachel remembered she still needed to deal with the roller bag under her foyer table. "Didn't you learn anything from what happened when we went to Sauveterre?"

Magda thinned her lips. "If we want to know anything, we need to talk to a source that might know."

"Well, then, what about Dolly? What about Boussicault? Either of them would be a good source."

"Okay," Magda said so swiftly that Rachel realized she'd been lured into a trap. "How about Boussicault *and* Mrs. Ochs?" She added graciously, "And Dolly, if you think she can help. In whatever order they call you back."

* * *

Counting on the complexities of distance, time zones, and the personal interconnections involved, Rachel assumed that she would speak to Mrs. Ochs last, if at all. But Boussicault was closeted once more with his inter-arrondissement liaison committee, Dolly didn't respond to Rachel's voice mail, and most surprising of all, Alan told her that Ellen Ochs was eager to help. So two days later at seven PM, she clicked on the Skype camera icon and found herself staring at an unknown woman seated on her in-laws' sofa, Alan sitting next to her.

Because her mother-in-law had described Mrs. Ochs as "my friend from the community center," Rachel had expected a woman of Jean's own age, a well-preserved septuagenarian or the more dowdy, white-haired figure she associated with the words "community center." But her mother-in-law's friend seemed to be around Rachel's age. Stray strands had escaped her blonde ponytail and hung lank around her face. Her eyes were ringed with shadows, and Rachel recognized in them the same sheen of shed and not-yet-shed tears that she'd seen in Antoinette Guipure's. Still, when Rachel asked if she was sure she wanted to go through with the interview, Mrs. Ochs nodded firmly. "Alan tells me you're a detective, and I want to help."

Rachel caught her husband's eye for a moment and flashed a look of gratitude. Then she began in the way she thought might make it easiest for Mrs. Ochs to talk without pain: by making her feel she was being of help without bringing up her husband's death directly.

"Thank you so much for agreeing to do this. I don't know if Alan told you, but at the moment I'm investigating another death, also in Paris. Going through the victim's calendar, I came across your husband's name. Apparently they had a meeting scheduled for April fifteenth.

"So what I'm wondering is, did your husband ever mention the name Roland Guipure to you?"

Ellen Ochs looked—what? Wary? Doubtful? Unnerved, Rachel decided.

"Roland Guipure is the man Jack said he needed to see while we were in Paris." Guipure is the man Jack said he needed to see while we were in Paris."

"We? You were supposed to be in Paris with him?"

The other woman nodded. "Originally it was a trip for the two of us." She smiled, remembering. "While we were clearing up from dinner one night, Jack asked me out of the blue, what would I say to a long weekend in Paris? He needed to go there to see someone, but he said that except for a couple of hours while he was doing that, we could spend all the time together." Rachel could see that she was twisting her hands in her lap. "I asked him who he needed to see in Paris. We've never been abroad in our lives, and the companies Jack does accounting for don't do any international business. He told me the meeting wasn't about business; he had to go see someone named Roland Guipure about his grandfather."

"I'm sorry." She really was. But— "His own grandfather, or Guipure's grandfather?"

Just for a second, Ellen Ochs grinned. "Both, actually. He said, 'I need to go see a fashion designer named Roland Guipure about my grandfather.' And when I asked what on earth his grandfather could have to do with a Parisian fashion designer, he said no, no, the connection was between his grandfather and the designer's grandfather. He said it was about someone they both knew before the war. And then he laughed and said he wasn't going to tell me anything else until he was sure there was something to tell. That was *so Jack*." She teared up again. "He always loved to make a mystery."

Rachel waited while Mrs. Ochs dried her eyes with the end of her sweater sleeve, but once she seemed to have collected herself, Rachel pressed on. "Why did he end up making the trip alone?" She didn't add that by not going Ellen had quite literally dodged a bullet.

"We were just about to make the reservations when our son broke his leg." She shook her head. "He fell out of a tree, of all things. We couldn't leave him on his own, so I said I'd stay and Jack should go. After all, he had an actual reason."

"Do you by any chance remember when he first suggested the trip?" Had it been before he'd even spoken to Guipure, or had the phone conversation on Guipure's calendar given Ochs a reason to visit Paris?

"Uh, well, let me think. Bert broke his leg in early March, and it would have been around ten days before that." She gave a watery smile. "That's a terrible name for a fifteen-year-old in this day and age, I know. He hates it. But he's named after Jack's grandfather, actually. He's Albert Ochs the second."

Mntiond trip rt. afr date of S'terre call, Rachel jotted on a piece of paper next to the computer. And just in case she would need reminding, *Grandfather Albert Ochs.*

"Had he been acting differently during the period before that? Had anything changed?"

"No, not that I—oh, wait, yes. He'd started going through his father's books. My father-in-law died two years ago, and we boxed up his books and brought them here. We put them in the garage for Jack to sort through when he had the time, and, well, you know how that goes. It was only this January that he finally made a start."

"What kind of books are they?"

She tried to remember, but all she could come up with was, "Just ordinary books, I think. I haven't seen them for two years, but I don't remember any that looked especially odd. My father-in-law tended to read Dick Francis–type things."

"Would it be all right if Alan came over and had a look? And maybe made a list of the titles for me?" Sorry, Alan.

"Yes, sure." The various looks of worry, concern, and sorrow had now ceded to confusion. "Do you think my husband was killed over a book?"

It wouldn't be the first time, Rachel wanted to say. But instead she answered straightforwardly, "I really don't know. I'm just trying to explore every avenue." She took a deep breath. "And in light of that, your husband didn't mention talking to anyone at Sauveterre named Gabrielle, did he?" She shifted in her chair. "Or even just mention the name?"

Ellen's blank expression provided the answer before she spoke. "No. Who's that?"

"She's the assistant of Roland Guipure's sister." Then, realizing that would make no sense to someone unaware of the link, she added, "The assistant to the chief financial officer of Guipure's company."

"What's her last name? Maybe he mentioned her by that."

"Aubert. She's Gabrielle Aubert."

Once again Ellen Ochs looked blank. "No. I've never heard that name before. I'm sorry."

"Oh, please don't trouble yourself. But just let me ask you one more time . . . you're quite sure your husband didn't say anything, anything at all, about why he was meeting with Guipure?"

The other woman shook her head. "No. I'm sorry. He just promised that he'd explain everything when he came back." She began to cry, then apologized in an almost exact echo of Antoinette Guipure three weeks before. "Oh, I'm sorry; please forgive me. It's just . . . I can't get used to the idea that he's never coming back. I bought mint chocolate chip ice cream for us all to eat together."

A great detective might have pressed on, but if so Rachel was no great detective. She was tired of intruding on women in pain, tired of making them seek forgiveness for their perfectly natural reactions. So she apologized, apologized again, thanked Ellen Ochs for her time, and ended the call.

*　*　*

The next day brought a call from Boussicault. He would have time to meet Rachel that afternoon. But could she come to his office? He had only the afternoon free from attempting to deal with the mess at Rue du Faubourg-St. Honoré, and he needed it to go through his own paperwork.

Boussicault's home police commissariat on the Rue Vaugirard looked just as sad as it had the previous summer, when Rachel had last seen it. If she wasn't much mistaken, she thought as she waited in the gray and wood-grain veneer lobby, the copies of *Voici* and *Closer* on the table were the same ones she had flipped through before their first meeting in 2013. As Boussicault had done that time and all the times after, he collected her at reception, then led her through the labyrinth of corridors to his own office, a strange three-sided glass box jammed up against one edge of a squad room. He gestured at her to sit down in front of the desk, then sat down behind it.

The desktop was covered in open and closed files; in front of his desk chair lay a stack of sheets with a fountain pen on top. He picked it up and used it to point to the stack. "Incident logs." From underneath them he pulled out a beige manilla folder.

"There isn't much progress on Ochs," he said. "Just the autopsy results, which came in last week, and the crime scene report."

"May I read them?"

As he had also done before, many times, he put his elbows on his desk, steepled his fingers, and held them over his mouth, staring at nothing. After a few minutes in that position, he stood up, walked to one side of his aquarium and pulled the gray vertical blinds closed.

"They'll think we're having an affair," Rachel joked.

"Better that than thinking I'm sharing information with a civilian. Again." He sat back down at the desk and lifted the folder. When he spoke, his voice was very precise. "Madame Ochs asked you for this information, is that correct? She asked you to act as her liaison with the police because she feels the investigation is proceeding too slowly for her liking."

Rachel bit her lip for a moment. "Absolutely," she said stoutly. She leaned forward and took the folder.

The crime scene report was on top. The police had received a call to the Holiday Inn Elysées at eleven thirty PM on Friday, April 16. Shortly after eleven, the occupants of room 318 had called the front desk to report a loud noise in the room next door. Twenty minutes later the hotel had sent someone up, and when no one responded to their knocks they opened the door and found a white male lying across the room's writing desk, the remains of a cushion and its stuffing discarded on the floor. The man was dead. The report stated that his suitcase hadn't been unpacked, and he was fully clothed.

"His wallet was gone," Rachel said.

"As you might expect from a robbery."

Or a murder staged to look like a robbery. Rachel turned to the autopsy report. Jacques Ochs, as the coroner spelled it, had been a healthy male between forty-five and sixty years old, a touch overweight for his five feet nine inches. He had been killed sometime between nine and eleven PM by one shot from behind. The killer had used a 9mm bullet and shot from a distance of forty centimeters or more. When shot, the victim was standing fully clothed at the desk, onto which he collapsed, as shown by postmortem blood pooling in the arms and forehead. The shooter was either a very good shot or standing very close or both, because the bullet hit Ochs almost dead center at the base of the skull. It had a slightly upward trajectory, and it had not exited. The victim died instantly.

In the space below the autopsy diagram, with its neat little dot drawn at the base of the male figure's skull, was a box headed "Stomach Contents." Ochs's last meal had been shredded pork with some sort of sauce, bread, *pommes frites*, and about two liters of water.

Rehydrating, Rachel thought. Then, darkly, *Not that it did him any good.*

There were no more pages. Rachel finished making notes and handed the folder back to Boussicault. He tossed it onto a pile next to him, then steepled his fingers once again. He leaned backward in his chair. "Rachel." He spoke seriously. "This information is confidential, and this crime did not occur in my *compétence*. You and I both know that this is—" he nodded at the closed blinds. "But you must also know that I can be of limited help to you if you—er—if Madame Ochs finds herself in any kind of difficulty."

Rachel nodded. "I understand." She smiled reassuringly. "I don't see that happening."

Boussicault didn't look as sure, but he said nothing.

She met Dolly at Le Grand Comptoir d'Anvers a couple of hours later. Each ordered a glass of wine, but only Dolly drank from hers: Rachel was too focused on the task at hand to pay attention to anything else.

Dolly did remember arranging the phone call between Guipure and Ochs. In fact, she even remembered Ochs's initial contact. He had sent Guipure a letter in early February. She remembered because it was marked "Personal and

Confidential" and had a US stamp. She hadn't read it, hadn't even opened the envelope, but simply placed it in with the rest of the mail she gave to Guipure in the morning. A few hours later he had emerged from his *atelier* and asked her to put a telephone call with a Monsieur Jack Ochs on his calendar for five pm that Friday. He had still been on that call when Dolly left the office at six; she had seen the red light next to his extension number. But she knew nothing about the conversation. She hadn't heard Ochs's name again until a month later, when Guipure asked her to add a meeting with Ochs to the calendar for Saturday, April 16, at two in the afternoon. She remembered the time because, as was Sauveterre policy, she'd called Monsieur Ochs to confirm two days before the meeting. She'd spoken to him in his room at the Holiday Inn Elysées.

"I think I woke him up. He sounded very tired. And he had a Southern accent."

But these crumbs were an embarrassment of riches compared to what she could offer about Gabrielle. "She was already working for Antoinette when I arrived. Even then she ran that office like a Swiss watch."

"But she would've had access to Guipure's calendar?" Rachel was already sure of the answer but, as with Ellen Ochs, she wanted to be doubly sure.

"Of course." Dolly was dismissive. "Everyone at the company's top tier could see everyone else's appointments: Keteb, our office, Antoinette's office, the head seamstress . . ."

"So she would've seen that Guipure had a meeting with Jack Ochs."

"Yes, but she never said anything about it to me. And she would have. She loved America. She studied at the Fashion Institute of Technology in Manhattan, and any time anything to do with America came up, she loved to linger over it." She snorted. "Once, we were working together on the arrangements for the banquet to follow spring/summer haute couture 2012. That was the 'Pearls' collection, and the banquet was pearl themed. We were trying to calculate how much white caviar to order, and of all things, she told me *caviar* always made her think of America. She had this great-great-uncle or something, Septime—I remembered the name because it was so old-fashioned; you don't hear names like that anymore. Anyway, *Oncle* Septime had moved to America right before the war, she said, and on the ship over they'd had caviar at dinner. Septime had never even seen caviar before, never mind eaten it, and the story was that after dinner, he'd taken the steward aside to warn him that someone in the kitchen had added too much salt to the black beans. This was a famous story in her family, apparently. She told me he'd been dead for years, but they still told it." Dolly took a sip of wine. "So, you see: anything that would allow her to squeeze in the US."

It seemed to Rachel that the story had been more about Gabrielle's relative than about the United States, but she got Dolly's point. Gabrielle would have mentioned seeing Jack Ochs's name, if only for the connection it made to America. She shook her head and tried her last possible avenue. "I don't suppose you ever saw her talking with Keteb, by any chance? Were they work friends, like you and he were?"

Dolly frowned. "They often talked in the period before Monsieur Guipure entered *désintox*. We all talked to each other quite a bit then. We used to try to figure out how to unhook him from Thieriot, until Antoinette realized the reviews were our best chance. I ran into them discussing that a few times in Gabrielle's office while Keteb was waiting to see Antoinette."

"But nothing after Guipure returned?"

"Oh." This time Dolly's laugh was bitter. "After Monsieur Guipure returned, Keteb wasn't talking to *anybody*. You couldn't get past his rage to talk to him." She looked at Rachel, her face crumpling. "You're not thinking that Gabrielle and Keteb connived to kill Monsieur Guipure?" She gave a real laugh. "Gabrielle spent all her time organizing Antoinette's life. She didn't have any time left over to have a social life, never mind arrange a murder plot. Besides, it's just . . ." She shook her head. "No."

"She bought heroin on the night of his party," Rachel said.

"What?" For the first time in their acquaintance, Dolly looked less than fully in control. *"What?"* she said again. This time what she drank from her glass was not a sip, but a slug.

Rachel told her a version of what she'd learned from Mediouri and his associate, leaving out the source of the information. When she finished, Dolly sat back hard in her chair.

"I don't believe it. Your information is wrong, or the real explanation is missing, or—" She ran out of breath. "Or there's something else going on that you don't know yet."

"From your mouth to God's ear," Rachel said. Then she realized she'd spoken in English. For the first time in decades, she didn't know the equivalent phrase in French.

The next morning brought Alan's neatly typed list of book titles. Jack Ochs's father certainly had liked Dick Francis. He owned every one of his mysteries. Also on the list were classics of the type that might have been read in high school or college sixty years before—Shakespeare's *Julius Caesar*, Dickens's *A Tale of Two Cities*, an anthology of English and American poetry, a copy of *Catcher in the Rye* (second edition, Alan had noted in parentheses), and several coffee table books on modern art—although none, Alan added, published after 1970. This, plus a history of the twentieth century up to 1950 and a glossy color photo book of horse paintings by the eighteenth-century artist George Stubbs, was the sum total of the ten boxes of books in the Ochs's garage. Alan signed off by reminding her that he would be home the following week.

As if I could forget! Rachel thought. Always by the end of his month away, a month seemed too long to be apart. She remembered Ellen Ochs's mint chocolate chip ice cream and winced.

*   *   *

"Well, no one's going to kill two people over a second edition of *Catcher in the Rye*," said Magda when Rachel finished her update. "So let's see what else we have." In the silence over the phone line Rachel could hear her tapping her thumb against something in the background. "If we put together what they all told you, we know that, first, sometime in early or mid-February Guipure received a letter from Ochs. And, second, after it arrived, Guipure telephoned Ochs at least once."

Rachel pressed her head against her *séjour* window and watched a pigeon peck at what looked like some bread on the pavement below. "And we can assume that whatever the letter was about, and whatever they talked about, was somehow connected to the Second World War. Or rather 'about someone they both knew before the war,' to quote Ochs."

"But who knows what that means?" As Magda spoke, the pigeon was joined by another, identical in every way. "His wife also said he liked to make a mystery. Did he mean someone they both knew at the same time? Someone one knew in France and one in the US? Had Ochs's grandfather even been to France?"

"No idea."

"Right. So, let's work with what we do know. After the call or calls, Guipure and Ochs arranged a meeting, a meeting that we know was still scheduled to go ahead the day Guipure died. Which we know because Dolly called Ochs at the hotel that day to confirm."

"And we know that even though Guipure's death meant they wouldn't meet, Ochs was killed too."

"Which suggests that whatever Guipure was killed over, Ochs was somehow involved with it."

Neither woman spoke. They had come to the end of the known facts and the fact-based assumptions.

Magda heaved a sigh. "We should pay another visit to the Maison Sauveterre."

Rachel sighed in return. "I think I've used up my one chip there. Why would banker's wife and charity organizer Rachel Field pay a second visit?"

"Because this time it's about another matter entirely. You're a friend of Jack Ochs's family, attempting to assist his grieving widow in understanding his death. Okay, it's a coincidence that you know both Antoinette Guipure and Jack Ochs, but it actually *is* a coincidence, if you understand what I mean."

Rachel understood what she meant.

"You're searching for information on Albert Ochs's connection to the Sauveterre family," Magda went on, "not information about Roland Guipure."

Rachel sighed again, although she wasn't sure why. Down below, only one pigeon remained, pecking at the food on the pavement. "Okay," she said. "I'll call right away. Hopefully we can get in before the memorial service."

"And if we get a chance, maybe we can find some way to question Gabrielle at the same time."

Chapter Twenty-Three

Once more Gabrielle came to greet them in the foyer. As she descended the stairs, Rachel considered her legs. They were long and shapely, and the stiletto heels made them seem longer and shapelier still. Maybe they *could* wrap around someone twice.

"We're so grateful to Antoinette for agreeing to see us so quickly," she said as the girl led them up the steps.

"And in the middle of such big changes," Magda added from behind her.

"She was eager to help. She's very interested in anything to do with her grandpère. And with Monsieur Guipure, of course."

It seemed to Rachel that this was as close to an opening to question Gabrielle as she and Magda were likely to get. "Yes." She made her voice solemn. "How is she adjusting to his . . . absence?"

"She's managing well."

"And all the rest of you?" Rachel made her tone carefully sympathetic. "Antoinette told us Sauveterre is like a family. Losing Monsieur Guipure and having Monsieur Lellouch take his place so quickly must be hard for you."

"Well, we knew Monsieur Guipure would need to be replaced quickly if the house was to continue. And Monsieur Lellouch is already familiar with Monsieur Guipure's language and aware of his legacy, so in many ways he's an ideal choice." Gabrielle's voice sounded normal, Rachel thought, but who knew what was going on in the face she couldn't see?

"And it works out well for you." Was it her imagination, or did one of Gabrielle's heels stutter for a moment on the steps? She kept her voice neutral. "I mean, because you already know Monsieur Lellouch so well. I remember that when we were here before you were going into a meeting with him. As Madame Guipure's assistant, you must spend a lot of time with him."

"Yes. We've worked together occasionally." Now she knew she wasn't imagining: the girl's voice had become very careful. "And I'm sure we'll continue to work together in the future."

With this bland remark, they reached the door to the business offices. Gabrielle turned around and gave a smile that didn't reach her eyes. "Here we are, then. Antoinette is expecting you, so please follow me."

Even in mid-May the interior decoration of Maison Sauveterre made the rooms feel cold, so Rachel wasn't surprised to find a fire burning in the fireplace of Antoinette's white office once again. She was interested, though, to see that both the desk and the windowsill now held vases of flowers, although the effect of the purple tulips and daffodils merely enhanced their icy backdrop.

"Madame Field and Madame Stevens," Gabrielle announced, and as Antoinette came forward, she detached a sheet of paper from her clipboard and held it out. "I've also heard back from Saint Roch. They said yes about the cameras, and this is their suggestion for pew allocations."

"Superb." Antoinette smiled at Rachel and Magda. "Gabrielle is handling the logistics of the memorial service." She nodded her thanks. The girl slipped noiselessly from the room.

Like the room, Antoinette had begun to take on color. She wore a soft top of very finely woven gray wool with a pleated linen collar that stretched over the shoulders and chest, which she had tucked into a calf-length magenta skirt that fastened at the waist with a huge gray button. *Sauveterre prêt-à-porter autumn/winter 2013 and autumn/winter 2006,* Rachel identified silently.

Antoinette's manner was as different as her clothes. No longer a pathetic figure, she walked briskly to the little island of furniture and sat forward on a chair. Even her posture telegraphed intense focus and a limited amount of available time.

Her smile was quick. "It's good to see you again. Gabrielle tells me this time you come on behalf of an American friend?"

"Remarkable," she said as Rachel finished her explanation. "When Gabrielle told me about the situation, I had her print out the relevant calendar pages, and I still had trouble believing it." She shook her head. "Still, coincidence is more common in real life than we think." She hesitated for a moment. "But forgive me . . . you say the police told Madame Ochs that her husband was killed during a robbery. So she has been in contact with them. Is there a reason she asked you to step in? Does she not trust their conclusions?"

Rachel had anticipated this question. "It isn't that. But the police investigation of the robbery is progressing very slowly, and . . ." she sighed, "Madame Ochs is an American." She met Antoinette's eyes and smiled apologetically.

The other woman smiled back. "She wants everything done faster, *hein*? And she wants—" she suddenly broke into perfect, unaccented English—"every avenue explored."

Rachel grinned. "Exactly."

"And you've already been to the hotel? You've asked about people who might have requested Monsieur Ochs's room number, or anyone suspicious that night?" Then she shook her head. "I'm sorry; I shouldn't tell you how to handle things. It's a bad habit you get into when you run a company."

"It's fine." Rachel shifted awkwardly. "As it happens, we haven't been to the hotel yet. That's our next stop after talking to you." She shot a surreptitious glance at Magda to remind her that they needed to check out the hotel.

"But for now this connection to my brother is an avenue in its own right."

"Exactly," Rachel said, glad that Antoinette had relieved her of having to make the connection.

"And Madame Ochs told you her husband's conversations with Rolé had to do with my grandfather?" Rachel nodded. Antoinette moved a little further forward. "Did she say with what, specifically?"

"He only said that it was about someone both his grandfather and yours had known 'before the war.'" She added apologetically, "His wife says he loved to be mysterious."

Antoinette sat back in the chair for a moment as if winded by frustration. Then she straightened and shook her head again. "Unfortunately, there's no way for me to know what my brother and Monsieur Ochs spoke about now that Rolé is . . . gone. We worked under the 'divide and conquer' model: we didn't discuss our meetings unless they were relevant to both of us. And I don't remember ever hearing the name Albert Ochs from my grandparents. Or my mother, for that matter."

"Well, we wondered . . ." Rachel felt Magda shift beside her, ready to jump in if she delayed. "Ochs is a Jewish name, so we thought perhaps the connection to your grandfather lay in a mutual friend your grandfather had helped?"

Antoinette exhaled in a little puff. "I don't recall seeing the name on any of my grandfather's receipts. But then there are a lot of receipts; he helped many people, even before the war. You are welcome to look in our archive." She gave a little smile, and Rachel remembered Naquet saying Sauveterre was justly proud of its archive. "We have the records from all of Grandpère's transactions."

"Yes, that would be terrific. Thank you."

"Not a problem. Gabrielle!" The girl appeared again. "Gabrielle organized the renovations of the archive last year. Gabrielle, please take Madame Levis and Madame Stevens down and help them find what they need. She'll have to stay with you while you look." Antoinette's smile was apologetic. "Nothing personal; it's company policy."

* * *

On the way downstairs Rachel tried once again with Gabrielle.

"You seem to handle everything that needs organizing at Sauveterre, Gabrielle," she said mildly.

"Yes. I'm fortunate that Antoinette trusts me enough to give me so much responsibility."

"That must interfere with your social life. Do you have to spend a lot of time here after hours?" That would be the ideal time to arrange a delivery better left unseen.

"Monsieur Guipure used to say that fashion has no clock. I usually stay until I'm done working on whatever needs to be finished."

"So in the days before a show, or in the run-up to something like Roland's birthday party, that could mean being here until quite late."

"Well, the shows are handled by creative, so they don't involve me very much. But when we're preparing the annual report, or in the run-up to one of the quarterly financial meetings, I do stay late, yes. I was here very late sometimes while Antoinette was working on the licensing agreement."

"Well"—Rachel gave a little laugh—"I suppose what you lose in a social life outside you gain in a social life inside. You must have made a lot of friends in the company, spending so much time here." Perhaps the girl could be led into revealing her connection to Lellouch.

"Not so many. The offices are quite separate from the *ateliers*. I do see some of the seamstresses sometimes."

Gabrielle walked toward the back of the foyer. "The archive is just down here."

They followed her into the shadows. Here the marble banister became a cheap iron railing, the stairs ordinary metal ones with nonslip cross-hatching. Even Rachel's practical flats made noise on these. At their bottom was a metal door locked by a deadbolt, an ugly gray contraption with a knob sticking out of its right side. Gabrielle tucked the ever-present clipboard under one arm and used that hand to put a key in the lock. As she turned it, she simultaneously pulled the knob to the right. A long iron bar emerged—a second bolt under the first. Rachel the lockpick was impressed.

"It seems old-fashioned, but it's more secure than even the best digital lock." Gabrielle's voice was proud. "No malfunctions, no possibility of overrides." She turned the doorknob and pushed.

As they crossed the threshold, fluorescent lights flickered on. They stood at one end of a huge room, its white walls lined with filing cabinets occasionally interspersed with chests of deep drawers. From her experience at the Bibliothèque Nationale the previous summer, Rachel recognized these as map cabinets, used to hold items that needed to lie flat. In the center of the room were two tables with white Formica tops, two chairs tucked under each, and each with a box of white cotton gloves in the center. Gabrielle crossed to the fourth filing cabinet, opened the top drawer, and removed all the folders it held, putting them on the closest table. Then she did the same with the folders in the top drawer of the fifth cabinet, a much smaller number.

"Those are all the Galerie Sauveterre's bills of sale and purchase receipts for the years 1936 to 1946. Please wear gloves as you look at them." She pulled out a chair and sat down at the far table, frowning at something on the clipboard.

The gloves snagged slightly on the skin of Rachel's hands, and as Magda finished pulling hers on, she whispered, "I feel like Mickey Mouse!" When Rachel began opening the folders, though, she saw the wisdom of them. Some of the documents already had crumbling edges; some were so damaged that they'd been slipped into protective plastic sleeves. Even with the gloves on she was careful to handle them gingerly.

The folders were organized by year and month, January to December, and the sheer number of receipts suggested that every one had been preserved. No wonder Gédéon Naquet had praised the archive: it was a researcher's dream.

But in the entire collection of thin yellowing sheets spanning 1936 to 1940 there was no mention of anyone named Ochs, as buyer or seller. She started on the smaller pile of 1940 to 1946. Whereas the folders for the years preceding the German invasion showed a roughly equal division of buying and selling, in the 1940 to 1946 grouping, buying predominated. And the names of the sellers were all similar: *Pierre Goldman: Marc Chagall, The Drunken Fiddler, 112,000ff; Hélène Dreyfus: Paul Klee, Tale à la Hoffman, 105,000ff; Maurice Ephrussi: Jean Metzinger, Two Nudes Asleep in a Garden, 190,000ff.* As she flipped through this history of Sauveterre's decency she felt her throat tighten. Something about the recognizably Jewish names, each following the next in neat handwriting on identical carbons, brought home to her the desperation, and the hope, of the Jews in occupied France in a way that no book or museum exhibition ever had. How many of these people made it out, and how many sold their treasured art in attempts to fund escapes that never came to pass? Seventy-three thousand

French Jews died in the camps during the war. How many of those had their names preserved only in the purchase receipts of the Galerie Sauveterre?

After an hour of flipping through folders, though, such thoughts had been driven from her mind by the aching muscles between her shoulder blades, and by one simple certainty: however many of Sauveterre's customers had succeeded in fleeing and however many had failed, the receipts showed that none of them had been an Albert Ochs. Across the table from her, Magda closed her final folder and massaged her lower back. She looked at Rachel and shook her head. No luck there either.

Outside on the pavement once more, Rachel ran a hand through her hair, dislodging imaginary dust that could never have hidden in an archive as clean as Sauveterre's. But just as she was about to sigh, she stopped herself. If she knew from experience that there came a moment in each investigation where the case took over, didn't she also know that there came a moment when the case seemed hopeless? And hadn't experience shown her that such appearances were wrong? Neither of her previous hopeless cases had turned out to be hopeless. It turned out that the secret to solving a mystery was the same as the secret to any other success: just keep going.

"Let's check out the hotel."

Chapter
Twenty-Four

⁓

It was one of Rachel's firmest convictions that you could judge a mid-level hotel by its lobby floor. Hotels with carpeted lobbies invariably turned out to be two stars or below; hotels with marble or granite floors equally invariably turned out to be three stars or above. The Holiday Inn Elysées bore out this conviction. A three-star hotel, it had a stone lobby floor laid out in a pattern of alternating brown and cream-colored tiles. The lobby itself was immaculate and hushed, accessed by front doors that slid open and closed silently, shutting out the noises of the street outside. In fact only its reception desk, a construction of wood veneer and beige Formica, marked it out as three stars rather than four.

As they approached the counter, the woman behind it looked up from the computer terminal she'd been reading and smiled broadly. Her teeth were dazzling. *"Bonjour!* Can I help you?"

Rachel smiled back. "I hope so. We're looking for information about one of your guests, Jack Ochs."

"I'm sorry, the hotel doesn't give out information about guests."

"Well, he's really a former guest. He stayed here in April."

The smile remained in place. "As I said, the hotel takes the privacy of its guests very seriously. Even when they're no longer in residence."

"Monsieur Ochs is no longer in residence because he's dead. He is the man who was killed in his room here a month ago. You may remember? We're connected to his family, and we're hoping to get answers to a couple of questions."

"I'm very sorry, but as I said, the hotel won't be able to answer them. If you wish to submit a complaint about our policies, I can direct you to the appropriate page on our website."

Magda nudged Rachel aside. She had her wallet out and open, and she snapped down onto the counter one of the mocked-up business cards Rachel had made her at the end of their previous investigation. She rested her thumb so it covered the company motto Rachel had added as a joke.

"Stevens and Levis, Private Investigators. We've been retained by the family to look into the circumstances surrounding Monsieur Ochs's murder. Working in conjunction with the police, we're exploring the possibility that there is more to this situation than meets the eye. Now, I can call my associate Capitaine Guillaume Boussicault from the Commissariat Vaugirard, and he and his men can come down here with a warrant to commandeer your computers for as long as it takes to check every single file and find those that pertain to Monsieur Ochs, or you can help us out of your own accord, and no one will have to tell your *gérante* who caused all of that to happen."

It was as if she had set herself the task of using every police show cliché in a single speech. Yet it worked. The woman's smile wavered. She glanced quickly at the card, then toward the open office door behind her, and then back at Magda. "All right, all right." She kept her voice low. "What do you need?"

"When did Monsieur Ochs check in?"

A quick clicking of the keys. "He arrived at ten AM on Thursday, the fourteenth of April. He'd arranged an early check-in."

"And did he receive any telephone calls or messages while he was here?"

More clicking. "There were three phone calls. All were put through to the room and there were no messages left on room voice mail. One call the morning of his arrival from the USA, another one later that afternoon from 1 4076 85 85. Then another the next day"—she glanced up briefly—"that's Friday the fifteenth, in the afternoon, from 1 4076 85 90."

Rachel jumped. Magda half turned. "What?"

"Nothing, nothing." She waved a hand. "It's just that 4076 is the first four digits of Sauveterre's general number. That must have been when Dolly called to confirm the meeting."

But the other call had come after Guipure was dead. Had someone called to cancel the appointment? She pulled a piece of paper from her bag and wrote both numbers down. She would check later.

Magda had returned to the task at hand. "Were there any outgoing phone calls *from* the room?"

The woman scrolled down, then shook her head. "No. Although Monsieur Ochs did call down and ask for a wake-up call at six PM on Friday evening."

"Any visitors?"

"We don't record visitors."

Magda sighed in a way that suggested this was a grave and outrageous failing. "Were you personally on duty for any portion of his stay?"

The woman glanced at the computer to check the dates. "Some of it, but I didn't—that is, I wouldn't have known who Monsieur Ochs wa—"

"Thank you." Magda reached into her bag and brought out her case folder. She opened it and took out an enlargement of Gabrielle's LinkedIn photo, which she put on the counter on top of the business card. "Have you ever seen this woman?"

A shake of her head—*No.*

"What about this man?"

Naquet's author photo earned another shake.

"Or these?"

She laid down a photo of Lellouch and Guipure standing next to each other and grinning fixedly, obviously cropped from some larger publicity photo. The woman began to shake her for a third time, then leaned in closer.

"Is that Roland Guipure, the *couturier*?" Magda nodded. "Well, no, I didn't see either of them, but why would Roland Guipure come to our hotel?"

Magda acted as if she hadn't heard the question. "We'd like to see Monsieur Ochs's room, please." She stared at the receptionist, daring her to refuse.

Rachel held her breath. Surely, surely a moment would come when the bluff would stop working.

This was not that moment. "Well, I, uh—" Another furtive glance toward the office door. "Well, we can only allow that if the room is unoccupied." Typing again, she frowned at the monitor. Then her face cleared. "Fortunately, room 532 is currently empty. I can—" She reached for the universal key card that lay on the desk in front of her.

Magda held up a hand. "No, thank you. We work better on our own. Faster." As they waited for the key, she slid the fake business card back into her wallet before the receptionist could see the motto: *We are shameless in the service of detection.*

In the elevator Magda idly scanned the breakfast menu posted on the wall next to her. Rachel studied her face.

"How do you do that? How do you just . . . get people to go along with you?"

Magda shrugged. "It's another version of what you do. You see that people have things they want to say, and you move them into a position where they feel they can say them. Like with Cyrille Thieriot. I do that with actions rather than words: I make it easy for people to feel okay about doing things to help us. Most people instinctively want to help; that's why there are so many rules to keep them from doing it. I just do what it takes to make them feel comfortable breaking those rules. You're patient, I'm aggressive, but it's the same essential result."

Rachel was still evaluating the truth of these statements when the elevator doors slid open. They stepped out onto a corridor papered in cream, with a thick green carpet underfoot. A sign on the wall said "502–540," with an arrow pointing left.

Ochs's former room was a model of bland luxury. Decorated in brown and beige, it had a thick carpet, plump pillows, and a lustrous chenille spread artfully draped across its snowy, wrinkle-free duvet. Everything about it said that it was interchangeable with hundreds of other rooms in this building, and countless others around the world. It was a good choice for a modest traveler, though, one who valued comfort over individuality and neutral familiarity over artistic exuberance—which made Rachel all the more confused about how its occupant connected to the life of a man like Guipure.

"I really don't think we're going to find anything. The place has obviously been cleaned within an inch of its life."

"No pun intended." Magda's voice sounded hollowly from behind the open door of the narrow wardrobe. "No, probably not, but . . ." She closed the door and headed for the bathroom. "Check under the bed. I know it's one of your favorite places."

"Ha ha." The last time she and Magda had searched a hotel room, they had been forced to hide under a bed when housekeeping arrived unexpectedly. She thought of this as she crouched down and lifted the suede fabric bed skirt, and specifically of the used Band-Aid that had been inches from her nose while she lay on that room's grubby carpet.

Fortunately, there was no Band-Aid. Less fortunately, there was nothing else either. The rug under the bed was a bit dusty, but that was all. She used a hand to lever herself up to a standing crouch, then ran the other between the mattress and the large wood-framed mirror that served as the headboard. She had once found a clue in the back of a locker, so she knew where things might get stuck, but this time there was nothing. She straightened up.

"Nothing here." Magda emerged from the bathroom.

"Or here."

Magda raised her eyebrows. "So much for the good omen of the granite floor."

"That's about the quality of the hotel, not the number of clues." But Rachel said this distractedly. She was thinking that if Ochs had arrived on the morning of the fourteenth and told his wife he hadn't left the hotel when they spoke on the fifteenth, that meant he must have either ordered room service or eaten at the in-house restaurant.

"Come on," she beckoned Magda. "One more stop, just to be sure. Let's go have something in the restaurant."

Chapter Twenty-Five

The hotel's restaurant was open only for breakfast and dinner, explained a young man in a black vest who seemed to be standing guard on the dining room, but the bar was open. If they took a seat there, he would send someone to take their order.

Rachel smiled her thanks. "Could I see a dinner menu while we wait, please?"

"We don't begin serving dinner until seven."

Taking a lesson from the receptionist, she kept the smile on her face. "Still, if you wouldn't mind."

Whether he minded or not, he retreated to the dining area and, after some shifting and searching, returned with a dinner menu.

"What are you doing?" Magda asked as they settled at a table near the glass and wood bar and the young man went off to find a waiter for them.

"I'm looking for . . ." Rachel said, running her eyes down the first page of the menu, flipping it over, then laying it crosswise on the table, resting her finger halfway down the laminated page, ". . . this."

Magda craned her neck to the side. "'Delicious pork, slow-cooked, shredded, then mixed with a barbecue sauce, served on a brioche grilled golden-brown, with pommes frites.' It's a pulled pork sandwich—so what? They can't make it for you now. The man just said they don't serve dinner until seven."

"It's a pulled pork sandwich, but it's also an almost exact description of what Jack Ochs had in his stomach. Remember, the autopsy showed that Ochs's last meal was shredded pork, sauce, some kind of bread, and *pommes frites*. Not too many restaurants in Paris serve any form of shredded pork, never mind with sauce, on a bun, and with french fries. That's food designed to appeal to Americans. I think this is where he ate his last meal."

A young blond man, also in a vest but tying a long gray apron around his waist, approached their table. "*Bonjour, mesdames.* What can I get for you?"

Rachel ordered a coffee for Magda and a Coke Light for herself. "And may I ask you a question?"

He looked wary but nodded.

"Do you remember that a guest here died in his room last month?"

Another nod, firmer this time. "He was killed in a robbery, yes? I remember hearing about it when I came in for my shift."

"We're making some inquiries on behalf of the family. Do you know if anyone who was working then is here right now?"

"I will go and ask in the kitchen." His eyes lit up as he hurried off.

Watching him, Rachel wondered why people were so eager to associate themselves with violent death. But she knew the answer. It was a form of celebrity, and who didn't yearn for even the slightest brush with fame?

In a few moments the waiter returned, bringing with him their order and a small Asian man whose broad face was lightly marked with acne scars and whose hair, otherwise deepest black, stood up in small bleached spikes at the top of his head. Their waiter introduced him as Kento. He had been waiting on tables on Friday night, their waiter explained, and had served the man who had died. He would answer their questions.

Rachel tapped her *portable* screen, tapped it again, made the expanding pinch that magnified the display, and held it up. It showed Ochs's photo from the passport Alan had scanned to her earlier. "First, is this the man you waited on?"

Kento leaned forward to look, then nodded vigorously.

"Thank you. Okay, can you tell me everything you remember?"

In a thick Parisian accent, Kento explained that Monsieur Ochs had come into the restaurant at around eight on Friday night. Yes, he had ordered the pulled pork sandwich—he remembered because in his experience only American customers ordered it, and sure enough when he switched into English after Monsieur had placed his order, Monsieur had obviously been relieved. He had asked Kento if he could recommend a restaurant near the hotel that was open late and reasonably quiet. Kento had recommended La Traboule, just around the corner on the Rue de Penthièvre, which was not quiet but was managed by Kento's brother-in-law. In Kento's experience tired people didn't look for a second option no matter how unsuitable the first, and since Monsieur looked fairly tired, he figured this was a chance to send a bit of business his brother-in-law's way. He gave him directions to La Traboule, and Monsieur had thanked him and given him an enormous tip. The last Kento had seen of him, Monsieur was heading toward the bank of elevators in the lobby.

"He asked for somewhere that would be open very late that night, Friday night? Not the next night, Saturday night?"

No, that night. "He never said anything about Saturday."

"Thank you. That's very, very helpful." Rachel dug out her wallet and gave him her own enormous tip, along with fulsome compliments on his excellent English.

"What do you mean 'very, very helpful'?" Magda asked when their own waiter had gone off to fetch their bill. "All he did was confirm that Ochs had the sandwich and tell us he tried to con him into going to the wrong kind of restaurant."

Rachel put a finger to her lips. She felt certainty and its accompanying confidence rising inside her. "Wait, I'll explain. But first I need to talk to the receptionist."

She left their waiter a gigantic tip of his own, then crossed the four-star lobby to the three-star reception desk. The brunette was frowning at the computer screen once more.

"Excuse me."

The receptionist looked up, and after thanking her for her help—yes, seeing the room had been very helpful, absolutely—Rachel wondered if she'd be willing to answer just one more question. Well, re-answer it, really.

"I'm sorry to ask this again, but we need to be absolutely certain. Are you sure no one telephoned and asked to speak to Monsieur Ochs after the call on Friday afternoon? No one called on Friday night? Or on Saturday morning?"

The receptionist checked again. A shake of the head. No, there had been only the calls on Thursday and on Friday afternoon. By Saturday, of course, Monsieur Ochs was no longer—she shifted uncomfortably—using his room, but if any calls had come they would have been logged by the police.

Boussicault hadn't mentioned any.

"And I'm sorry again—we should have asked you this before—but do you remember anyone coming in and asking for Ochs late on Friday night or on Saturday morning? Not just the people we showed you, but anyone at all?"

She looked upward, casting her mind back. No. Of course, once Monsieur Ochs's body had been discovered, things had become very crowded and very busy, but exactly because of that she thought she would have remembered anyone asking for him, and she couldn't. She was sorry she couldn't be more helpful.

The twenty-euro note Rachel slipped across the counter seemed to cheer her up.

The pneumatic doors swept open, and once more there they were on the pavement. Rachel waited for the doors to close again before she spoke.

"He was killed before his meeting, and he was killed by whomever he was supposed to be meeting."

Magda made a dismissive face. "How do you figure that, Sherlock Holmes?"

"You mock, but you are about to eat your words as surely as Jack Ochs ate a pulled pork sandwich. First, we know that Ochs received a call from his wife after his arrival on Thursday, then one from Dolly later the same day. Then there was a second call from Sauveterre on Friday afternoon. I think that second call was to move the meeting to Friday night. He was asking at dinner for somewhere quiet he could go later, and quiet suggests he was going to be having a conversation, which suggests a meeting. Second, he asked Kento for somewhere that would be open late. By eight at night, nine or ten isn't late. So he must have been expecting to meet later than that."

Magda caught on. "And Boussicault said time of death was in between nine and eleven. If later was later than ten, he must have been killed before he left for the meeting." Rachel nodded. "Okay, but that only tells us that he was killed before the meeting. How do you figure it wasn't by a thief?"

"Because we know no one called or came to the desk to ask for him. If you were supposed to be meeting someone and he didn't show up, wouldn't you wonder where he was? And if you knew what hotel he was staying in, or if you'd arranged to meet him there in the first place, wouldn't you ask the desk to call up, or maybe ask for the room number so you could go up yourself? Or let's say the person he was meeting figured he'd fallen asleep— it was late; he was jet-lagged—and they didn't want to wake him by phoning or going up to his room. If that was the case, they'd call the next day, or maybe even stop by, to reschedule. But now we know no one did either of those things. Whoever was meeting him knew there would be no point in calling or stopping by to reschedule. Which means they knew he was dead."

"Which means they killed him." Magda looked impressed.

"Or paid someone else to do it."

"Gabrielle." Magda was firm. "It must be her. She bought the heroin. And those two phone calls Ochs got from Paris were from Sauveterre. One was probably Dolly calling to confirm, but the other one came after Guipure was dead."

"So you caught that, too."

Magda nodded. For a second they grinned in mutual admiration, then she went on. "The second phone call could have been Gabrielle. It would have been very easy for her to call from Sauveterre and arrange to meet Ochs herself. To head him off."

"But *why?*"

"Well, that's the big question, isn't it?" Magda started buttoning her jacket. "We already know there are connections here that we don't know anything about, and the Sauveterre archive was no help. I think this is my cue to go home and do a little digital digging."

Rachel settled her bag on her shoulder. "I'm going to call Dolly again. She'll be able to tell us for sure who's attached to the extension number of that second call from Sauveterre." Magda's fingers paused for a split second. "What?"

She started buttoning again. "Nothing." She finished. "Only . . . she worked for Roland, and we never looked into her very deeply. And we have only her word for why she was let go. Should we really feel sure about trusting her?"

Rachel considered this. It was true that they'd made no effort to check out Dolly, or to double-check her stories, and it was true that such lack of verification would be a murderer's best friend. But on the other hand . . .

"Who else do we have?"

Chapter
Twenty-Six

Once again Dolly wasn't home. Was Dolly *ever* home? Rachel tried to imagine her life and came up with days filled with complex exercise classes that nonetheless did not require perspiration, wine in various colors sipped from glasses of various shapes with various friends, and evenings spent flicking through books with those heavy pages that smelled like museum gift shops.

Emerging from this daydream, she realized that she had based it all on Dolly's immaculate and unwrinkled brown silk shirt; from this she had extrapolated a life of ease and elegance. She remembered Magda's earlier remark. Fine, since she had nothing to do but wait for one woman or the other to call her, why not use the time to do a little background research?

If Dolly's LinkedIn profile was to be believed, she had indeed been born in Nancy, and on September 11, 1960. She had been working as an assistant since 1982, working her way up through the ranks at a series of magazines before moving to Givenchy. When Hubert Givenchy left in 1995, so did she, moving first to work at Louis Vuitton and then, in 2013, to Sauveterre. Her profile listed that job as ending on April 22, which made her story about being let go after Guipure's death plausible.

Oh for a copy of *How to Hack Like a BOSS*! Or even just *How to Hack*. Like everyone else, Rachel was automatically inclined to believe what appeared in print, but this case had shown her clearly that there could be much more to someone than the bits the media offered. If she were Magda, she would probably have peered behind some firewall by now and learned that Dolly was a lost Romanov grandchild or a spy from Balenciaga sent to infiltrate other fashion houses and report back on their secrets.

On cue, her doorbell rang. Of course it was Magda. "God bless the Mormons for their belief in baptism of the dead. They're out there trying to find every person ever born, and they've put their records online, for everyone to use, on something called FamilySearch. They've digitized every state census in the US. Including Florida, which is where I started looking for Albert Ochs."

"And?"

Magda's story was one of many leads and few results. She had found an Albert Ochs in the Florida 1945 census, living in Daytona and married to Muriel, with a two-year-old son named Paul. "But he wasn't in the state census they did in 1935, or in 1925, and Florida birth certificates aren't digitized that far back. So I used the FamilySearch website to find his death certificate, which showed he was born in Hypoluxo, Florida, on June 24, 1905. But I checked every census from 1890 to 1925, and *no one* with the last name Ochs is listed as living in Hypoluxo during that period." She sighed, then added, "The nationwide census from 1940, however, did tell me that one thousand one hundred and seventy-six people named Albert Ochs lived in the United States in 1940. I suppose he could be one of those."

"What about searching birth certificates?"

Magda shook her head. "Those aren't accessible digitally. A relative of the deceased has to write or go in person to request."

That left them with only a deep dive into the 1940 national census. Better to try every other avenue before attempting to track down 1,176 Albert Ochses. Rachel bit her lip and thought. If Albert Ochs had been born in Hypoluxo but was never listed as living there, what were the possible explanations? Could he have been an emergency birth to parents visiting the town? In that case, there would be a birth certificate on file. Her mind began to race. Perhaps her in-laws could be persuaded to visit Hypoluxo, wherever it was, to look through the birth certificates for 1905, to see if there had been an oversight? Maybe Ellen Ochs could appoint them her proxies in an attempt to locate the misplaced birth certificate of their Albert Ochs? But no, in order to do that they would need to know his place of birth.

"Stop thinking," Magda broke in, "because I already did. I remembered what you said about Ochs being a Jewish name. And I thought . . . I know it sound far-fetched, but nineteen forty-five the tail end of the war. What if Ochs isn't in any census before 1945 because he wasn't in Florida before then? Because he wasn't in the *country* before then?"

Rachel turned this over in her mind. "You're saying that he came from somewhere else and just pretended to be a Florida native?" Magda nodded. "But why?"

"Well, someone who arrived in the US between 1935 and 1945 might have memories he didn't want to talk about. He might try to suppress his past, try to deny it. He might even do that to the extent of pretending that he was just an ordinary American, born and raised. Remember that documentary we watched last year about that Clark Rockefeller man?"

Rachel nodded, unfazed by this apparent detour. She and Magda had both been fascinated by the case of the imposter who had pretended to be a Rockefeller. She knew where her friend was going. "You're thinking of the way he changed his accent."

"Lost it. Completely. We heard him interviewed, remember? No one would have guessed that he was actually German. And there are all those English actors who do flawless American accents. It can be done. Ochs would have needed to work hard to get rid of his original accent, but once he did that, he could pick a place and tell people he was born there, make up some stories about his childhood." She held out a hand. "And then that becomes your life. Of course, if you don't tell anyone that you've lied about those things, when you die, people think you were born where you said you were born, and they put that on your death certificate."

It was the perfect explanation, so perfect that Rachel could scarcely bring herself to ask, "Do you have evidence to back any of this up?"

"I think I do." Magda opened the folder and laid a sheet on the coffee table. "I went to the Ellis Island website. They have a database with the name of everyone who passed through from 1820 to 1957—really, the internet is fantastic. I searched 'Albert Ochs,' and I found this."

The sheet was a printout of a screen shot. *Purchase Passenger Record* it said at the top. Beneath that was what looked like a graduation certificate, albeit one with *SAMPLE* written all over it in gray letters. Through those letters it was possible to see that it certified the arrival of one Albert Ochs, thirty-five years old, at Ellis Island. This Albert Ochs had been born on June 25, 1905, in Alsace, and had arrived in New York on the SS *Pennland* on January 4, 1940, having embarked at Le Havre.

"My God." Rachel realized she hadn't quite believed Magda's theory until then. She reached out and rested an index finger on the printout. "There he is. Albert Ochs, supposed Florida native, arriving on the boat from France."

"Wait. It gets more interesting." Magda took out some stapled pages. "The *Pennland* is a ship with a history. It carried troops in the Second World War and was bombed by the Germans. That makes it of interest to World War II buffs, and one of them digitized its passenger lists—*all* of its passenger lists, including the one for the passengers embarking on the January 1940 Le Havre to New York crossing." She put the sheets on the coffee table. "Here are passengers *N* through *P*."

Rev. J. L. R. Nisbett, Mrs. Nisbett, Mrs. Northacker, Master Northacker, Mrs. Emily Offutt, Miss Nancy Offutt, Miss Frances O'N—

"He isn't listed."

"No, he isn't. No Ochs at all is listed as embarking on that voyage. But"—a small smile twitched Magda's lips—"these people are."

She laid another sheet on the table. It was a different portion of the passenger list, but here she had highlighted two names. Rachel squinted at the yellow stripes. *Mr. Septime Aubert, Mr. Jacques Aubert.*

Magda took Rachel's silence for forgetfulness. "Aubert. Aubert as in Gabrielle Aubert. Remember?" she prompted, "You said that Gabrielle told Dolly about a relative named Septime Aubert." When Rachel still didn't say anything, she prodded again. "The one who had caviar on a boat to America just before the war?"

"Yes, I remember." Rachel picked up the stapled sheets. "I'm just trying to put it all together." She bit her lip again. "So you're saying that you think Albert Ochs, the grandfather of Jack Ochs, was also one of these Auberts?"

Magda nodded. "The younger one."

Rachel nodded back. "And that for some reason he left France and went to America, changing his name on the ship that took him there?"

Magda nodded again. "Or he changed it when he got off the ship and entered the US." She pushed the printouts closer to Rachel, as if she was emphasizing their evidence.

Rachel squinted, calculating. "Okay . . ." She wanted to believe—she was almost willing to believe—but, "Did both Auberts disembark at Ellis Island too? That's what we would need to know to make the hypothesis plausible."

Now Magda broke into a grin. "That's the very question I asked myself. So I went back and looked, and I found this." She put down another sheet. Again Rachel saw the certificate template, again the *SAMPLE* watermark, but this one certified the arrival of Septime Aubert and Jacques Aubert, born in Paris on January 8, 1880, and June 2, 1905, respectively, at Ellis Island, both arriving on the same ship as Ochs.

"Well," Rachel felt her excitement ebbing away, "that takes care of that. Both of them are listed, so they both got off."

"I disagree." Magda held up a finger. "I went through all the passenger records of entry for this ship—five hundred and seventy-three of them. Every single other record looks like the one for Albert Ochs, with just one person on it. This is the only one that has two people together."

"No one else was listed together? No husbands and wives, no families . . . What about this"—Rachel looked at the passenger lists—"Master Northacker? He wasn't listed on a certificate of arrival with his mother?"

Magda shook her head. "This is the only one." Then, as if to make sure Rachel understood what she meant: "Septime Aubert and Jacques Aubert are the only two passengers listed on the same record of entry. That suggests that at least *something* odd was going on." She sat back, satisfied.

Rachel didn't know if she felt the same. She decided to push back. What if another explanation fit? "Maybe one of the two Auberts was sick. Maybe he went to the bathroom. So the other had to fill out the certificate for both of them."

"That would mean that the missing Monsieur Aubert was the only person out of five hundred and seventy-three people who was sick or needed to use the bathroom. That seems like an unlikely explanation to me."

This time, Rachel agreed. And it did look convincing, this link between Jacques Aubert and Albert Ochs. There was no

Albert Ochs in any Florida census before 1945, even the census in his supposed hometown. How could that be squared with his insistence that he was from Florida? And Jacques Aubert's birth date was so close to Albert Ochs's—the only difference between them was one missing digit, exactly the kind you might take out if you wanted a different birth date, but one that you could still remember easily. Plus, of course Gabrielle had told Dolly that her great-uncle—or whatever he was—had made a journey to America. Okay, she'd said he'd moved before the war, but strictly speaking the Second World War hadn't come to France until 1940, which was the year of this *Pennland* sailing. And Septime was such an unusual name! Could there really be two Septime Auberts? Then there were the passenger lists, Rachel thought. One man named Aubert got on the ship but didn't get off, while Albert Ochs got off the ship but hadn't gotten on . . . If you put it all together, it made a very suggestive story.

Except what was the reason? Why would Jacques Aubert have decided to eradicate himself and become Albert Ochs?

She asked Magda. Magda, of course, had an answer. "I thought about that all the way over, and I think it's connected to Judaism."

She paused. "Go on," Rachel said.

"I can't figure it out completely, but I thought maybe something like this. This Septime Aubert is Gabrielle's great-great-uncle, or whatever relative he was. What if Jacques Aubert is . . . his son? Or someone close to him who needs to leave France because he's Jewish."

Rachel interrupted. "Aubert isn't a Jewish name."

"But it doesn't need to be, right? Judaism is carried maternally. It could be that Septime Aubert married a Jewish woman. Then he wouldn't be Jewish, but his son would count as Jewish to the Nazis."

Rachel nodded, but Maga had already moved on. "Or maybe Jacques Aubert was in the Resistance, or he was a communist or a criminal or someone else the Nazis would have wanted to kill. I did some research about people-smuggling during the war, and it did happen. Not just people high up, like Raoul Wallenberg, issuing passports or hiding people in embassies, but ordinary people too. There was one couple who saved Jewish children by planting them with Christian families, and they made them new birth certificates—everything."

"The *Réseau Marcel*." Rachel's mother had told her about them when she'd first moved to France.

"That's it. We know Maximilien Sauveterre helped Jews one way; why not another? Or why not more people than just Jews? Maybe he helped Aubert get a new passport for his son, and on the ship Monsieur Aubert becomes Mister Albert Ochs, who disembarks at Ellis Island."

"But then why kill a descendant of that person eighty years later? If Sauveterre smuggled out a Jewish friend, or even a member of the Resistance, surely that person's family would have been *thankful*. How do we get from that to Gabrielle murdering members of both families seventy years later?"

"I don't know; that's the part I couldn't figure out. I was hoping you might have some ideas."

Rachel was about to suggest that they could have some tea and brainstorm together, when her phone rang. It was Dolly.

She had been out for a drink with friends after her yoga class, but now that she was home, her time was all Rachel's. How could she help? Yes, as she had said, she phoned Ochs on the afternoon of his arrival, to confirm the meeting on Saturday. No, she hadn't called him again after that. She was absolutely certain because the rest of the afternoon and evening had been taken up with managing Monsieur Guipure's party, "and on Friday I was with Antoinette all day." After Antoinette had finally fallen asleep on Friday, Dolly herself had been so exhausted that she'd headed straight home and gone to bed. She had slept from six PM until seven the next morning. But if there was a second call from a Sauveterre number . . . She had called nearly every extension in the company for one reason or another during her time there, so she might well recognize the number. Would Rachel read it to her?

Rachel read it, pausing between each numeral. When she'd finished, there was a hesitation, and then Dolly said, "That's Keteb's office extension."

*   *   *

"Did she say he made the call, or did she say it came from his extension?" Magda took a swig from her mug of tea. "There's a difference. Gabrielle told us she stayed late at company headquarters if she needed to. It would have been easy for her to stay late the night after Guipure died, when there were a million things to do, then purposefully use the phone in Lellouch's office in order to implicate him."

"That's perfectly true. But it's also true that we haven't figured out why Gabrielle would want to kill Guipure, whereas with Lellouch we have a motive."

"We haven't found a motive for Gabrielle *yet*. We're working on it."

"But in the meantime, we have a phone call that was made from the office of a man who had a reason to kill at least one of our victims."

"Was Lellouch even in the office the night that call was made to Ochs? Do we know that?"

"Do we know that Gabrielle was?"

They had reached an impasse. Without access to Gabrielle or Lellouch, or preferably both, they couldn't get any further than speculation and theories about why Gabrielle might want to kill Jack Ochs, how her motive for killing Guipure was more credible than Lellouch's, or why Lellouch's might be more believable than hers. Really, Rachel said to herself, they'd done an exceptional job. Starting from nothing, they'd managed to discover evidence, put together a time line, and identify two plausible suspects, with no outside assistance. But as much as it pained her to admit, it seemed they'd reached the end of what they could do alone. Now only one collaboration could take them forward.

"We need to call the police."

Chapter
Twenty-Seven

Boussicault looked carefully through their folders and read the transcribed notes that Rachel had typed up the previous night. He listened to their story, interrupting only to ask for confirmation or clarification. When they finished, he steepled his fingers together for a long minute before he spoke.

"Of course, the police in the third arrondissement know a large part of this. They've already interviewed everyone at Sauveterre, and they talked to the former assistant, Madame Fauré, as well. They were also very interested in the recent announcement by Sauveterre that you've noted—they were made aware of Monsieur Lellouch's arrangement with Madame Guipure, so the significance of his promotion was clear to them. But I know they don't know anything about Mademoiselle Aubert's adventure in buying heroin. Your connections are better than those of the police, Rachel." He tipped his head. "And the police in the eighth—they're no further along than I thought they'd be. I don't believe they've abandoned their robbery theory yet, although I have few friends over there, so I'm less informed. I'll telephone that commissariat and see what I can find out. And then I think I'll suggest to the third that they bring Monsieur

Lellouch and Mademoiselle Aubert in to be interviewed. Monsieur Thieriot too, I think, since both buying heroin and appropriating potentially valuable drawings without permission are crimes. Monsieur Naquet has yet to do anything really suspicious, so we shall leave him to his own devices for now."

"How soon will you have them in?" Magda had always been more brusque with Boussicault than Rachel was.

But he just smiled politely.

"Well, if you'll permit us a few days for background work, based on your excellent notes, of course, I would say within a week."

"And can we sit in on the interviews?"

"Oh no. No. I allowed Rachel to do that before everyone objected. But I promise to let you know what is said. And when transcripts are available, I'll make sure you're sent one."

Magda was about to object that they should be allowed better access to the activity on a case to which they had, as Boussicault himself had just pointed out, made a substantial contribution, when Boussicault's phone rang. He held up a finger to indicate a break, and picked up the receiver. "Boussicault. Where? I see. What name? Really? All right, I'm on my way."

He put the phone down and stood, reaching for his jacket where it hung on the back of the chair. "That was the local police of the Marais. A young man has just been found stabbed to death in his apartment. According to his *carte d'identité*, he is Cyrille Thieriot."

Rachel and Magda both started to speak at the same time, but Boussicault shook his head. "No. No, you can't."

* * *

They watched the news together that evening. Or, as Magda insisted on putting it, they were *reduced* to watching the news. Rachel, who had in the previous two years discovered three bodies murdered in different ways, attempted several times to convince her friend that she truly did not want to see a freshly murdered corpse, but Magda was determined to view Boussicault's order as a professional discourtesy despite the fact that they had no profession and that, after the initial firm refusal, he had been quite courteous. He'd accompanied them outside the commissariat and, putting them in a taxi, promised that they would be the first to know if he learned anything significant.

On the television screen, the newscaster was announcing a tragic discovery in the Marais. Seeing his neighbor's door unlocked and open, a man had entered the apartment to check and discovered the body of the occupant, Cyrille Thieriot, face down on the bed, several stab wounds in his back. A picture of Thieriot, one Rachel recognized as having hung on the wall behind him, flashed up as the announcer said that the victim, twenty-six, had been a waiter at the LaLa Lounge and had lived in the apartment for several years.

Suddenly the program cut away from the studio, and Rachel found herself looking at a crying woman with a microphone in her face. *La mère de la victime,* said the subtitle.

"Who would do something like this?" the woman asked, sobbing. "My son was a good boy. We were proud of him! The police say nothing was touched, and none of the neighbors heard a fight. It was just a senseless act! My wonderful boy!"

A young man appeared on the screen next to her. He had the same full lips and doe eyes as Thieriot. "My mother doesn't want to answer any more questions." He moved her gently out of the frame. Without missing a beat, the picture cut back to the anchor in the studio. "The police say they are exploring several possible leads. More on this story as it develops."

Rachel reached for the remote and clicked off the set. "It's only a matter of time until they figure out he was once Guipure's *compagnon*, and then they're going to go crazy."

Bu Magda didn't reply. Instead, she sat thoughtful for a few seconds, then said, "It must be related to our murders." She looked Rachel. "Don't you think?"

Rachel raised her eyebrows and inhaled. "It feels like it has to be. Although that undermines our hypothesis about the connection between the first two murders. I don't see how Cyrille could link to Ochs's and Guipure's grandfathers." She thought again. "Even through Guipure." She frowned. "You don't suppose we have it wrong and the *first* two deaths were coincidences, but this one is somehow linked to Guipure? That's all I can think of. Unless . . . " She bit her thumbnail. "Unless Thieriot's *is* a coincidence after all. Parts of the Marais are very rough."

"But not that part." Magda made a disbelieving face. "There was a sign for a new luxury development just down the street from his building. Anyway," she said, and waved toward the blank TV screen, "the police said nothing was taken."

They sat silent for a long while. The various possible coincidences whirled in Rachel's head, but it couldn't be that *all* the deaths were coincidental: there were too many murders and too many connections for that to be the case. But which two were connected, and how? She felt as if her brain were a sliding puzzle, one of those where, if she could just move the right piece, she would be able to make a pattern. Only she didn't know which was the right piece, and she was beginning to think a piece was missing altogether.

At last Magda said, "Do we know Thieriot wasn't Jewish? We never asked. And we don't know his mother's last name."

"Could you drop the Jewish thing?" Rachel was startled by the harshness of her own voice. "I'm sorry, I'm sorry. It's just . . . I don't think Judaism is the answer here."

Magda would have been within her rights to say that at this stage it was just as likely to be the answer as anything else was, but with the patience of long friendship she didn't. She picked up her mug from the coffee table and took a sip, then held it between her hands and waited.

There is something, Rachel thought. *There is something that binds all three of these men together, that would bind all three of their deaths together.* She felt it scratching at the back of her mind. She closed her eyes and focused, trying to pull herself back into what she envisioned as a dark space where her subconscious knowledge lay.

In the silence, a key scraped in the lock, then turned. Rachel opened her eyes as the door opened. Alan was home.

"You're here! I thought you were coming tomorrow!" She said the first thing that came into her head. "I haven't cleaned!"

"They offered me an earlier flight, and I took it so I could see you sooner." He took a half step back. "I can stay at a hotel until tomorrow, if you want."

"Oh, don't be silly!" She kissed him.

Magda gathered her bag. "I better go. We're at another dead end anyway."

"No, no." Alex pulled his suitcase into the hall. "You don't have to. I can just go right to sleep."

"Your lips say, 'Don't go,' but your sagging shoulders say, 'Please leave.' We were just talking about the case, and we can finish that tomorrow." Magda put her arms around him and pulled him into a close hug. "I'm so glad you're back. Your wife missed you, and so did I. Let me know when your jet lag's passed, and I'll have the two of you over for dinner." She kissed him on the cheek. "I can't wait to hear about your adventures in Miami."

"My adventures in Miami can't begin to compare with your adventures here," Alan said after she'd left. "You've reached another dead end with Ochs and Guipure?"

"Yes, only now Cyrille Thieriot has been—" She stopped herself. "It doesn't matter. Nothing matters except that you took an earlier flight to surprise me. And I am surprised. I'm sorry that the place is a mess, though. I really was going to clean tonight. Go sit down and I'll get you something to drink. Do you want tea?"

He took off his jacket and hung it on the hook next to the door. "I don't care that the place is a mess, I don't want to sit down, and I don't want a cup of tea. I want a huge glass of water, and then I want to go to bed with my wife."

He didn't finish the water.

Chapter
Twenty-Eight

The next morning they made love a second time, then a third for good measure. Afterward, Rachel went out for croissants while Alan had a shower. When she arrived back, he had laid her newspaper next to her plate, folded so the lower right-hand column showed. She found herself looking at what must have been Cyrille Thieriot's *carte d'identité* photo: his lips were in their recognizable pout, his chin tilted at its familiar angle, but he wore no makeup. His face looked vulnerable without it. She read the article underneath the picture.

Fashion Designer's Former Partner Found Dead
Late yesterday afternoon, police were called to an address in the Marais district of Paris, where they found the body of Cyrille Thieriot, 26. Thieriot, who had been stabbed several times in the back, was the former *partenaire sentimentale* of fashion designer Roland Guipure, who himself died last month, after a heroin overdose, at his 40th birthday party.

"At the moment we know very little about the circumstances of M. Thieriot's death beyond being able to say that it wasn't suicide," said Attah Alboukhir, a police spokesman. "We ask people to remain calm and refrain from speculation. The police will release more details as they come in."

"Clearly, he correctly sees that conspiracy theories are about to start sprouting like grass seed," Rachel said to Alan once she'd finished reading the article.

"Does fashion do conspiracy theories?" His hair was still wet, and strands fell straight over his face as he read his iPad.

"Oh, I'd say so. These days conspiracy theories are in vogue."

As he lifted his head to grin at her, her *portable* pinged. She fished it out of her pocket and woke the screen.

Bookseller.fr

Editions Sapier has negotiated a six-figure deal for Gédéon Naquet's biography of couturier Roland Guipure. Fabric of Life is the first bio of the recently deceased designer and is tipped to offer "an in-depth look at the triumphs of his career and the squalid tragedy of his death."

Well, Rachel thought, *let that be your memorial, Cyrille. You were right about the motivations of Gédéon Naquet.* She turned the phone off.

But of course that wasn't his epitaph—the media weren't going to let a potential scandal go that easily. When she turned the volume on the phone back up after Alan had left for a run, its screen was crowded with alerts:

Police Investigating Murder of Roland Guipure's
    Former Partner
Murder Victim, 26, Was Lover of Fashion Designer
Late Fashion Designer's Lover Found Murdered in
    the Marais
Sauveterre's Bad Season: Former Partner of
    Fashion House Head Killed
Marais Corpse Is Ex of Addict Designer
Ten Things You Need to Know About Cyrille
    Thieriot, Roland Guipure's Ex
Sad Last Days of Designer's Toy Boy

Death had brought Thieriot the celebrity he'd yearned for in life. Too bad he wasn't alive to revel in it.

The *portable*'s ringtone interrupted her thoughts.

"Have you seen the headlines?" Magda didn't even bother with a hello.

"And the article in this morning's *Parisien*."

"Have you heard from Boussicault?"

"Not yet. But according to that article, the police don't know much. I assumed that was why he hadn't been in touch yet."

"Well, we don't need to wait for him. We know where Thieriot lived. Let's go there."

"I'm not breaking into his apartment."

"I wasn't talking about breaking in." Magda's tone was injured. "I thought we could interview his neighbors. He *loved* to talk, especially about himself. I bet he told them all sorts of things that could be useful."

"Oh. Okay—" But Magda had hung up, and Rachel was left with only the blank silence of a broken connection.

Chapter
Twenty-Nine

～

The mid-morning sunshine bounced off the top branches of the tree outside Thieriot's building, turning its leaves bright green. In the hours since the news broadcast, the red-and-white striped tape marking off the building's front gate had torn, and someone had tied one portion around the linden's trunk. Now the two pieces rose on the spring breeze like lonely arms reaching for each other.

"What do you think, start there?" Magda gestured toward the red awning of the Bar du Marché Blancs Manteaux. "We know he was a customer."

But Rachel shook her head. "No one there paid any attention to him. He was made up like Lola at the Copacabana when we met him there, and no one even did a double take. He would have had no time for them." If Thieriot was going to share confidences, it would be with people who performed their appreciation of him, somewhere that matched his sense of himself: opulent, lustrous, and (she thought of his peacock-colored bedspread) at least a little decadent.

"Let's start here." She pointed to the Marionnaud perfume shop that filled out the bottom floor of Thieriot's building.

"Bonjour, mesdames!" A small blonde saleswoman hurried toward them. She was thickly but not obtrusively made up, foundation, blush, and highlighter all combining to draw out what was best in a sweet, snub-nosed face. Her blue eyeshadow made her eyes gleam, and her berry-colored lips curved into an eager smile. "Can I help you?"

"I hope so." Rachel reached into her bag and pulled out a copy of the photo of Cyrille Thieriot and Roland Guipure at Nüba. She rested her index finger on Thieriot's hair. "Do you know this man?"

The woman glanced at the photo. "Of course: that's Cyrille. He lives upstairs. He comes to see us almost every day. He hasn't been in yet today, though."

"Of course not. He's dead." The brunette standing behind the counter looked up from sorting perfume boxes as she said this. She had a face made for such pronouncements, Rachel thought. With a square jaw and high Slavic cheekbones, it was meant to look life directly in the eye.

"What?" The first woman turned her back on Rachel and Magda. "What are you talking about?"

The perfume sorter shrugged. "He was killed yesterday. Stabbed in his apartment."

"We've been here for two hours! Why didn't you tell me?"

She shrugged again. "I thought you knew. It was on the news."

"You know I don't watch the news! It upsets me too much." The first woman looked down and shook her head. "I can't believe it. He was in yesterday. He showed me how to do a cat eye." The tip of her upturned nose reddened; tears welled and began to run down her cheeks.

"Oh, Miriam." The second woman came out from behind the counter and handed her a tissue plucked from one of the cosmetics stands. "It's important to watch the news, even if it does upset you. And as for his coming in yesterday, you might as well say he was breathing yesterday. Everyone who dies was living their ordinary life the day before." She put out her hand and Rachel, knocked off her stride to discover a philosopher in a perfume shop, handed over the printout without thinking.

The brunette looked at it and confirmed briskly, "Yes, that's Cyrille. That's him with Roland when they went to Nüba."

"You know Roland Guipure?"

"Not personally. But—"

"Cyrille told us all about him when they were involved," the first woman broke in. "Where they went, what they did, what he said . . ."

"You were close to Cyrille."

Something about this sentence put the second woman on alert. Before her friend could answer, she said, "Why do you want to know?" She stepped forward so she was standing slightly in front of her colleague. "Who are you?"

"My name is Rachel Levis. And this is my partner, Magda Stevens. We're private detectives, and we've been hired by Cyrille Thieriot's family to investigate his murder." Oh, how easily the lie came! "Would you like to see my *carte d'identification*?" Not that this would provide any evidence that she was a detective of any sort, but previous investigations had taught Rachel that an offer to show ID made most people believe you were trustworthy.

"That's all right." The second woman shook her head. "As long as you're not reporters or loan sharks or something like that."

Why would she think of loan sharks? But Rachel decided to hold that question. Instead, she simply said, "Your colleague was saying that Cyrille talked to you about Roland Guipure. So you must have been good friends?"

The first woman, Miriam, spoke again. "Oh yes. I mean, not at first. At first he just came in as a customer. He was our first man. We still don't get many, at least not for *maquillage*, but I think he made such an impact on us at first because he *was* the first. Isn't that right, Carla?"

The other woman nodded, then picked up the thread. "After his first couple of visits he started coming in regularly because I told him we could do special orders. He knew exactly what he wanted, you see. He must have read every fashion magazine every month, because he knew the names of all the shades and exactly which *marque* did which one. We would place the orders, and when they came in, he picked them up on his way home. And we just got to chatting."

"He had a marvelous life!" Miriam teared up again. "He worked at Bespoke—you know, the restaurant—and the most amazing people used to come in . . . Or, at least, he made them sound amazing. He had a way of telling stories so that everything seemed exciting. And then he met Roland, and everything really *was* exciting. He told us how Roland wanted to introduce him to all his friends and how he made Cyrille come with him to all these trendy places so that he could show him off. Cyrille met Karl Lagerfeld—can you imagine?" Rachel remembered the photos on Thieriot's wall and nodded again.

"And he brought us the most amazing goody bag from one of Sauveterre's runway shows. Do you remember that bronzer, Carla? Much too expensive for Marionnaud to stock, and beautiful coverage. It went on like silk, didn't it?" Carla agreed that it did. "And of course we knew all about how he persuaded Roland to go into *désintoxification*—"

"And then what happened after he came out." Carla's tone made it plain what she thought of Guipure's post-rehab treatment of Thieriot.

"But he knew that might happen." Miriam switched her gaze back to Rachel. "He told us that even when he suggested Roland should go to the clinic in Greece, he'd known that often when people come out of *désintox*, they push away old friends and partners, but he'd been willing to accept that risk if it meant saving Roland's talent."

Carla pursed her lips and clicked her tongue disapprovingly. "Yes, but Roland could have at least acknowledged all Cyrille did for him. Introducing him to Cyrille's avant-garde friends, stimulating his imagination in new ways . . . But Roland just cut him off. No thanks, no support."

"Oh, Carla!" From Miriam's sigh of exasperation, Rachel understood that she was the soft heart to the other woman's hard head. "Love isn't about expecting payback or acknowledgment. Cyrille did those things because he wanted to share his life with Roland, just like he encouraged him to go to the *désintox* because he was genuinely worried about him. He didn't want anything in exchange."

Uh-huh, Rachel thought, irritated at Thieriot's self-serving restructuring of the story. But she felt a stab of sympathy too.

Having done it herself, she wasn't going to fault anyone who tried to smooth their path through a break-up; every jilted lover had the impulse to reconfigure their story so it became less painful. She drew the conversation back to a remark buried in Carla's complaint. "You say Guipure didn't offer Cyrille any kind of support when he ended the relationship. Do you mean financial support? Did Cyrille need money?"

Carla shrugged. "He was a waiter, poor boy. And special-order eyeshadows don't come cheap. Guipure paid for everything while they were together, and Cyrille became used to a nicer level of everything than he'd had before. It's hard to break that habit."

"He was having money troubles?"

"I couldn't say. But lately he'd been coming in to talk more than to buy."

"Until last week."

Miriam tightened her lips as Carla shot her a warning look, but it was too late: Magda had her in her sights. "What do you mean?"

"Well, only that last week he mentioned that he was think-ing of buying an apartment. They're building new ones for sale just down there"—she pointed in the direction of the Rue des Francs Bourgeois a block away—"and he told us he was plan-ning to view the show apartment. He said that the layout would be the same for all the *trois-pièces* units, and he thought he'd have a look."

"Trois pièces?" Three rooms plus a kitchen and bath in the Marais would cost much more than Thieriot's little studio.

"We were surprised too," Carla said. "We didn't know he had that kind of money."

"And when Carla said that," Miriam explained, "he said that he didn't have it *yet*. But he would have it by the time the apartment was finished. He said he'd been thinking since Roland died, and he had some things of his worth selling. Mementoes." Warmth flooded Rachel. The sketches. It had to be the sketches. "He said he'd held onto them for the sentimental value, but he knew Roland would have wanted him to be well cared for after his death, so he was going to sell them now."

"Did he say to whom?"

Miriam shook her head.

From behind her Carla said, "You could ask his friend Gabrielle."

"*GAB—*"

But Magda grabbed Rachel's arm and squeezed it. "Gabrielle?" Her voice was smooth. "We'll check with the family to see if they know anyone by that name. Do you know a surname?"

Carla shook her head. "Unfortunately not."

"What makes you think that this Gabrielle would know, in particular?"

"To be honest, I don't have a reason. The name just occurred to me because, well . . . last week Cyrille loaned me his *portable* to call my husband. We have to keep our phones in our lockers while we're on the shop floor, and I needed to tell him to pick up a *poulet roti* on his way home. Cyrille's phone was on the 'Recents' screen, and Gabrielle was the first name on the list. I'm just assuming they must be close because it showed he'd called her five times in a row."

Chapter Thirty

～

"Gabrielle is a very common name," Magda said when they were back out on the pavement. Her voice made it clear she was reminding herself as much as Rachel. "We need to bear in mind that the fact that he called *a* Gabrielle doesn't mean that he called *Sauveterre*'s Gabrielle."

"True, true. But bearing that in mind, how do we find out which Gabrielle he was calling?"

"Oh, I know how to do that." She waved a hand. "But before we do . . ." She turned and waited at the crossing onto the Rue des Francs Bourgeois. "Anyone can dream about buying an expensive apartment. You and I used to do it all the time when you lived in that little room, remember? Anyone can even go to see an apartment and pretend they're going to buy it. The question is whether he actually did anything material about it. Did he write a check or anything like that? That would show he was confident he was coming into some money." She took her phone out of her bag and started poking the screen.

"What are you doing?"

"Checking to see if there are specific hours for viewing or if we can just drop in."

It turned out that the viewing agent was at that very moment sitting in the building's lobby. When they arrived, she turned out to be as polished and gleaming as the decor that surrounded her. She nodded her smooth brown head when Rachel showed her the photo. Oh yes, Monsieur Thieriot. He'd come to tour the show apartment the previous week. She remembered because she'd enjoyed his tour so much. Most potential buyers didn't have much to say beyond asking about the various options for taps and kitchen appliances and wanting to know what the building maintenance fee would be, but he'd been full of conversation. Did they know he'd been the partner of the fashion designer Roland Guipure?

"Yes, we know." Once again Magda gave their story about being private detectives. Then she asked if Thieriot had said anything about moving forward with the sale after he'd finished his walk-through?

Oh, more than said: he'd filled out a formal declaration of intent. Seeing their blank expressions, she explained. Because they'd had so many walk-ins from the street, the company had started to ask each viewer who expressed interest to sign a formal declaration of intent. She looked slightly abashed. Of course it didn't really mean anything, but the word "formal" was very effective in scaring off dreamers and time wasters. But Monsieur Thieriot hadn't been scared off at all. He'd signed the document, given his contact details, and said he just needed to talk to his money manager and would be in touch. "In fact, I was going to call him today, to check in to see if he was ready to make an offer." She looked sad. "Is there somewhere I could send flowers?"

"I'm not sure when the funeral will be." Rachel thought of Jack Ochs, still lying in a drawer in the police mortuary, waiting for his case to be investigated and closed. Presumably Thieriot's funeral couldn't proceed either until his murder had been solved. "But if you give me your card, I'll contact you as soon as we know anything."

Magda slipped a brochure into her bag as they left.

"So he wasn't just dreaming," she said when they had settled at a table in a café down the block. "And look at this." She slid the brochure across the table, tapping the price list. *Trois Pièces: €500,000.*

"It must be the *croquis*," Rachel said, smiling at their server as she put a lemon tart on the table in front of her. "That must be why he was so intent on asking about them the last time we met. He must have decided to sell them."

"But to whom? Gabrielle doesn't have the kind of money he would've wanted. Maybe an art dealer? Would an art dealer be interested in a fashion designer's sketches?"

"Some would, I think, but I doubt they'd kill for them. And if he was trying to sell them to a dealer, what was he doing calling Gabrielle? He never mentioned that they had any kind of personal relationship."

"If it *was* her." Magda took a sip of her coffee. "Maybe he had a friend named Gabrielle, and he was calling her."

"Calling her five times in a row?"

"It's not outside the realm of possibility. But I grant you it's strange, so eat up and let's go back to my place."

Rachel didn't see the connection, and she said so.

"I said I could find out who he was calling, and I can. According to one of my books, all you need is the *portable* number and a computer, and it should be a straightforward process."

"'Should' like you should have been able to access Bespoke's reservations system, or 'should' like you should have been able to hack Sauveterre's e-mail?"

Magda looked around and signaled to their server for the bill. "We'll never know until we try."

On the métro heading toward Cadet, Rachel suddenly turned in her seat.

"You don't think it's my fault he's dead, do you?"

"What? What are you talking about?"

"He asked me if I thought the sketches would be worth anything, and I said they might. That makes *me* the reason he was trying to sell them, and if his trying to sell them is why someone killed him, that makes me the reason he's dead."

"I have some issues with that reasoning." But Magda's voice was kind. "If I tell you that you look good in red, then you buy a red dress and spill something on it, I'm not the reason you spilled something on your red dress. The chain of events is essentially the same. You told him a fact: the sketches probably are worth something. But you didn't make him go on and try to sell them. That was his choice."

"Okay." Rachel turned and looked out her window. She knew it was silly, but still she felt relieved.

"By the way," Magda said after a second, "you don't look good in red." She jabbed Rachel lightly with an elbow. "See? I just saved you from spilling something on a dress."

*　*　*

An hour later Magda was slumped over the laptop on her kitchen table, her elbow holding open one of her hacking

manuals, while Rachel sat across from her, researching art dealers on her *portable*. Tuning out Magda's soft mutterings, she
googled and scrolled to see if there were dealers or auction
houses who took consignment of design sketches.

There were several, but none of them were interested in a
croquis on its own. If there was a swatch of fabric attached, or
if the sketch had been made for a specific customer and included
a note addressed to them, or even if it had been done on the
maison's official stationery, a dealer was happy to take it and ask
for what seemed to her to be exorbitant price, but on no website
did she find a sketch that had been dashed off by a designer on
whatever paper was handy and sent off into the world unac-
companied by a textile. She was sure the drawings Cyrille collected didn't have swatches attached, but had they been made
on Sauveterre stationery? For a moment she regretted confront-
ing Naquet—he might have been able to tell them.

"Oop!" Magda sat up straight. "Here we go."

"It worked?"

Rachel moved to sit next to her. On the laptop's screen she
saw a column of numbers.

"What's Gabrielle's number at Sauveterre?"

It took her a few seconds to find the e-mail about the memorial service with Gabrielle's phone number at the bottom. She
watched as Magda typed it into the search box. A split second
later there it was, staring back at them from the computer screen,
highlighted in blue. Another tap of Magda's finger on the touch-
pad, and it was highlighted again, further down, five times in a
row. One more and there it was again, now four times in a row.

Rachel swallowed to wet her throat. "What dates?"

"Does it really matter?"

Before Rachel had a chance to say that if the most recent call was made on the day of Thieriot's death it might matter very much indeed, her own phone rang. The screen showed Boussicault's name.

"*Allo,* Capitaine *Ça va?*"

Boussicault apparently shared Magda's attitude toward phone etiquette, for he brushed right by the question. "I promised I would contact you when I had details. There hasn't been time for an autopsy, but the scene of crime officers had some preliminary findings. Monsieur Thieriot was found face down on his bed, with four wounds in his back. Nothing in the room was disturbed; there were no signs of any struggle. He had two wounds in his lower back, one on each side of the spine, puncturing his kidneys. The two in his upper back, again one on each side, punctured the lungs. All were clean stabs, quick in and out, made by an extremely sharp but shallow blade just long enough to puncture the organs."

"He was killed by someone he knew."

"That was my conclusion as well. He either turned his back on the killer or preceded them into the room, and that suggests he was comfortable with them. Moreover, you need to be very close to someone to stab them like that, and you need to be calm to be that precise. This wasn't a murder during a struggle or a frenzy. These two people knew each other well enough for Thieriot to have his guard down."

She glanced at Magda, whose face showed that she understood the gist of the conversation. *The sketches,* she mouthed at Rachel.

"Did the crime scene technicians catalogue the scene yet?"

"It wasn't very big, so . . . Just let me check . . ." She heard pages turning. "Yes, here's the inventory." Only then did he remember that he was a policeman and she was a member of the public. "Why? What was in there that I should know about?"

"Nothing. Or at least, not much. Guipure gave Thieriot some design sketches, and we wondered if they were still there. They're the kind of thing a thief wouldn't know to take, but someone close to him might."

"*D'acc.*" There was the sound of more pages turning. "It says 'twenty drawings of women.' Found in a drawer under the bed. Could that be them?"

It could. In fact, she couldn't see how it could be anything else, and she said as much to Magda after the capitaine hung up.

"So if Gabrielle killed Cyrille for the sketches," Magda said, seemingly dismissing the possibility even as she asked the question, "why would they still be in his apartment?"

Rachel tried to think of another connection between the *croquis* and the call. "Maybe he was calling her to see if he could get some money for giving them back to Sauveterre?"

But Magda didn't buy that either. "He wouldn't have called Gabrielle about that. He'd have called Antoinette. And look." She pointed at the digits next to Gabrielle's repeated number that indicated the length of each call: .15; .15; .45; 1.00; 1.00; 5.00. "He spoke to her for longer each time. That must mean som—"

There was a ping. Rachel looked around for her *portable*. This time, though, the noise came from Magda's phone. She glanced at her screen, frowned, tapped through, and after a moment handed it to Rachel, wearing what Rachel thought a novelist would call "a significant look."

BoF Careers: *Business of Fashion*

said the web page.

New Hires and Promotions, May 9–13
ALaMarche—Maude Benedet—VP Sales
Cecile Phan—JPC Charles Castelbjac—HPC
Maison Sauveterre—HPC Keteb Lellouch—CD
Maison Sauveterre—Gabrielle Aubert, PA to
     CEO—PA to incoming CD

So Lellouch wasn't the only one with a new position. Gabrielle had been appointed his assistant.

Rachel handed the phone back. Magda laid it carefully on the table, lined up its edges with those of the laptop, gave it a light tap to perfect the alignment, then looked up.

"Listen to me." She bit her bottom lip. "What if we were on the right track after we saw Mediouri and his friend? What if Guipure's death *was* a conspiracy between Gabrielle and Keteb, only with Cyrille too? Wait." She held up a hand as Rachel opened her mouth. "Just listen. We know that Keteb had something to gain by killing Guipure, and after what happened to him at AuSecours, he may have had enough rage and resentment to act on his feelings when he was denied the top spot again. We know that Gabrielle had a crush on

Guipure but *also* had reason to resent him—a fraught emotional combination at the best of times. Each has an ax to grind, they spend time together . . . it takes four months, but each eventually becomes aware of the other's anger. They hatch a mutually beneficial, theoretical plan, but there's a practical flaw: Gabrielle can buy the heroin, but they both know there's no way for her to get close enough to Guipure to administer it, never mind a way to maneuver him somewhere private enough to do it without anyone noticing. But who's been calling Guipure's office for months, trying to make contact with him? And who can they be pretty sure could use some money, since they know his financial habits? Cyrille. Maybe they don't make the connection at first. Maybe the plan even gets dropped. Until Gabrielle somehow finds out that Thieriot works at the LaLa Lounge. Which they know isn't enough to keep him in the style to which he was formerly accustomed. Plus, he's angry at being ghosted by the man he loves—who wouldn't be? So they approach him. And he agrees. At the party he accosts Guipure in the men's room and makes the injection. But then, being Thieriot, he spends the money, and he wants more. Like the woman said, special-order eye shadows don't come cheap. And now he's got something on them. It turns into a case of plain old blackmail. He calls and calls Gabrielle, threatening to tell all if they don't hand over some more money. After all, we know he could go to QuellesNouvelles with the info. Finally she says yes—that's the longest phone call—but when she goes to his apartment, or when Lellouch does, they kill him instead. We've seen that happen before."

They had indeed, when Edgar Bowen's butler had killed Bowen's blackmailing girlfriend. And everything they'd learned in the ten days since their meeting with Mediouri's associate made Magda's scenario plausible. Lellouch and Gabrielle did have reason to hate Guipure, and Thieriot was greedy and thoughtless enough to agree to help—and dumb enough to try to blackmail his more murderous co-conspirators when he ran out of money. It did fit. Except . . .

"How did they know Thieriot worked at the LaLa Lounge?"

"Well, somebody must have visited there before the party, to see whether it was a suitable venue at the very least. They could have seen Thieriot working."

"Obviously we need to check." Magda stood up and put her bag on her shoulder.

It took Rachel a second to understand what she meant. "Oh no. Please, not that. Please."

Chapter
Thirty-One

"Oh, it's you." The little man made it sound as if they were regular, if somewhat disappointing, visitors. He had the same peppering of stubble across his cheeks and chin and was wearing what appeared to be the same t-shirt, but today the sandwich he held seemed to be tuna rather than egg. He spoke to them as he swallowed a bite. "I've been wondering if you'd come back."

Rachel found this very hard to believe in light of their previous encounter. She stared at him disbelievingly. "Why?"

He took another bite of his sandwich. "I found something interesting. And the police haven't been back. The reporters haven't been back. So I found myself wondering if the two *culotté* detectives might come back."

"Why didn't you take this something interesting to the police or the reporters?"

He imitated her sarcastic stare, only with his tuna salad–filled mouth slightly agape. Then he said, "How successful do you think my trendy nightclub in a *louche* area would be if I got a reputation for taking things to the police or the press?" He swallowed. "But I like you two. You have balls."

"Vaginas, actually," said Rachel, making up for not speaking out in front of Mediouri's associate. "But thank you."

She smiled at him to take the sting out. He dipped his head and grinned back.

Magda took advantage of the détente. "*We* also have something to ask *you*."

He pulled the door open. "You better come in."

They stepped into a foyer backed by an old-fashioned box-office booth and a second door. This opened onto an area that split into two arms, raised seating areas that curved out and around a sunken wooden area that Rachel assumed was the dance floor. They were thickly carpeted in black, with black banquettes running along walls studded at even intervals with paintings of pouting showgirls wearing feathered headdresses and Victorian corsetry. At the dance floor's edge on the lower level, deep tufted chairs and couches surrounded small tables, all facing the floor. The two arms of the raised area met at the end of the room in a long bar, its top polished zinc and behind it a vast collection of alcohol. Bottles of every hue and design crowded shelves in front of a mirror that reflected them back at themselves—when she squinted, she saw that one ceiling-high section was devoted to vodka alone.

Despite its obvious newness and carefully curated luxury, the club had an air Rachel remembered from the bars she'd worked in when she was new to Paris: the stale beer scent and hollow atmosphere of daytime in a place meant for nights. Just as had been true then, the cash register behind the bar was open, the tongues that held the money in its sections raised.

The only difference was that the pile of bills on the bar-top was short, the pile of card receipts towering. In her day it was the other way around.

The man tapped it all into one pile, shoved it into the cash drawer, and locked the register. He put his hands on the bar. "What'll you have?"

Rachel didn't know what had caused his change in attitude since their first encounter, but it was another of her firm convictions that one should never turn down free food or drink. As he poured them two Coke Lights, he answered their questions. Certainly someone from Sauveterre had paid a visit to the club before booking it for Guipure's party. A girl had called and made an appointment with his partner, who had given them a tour. This had been around three months before the party. About a week later the same girl had called to make the booking, and a month before the party, a man and someone who he assumed was the same girl had come to take another tour and hammer out the final arrangements. That time he had done the showing around himself.

"Did you get their names?"

"He introduced himself as Roland Guipure, although I recognized him right away anyway. She didn't give a name. In fact, she hardly said anything. Just sort of hovered behind him all the time, taking notes on a clipboard."

Rachel exchanged a quick glance with Magda. *Bingo.*

"By any chance was Cyrille Thieriot here when they came?"

The man looked upward and squinted. At last he said, "Yeeees. Yes, because I remember that when the two of them came in, he took one look and scampered out like a rabbit. He was restocking the bar, and then half a second later he wasn't."

Rachel's heart pounded against her breastbone like a caged animal. She willed it to calm down.

"Come on," the man said abruptly. He nodded to his left, and Rachel suddenly became aware of a narrow, recessed staircase that led upstairs. "And don't bring your drinks. I don't like it when the equipment's sticky."

With this mysterious phrase he led them up the stairs and into a small room directly off the landing. The collection of stuffed notebooks on its shelves and papers all over its desk marked it out as the business office. He leaned over the computer monitor that stood on the desk and turned it to face them, brushing and setting in motion the head of a bobble doll designed to look like a grinning Nicolas Sarkozy wearing a sash that said "Grey Goose." He pushed a CD into the side of the monitor. "House copy."

The screen bloomed into life. After a few moments of desktop background, it began to run a film showing a large area filled with people. The dance floor was crowded, and at the far end of the room people packed a long bar. It took Rachel a moment to realize this was the room she had just been sitting in. On the screen, the carpet, the banquettes—in fact, everything she had just seen downstairs—were all white. Instead of the paintings of befeathered dancers, lengths of wide white fabric hung from ceiling to floor; instead of black seats, the bar stools now had white ones.

"You did this for one night?"

"Guipure had people come and do it. It was one of his questions when he came to look at the space: Would we be willing to let him make alterations if he agreed to change it back when he was done? I said sure, for an extra ten thousand euro and if he provided the labor." His voice said this wasn't the first time he'd made it worth his own while to oblige a rich man's whim.

On the monitor, people looked like marionettes moving to music the security camera didn't record, while others milled and chatted at the surrounding tables and on the raised plat-forms above. She recognized Keteb Lellouch, talking to a woman whose total lack of body fat and extreme height marked her out as a model. Over his left shoulder, she spotted Antoinette, gleaming in a white satin pantsuit as she watched the dancers. The rest of the crowd drank or posed or chatted with their eyes focused over each other's shoulders to check that there was no one better available. She began to see that her early concern over who had attended this party was irrelevant. It didn't matter that Guipure had had no friends to invite. This was an event designed for seeing and being seen.

The camera angle changed. Now the bar was directly in front of them, thronged with people waiting to order, and only the first few feet of the dance floor appeared. As she watched a man came onto the lower right-hand corner of the screen. Rachel recognized him as Guipure, less because of his face than because he was wearing white from head to foot—she was pretty sure she even made out the tips of white shoes beneath his trouser hems. He held some kind of tall glass with a straw in it in his left hand, and walked through the dance floor, arms snaking out to stop him every few steps for an exchange of cheek kisses or a short conversation. Then he vanished through an archway on the upper left.

"Men's room," said their host.

Now a woman appeared, this time from the top left side. It was Gabrielle. Rachel's heart leaped again. As the camera watched, she approached the bar, stopped, then spotted a gap in the crowd and began to walk toward it. A man suddenly entered the screen from the right, walking so fast he was nearly running. He slammed into her. She grabbed his upper arms to steady herself; he held her shoulders to assist her, but only for a split second before rushing off in the same direction as Guipure. His face was turned away from the camera, but there was no mistaking the long-fingered hand that gripped Gabrielle's shoulder, the extreme thinness of the man's body.

"That's Thieriot," said the club owner.

For a few seconds nothing happened. Gabrielle took up a place at the bar, leaning her arms on it. A woman wandered across the center of the dance floor, wearing what looked like a crocheted green short suit, cut down to her navel and accessorized with hip-high white patent boots. A man wearing a double-breasted suit followed, one arm stretched out toward her. The suit was lilac, and the lapel of its top side was ultramarine blue, but it was still a suit. Who was it who'd said, "Women's fashion changes every one hundred days; men's fashion changes every one hundred years"? Whoever it was, she wasn't sure they would have appreciated any of these particular changes.

Then Thieriot reappeared, still rushing, but this time from the direction of the men's room. He crossed in front the bar and disappeared from view. "Out my fucking back door in the middle of his shift," growled the man behind them.

A few more moments and Guipure also reappeared. His hair was slightly wet, as if he'd run his hands under a tap and pulled them over it, but otherwise he looked exactly as he had before. Once more he walked through the dancers. After a few steps, though, he stumbled, then righted himself by putting his hand on the back of a man near him. The man turned around and Guipure made a gesture of apology. He took another few steps, then stopped. He gave his head a quick shake. Then, walking carefully, he continued across the floor and out of the screen.

"Heading outside," the man said. "That's the last time security footage shows him."

Rachel looked at the bottom of the screen. The time stamp read 02:20.

* * *

"They bumped into each other," Magda said once they were outside again. She didn't need to say any more. They had both seen numberless films and television shows in which, by a seemingly accidental bump, pockets were picked or secrets were passed.

"But he hid when she came to the club with Guipure."

"He could have done that to be sure he didn't give anything away when they saw each other. You yourself said he's a bad liar. Or perhaps it's just difficult to be cool when you're face to face with someone you know you're going to kill in a month."

"It did look like Guipure had begun to feel the effects of the heroin when he crossed the floor after coming out of the men's room."

"Which was right after his encounter with Thieriot. An encounter Thieriot admitted to."

"And that happened right after Thieriot and Gabrielle slammed into each other."

"And *held* each other," Magda stressed. "They *touched* each other."

"She could've slipped him the syringe. She'd need to be quick, but she could have done it. We'd have to check the footage again—"

"But she could have done it, and she did buy heroin. That we know for sure."

"And she wanted that job, but Guipure didn't give it to her. She was also in love with him. Two good motives. And now the job is hers."

"True, Thieriot *was* her romantic rival in a way. But then Guipure dumped Thieriot. And the enemy of my enemy is my friend."

"Especially if that enemy needs money," Rachel pointed out.

They looked at each other. It worked; it actually worked. All the evidence was there, along with means and opportunity. They had done it.

"We better call Boussicault," Magda said.

Rachel almost agreed. "Could it wait until after I tell Alan? Just a couple of hours, so he feels in the loop. You know he's been upset about that before."

Magda nodded. She remembered Alan's rage when they'd investigated Edgar Bowen's death without telling him. "Okay. But only a couple of hours."

"I promise I'll call you as soon as I'm done."

Chapter
Thirty-Two

“What about Ochs?” Alan asked when she'd finished telling him about the nightclub video and Magda's idea. “That explains Guipure, but it doesn't explain why Keteb or Gabrielle would want to kill Ochs. According to what you described earlier, Ochs's grandfather was a member of Gabrielle's family. If he was Gabrielle's great-uncle, or great-great-uncle, that would make Jack Ochs her cousin in some way. It's hard to see why she would murder her long-lost cousin.”

“Not necessarily. Maybe Jack Ochs knew something about his grandfather that could be a threat to Gabrielle's family in some way.” Rachel felt herself growing hot, as she always did when Alan challenged one of her neatly constructed hypotheses. “Maybe Maximilien Sauveterre helped to smuggle him out because he was a threat.”

“Aubert isn't a Jewish name,” Alan pointed out.

“Well, the fact that Sauveterre helped Jews doesn't mean he *only* helped Jews.” Rachel realized she was echoing Magda, but it made sense. “He could have been doing a favor by removing the black sheep of a family he knew.”

"Which would mean all your ideas about thwarted love and being passed over for jobs would be irrelevant." Alan was calm. "I don't mean to be awkward, but this version makes much more sense to me. Guipure discovered something about the Aubert–Ochs incident that Gabrielle felt made him worth killing, and at the same time Ochs appeared, knowing or wanting something that made her feel the same about him. You still have the same murderer, just with a more logical scenario." He peered into her face. "After all, Guipure and Ochs did have a meeting arranged. There's a connection between them."

Rachel chewed her thumbnail and thought furiously. It did make better sense. And it did have precedent. "Magda thought something similar, originally."

"She thought Gabrielle killed Guipure and Ochs for the same reason?"

"She thought it was all connected to Judaism somehow."

"Well, now you can call her and tell her she might be right. She'll like that." He smiled. "But before you do that, could you do something else? I called my mother to let her know I'd made it home safely, and she asked me to remind you to send Ochs's stuff. Apparently Ellen has been asking after it. If I go find a box could you just gather it together? UPS will pick up tomorrow if I call them before five."

"Oh, I'm sorry. Right after I collected the suitcase from the commissariat everything started speeding up with Guipure, and I . . . yeah, let's do it now."

Alan reached for his keys. "I think I saved her box from Christmas in the storage cage downstairs. I'll be right back."

Rachel rolled the suitcase out from under the hall table, feeling guilty. Poor Ellen Ochs shouldn't have been made to wait three weeks to receive her dead husband's belongings. She would put a card in with the clothes, apologizing and inviting her to stay with them if she ever visited Paris. Although on second thought such a visit seemed unlikely . . .

She laid the suitcase flat on one of the dining chairs and unzipped it. The clothes, neatly folded to face upward when it lay horizontally, had slipped to the left during the three weeks it had been on end. She shifted them back and began to lift them out.

A sport coat, light brown tweed, with a collar label identifying it as Macy's brand. A royal-blue Oxford shirt. A long-sleeved brown polo shirt. A short-sleeved gray polo shirt. Under those, a pair of pale khaki chinos, and under that three pairs of tan socks, two undershirts, and four pairs of plain white boxers. Without all of this to prop it up, a paperback that had been pressing against the right side of the suitcase flopped over, revealing itself as something called *Fatherland*, by Robert Harris. A label stuck to the upper right corner said "Miami-Dade Public Library System."

Rachel could never resist a book. She flicked this one open to the first page, which had a diagonal "Canceled" stamp and a due date slip on which the last date was April 15, 2000. On the flyleaf someone had written *Paul Ochs* in cramped cursive script.

She flipped the book over to read the back cover, and as she did so a folded piece of paper fluttered out from between the pages, a thin grayish sheet, folded in half. She bent and picked it up, unfolding it. *Galerie Sauveterre,* it said across the top in a familiar elaborate font.

She went cold. Putting the book down, she held the piece of paper flat against the surface of the dining table with both hands. Its front side was slightly paler than its back and its central crease was sharp, as if it had been unfolded infrequently. It was the top copy of a receipt like those she had seen in Sauveterre's archive. In the top right-hand corner was printed "007892"—she recognized it as the receipt number, having spent one nightmarish summer working in the accounts office of her uncle's moving company. On the dateline underneath the scrollwork of the gallery name, someone had written *2 Novembre 1939*, and in the space given beneath for recording the sale, *Albert Ütz: Leger, Nature Morte*. She recognized the handwriting from the receipts she had viewed just a few days before in the Sauveterre archive. In the column indicating the amount paid, the same hand had written, *12000ff*.

That couldn't be right. She squeezed her eyes shut. She knew Leger's name: she and Alan had been to an exhibition of Cubism the previous spring, and a Leger had been part of the display. The plaque next to the painting had explained that Fernand Leger had been major figure in Cubism and was commonly considered a forerunner of pop art. The amount paid for a work by such an artist must have been 120,000 francs, not 12,000. Opening her eyes, she looked at the receipt again, more carefully this time.

She had been right. The amount was 12,000 francs. And who was this Albert Ütz? She had been through all the receipts in the folder for 1939, and she didn't remember that name. Had he sold Maximilien Sauveterre a still life so small and cheap that the man hadn't even bothered to retain a copy of the receipt?

She moved to her desk. She didn't need to hack anything to find what she wanted. Instead, she went right to the website of Christie's auction house, then to the page where they gave prices from their recent art sales. The lowest recent price for a Leger was $300,000.

She opened a second tab and found a site which told her that in 1940 a French franc had been worth two United States cents, then a second site that converted 1940s dollars into present-day dollars. Just as she heard Alan's key in the door, she was able to understand that in June of 1941 the Sauveterre Gallery had bought a Fernand Leger still life for the 2016 equivalent of $4,000.

She realized she was gripping her lips between her teeth. She tried to remember the prices on the Sauveterre receipts she'd seen. True, she'd been looking quickly, and her memory wasn't exact, but she couldn't remember any number lower than 100,000 flicking through her fingers in that icy basement room.

"Ready?" She turned to find Alan holding an empty cardboard box big enough for Ochs's suitcase to fit into. When he saw her face, he said, "What?"

"I found something strange." She explained about the price on the receipt and her painful mathematics, the comparison that didn't seem sensible or maybe even possible. "And who is this person anyway? I looked through all the receipts in that archive, and I didn't see one for an Albert Ütz."

As soon as she said the name out loud she understood. Of course! No wonder they hadn't been able to fit all the pieces together—they hadn't *had* all the pieces. She put the receipt down on the table in front of her and stood still for a moment. She needed her hands to stop shaking before she could call Magda.

*   *   *

Half an hour later the two of them sat in the *séjour*. Rachel had refused to tell Alan anything until she had told Magda, and he had sulkily sequestered himself in the bedroom to take a jet-lagged nap. As he slept, Magda listened while an excited Rachel gave a frenetic explanation of what she thought had happened, but now she said, "I couldn't follow that at all. Start again, and do it slowly."

Rachel took a deep breath. "Okay. Let's start with Jack Ochs. He was killed second, but he was really the start of everything. Or rather, his grandfather was."

"That's just as confusing." Magda leaned forward. *"Be clearer."*

Rachel gathered herself. "All right, let me start with this: you were right. Albert Ochs got on the SS *Pennland* as someone else. But he didn't get on as Septime Aubert or Jacques Aubert. He got on as Albert *Ütz*." Her computer sat on the coffee table, and she turned it so that Magda could see the passenger manifest for the SS *Pennland* on its screen. She scrolled down past the *O*s and the *P*s, nearly to the end of the list. *Dr. and Mrs. William Thomas, Mrs. Anna Titelbaum, Miss Frederika von Urlaub . . .* and there it was: *Mr. Albert Ütz.* "Maybe when Ütz said his name, the immigration heard officer heard *Ochs* and wrote that down instead. Listen." She said the two names one after the other. "Or maybe Ütz had had so many people on the boat mis-hear him that he just gave his name as Ochs.

Don't forget, he was leaving a Europe where it was dangerous for Albert Ütz, a Jew, to exist at all. Maybe he was relieved to leave that him behind and start over as Mr. Ochs."

"But Ochs is a Jewish name too."

Rachel nodded. "I thought about that. Being a Jew in Europe in 1939 was dangerous, but in a sense it was dangerous because it was important. It was an integral part of who you were. Just because he wanted to be safe, that doesn't mean Ütz wanted to stop being his essential self. So he became an American Jew from Florida instead of a Jew from France. Which explains why he made up that story about being born in Hypoluxo."

"But how do you know he made it up?" Magda stared at the computer screen. "How do you even know this is the same man? How do you know you aren't just making it up again?"

"I don't," Rachel admitted. "But thanks to the Mormons and their amazing record keeping, in the time it took you to arrive here, I was able to learn from the FamilySearch website that an Albert Ütz was born in Le Hohwald, Alsace, on July 25, 1905. And thanks to the search I did on Wikipedia in the minutes I had left over, I now know that between September 1939 and July 1940 all the Jews in Alsace were expelled." She sat back. "Which would give a wise Jew just enough time between July and December of 1940 to make his arrangements and get the hell out of France."

Magda pushed out her breath dismissively, but after a few seconds of consideration, she relented. "All right. It does line up. But I still don't understand what it has to do with Roland Guipure."

"It has to do with Roland Guipure because it has to do with Maximilien Sauveterre." Rachel pointed her chin at the yellowed receipt that lay in front of Magda on the coffee table. "That receipt is for a painting Jack Ochs's grandfather sold to Maximilien Sauveterre. I think Ochs found it when he started going through his father's books. Remember, Ellen Ochs said he'd started to do that right before he surprised her with the trip to Paris, and I found it in a book with Paul Ochs's name on the flyleaf. I think he found it and he did what anyone would do— he tried to use the internet to figure out what it was. It would have taken him very little time to figure out that Sauveterre had wildly underpaid Albert Ütz for a Fernand Leger painting, and I think he contacted Guipure because he found him on the internet connected to the name Sauveterre." She gestured to two-inch-high letters on the receipt. "There are a lot of Leger *Nature Morts* around, but not many Galeries Sauveterre. I think Ochs contacted Guipure to tell him about the receipt and ask for help tracking down the painting. He had an excellent case for restitution. And I think that's when Guipure first began to realize that Maximilien Sauveterre lied about paying Jews fair prices for their art. That he forged those famous receipts and used the money he made from reselling those paintings at huge profits to build the Sauveterre family fortune."

Magda gasped—as Rachel had hoped she would. Then she said triumphantly, "So it *was* about Judaism."

"Well," Rachel said, tilting her head slightly from side to side, "let's say it was about Jewish*ness*. It's a religion and an ethnicity, remember, and we're dealing with the ethnic aspect." Magda rolled her eyes. "But it was also about communication."

Magda made an uncomprehending face. "Which means what?"

"All the dead men had communicated with each other. Or, to be more accurate, the other two had been in communication with Guipure. He's the fulcrum here."

Magda frowned. "I can see that for Ochs, but Thieriot? Where does he fit in?"

Rachel wrinkled her nose. "I haven't figured that out yet. Not completely. But I'm sure about Albert Ochs and Albert Ütz. And I'm *sure* about the sales. However"—Rachel made a face that said Magda wasn't going to like what followed—"if Albert Ochs is Albert Ütz, that means he can't be Jacques Aubert. Which means there's no connection to Gabrielle."

"But Gabrielle bought the heroin!"

"I know, I know. I can't explain that. But I can't argue with the evidence either."

"Maybe she bought it for Lellouch." Magda considered. "So we were right; they're working together."

Rachel shook her head. "It can't be that either. Because if the murders are about Maximilien Sauveterre's falsifying receipts, Lellouch had nothing to lose or gain from that. He could find another job if the House of Sauveterre crumbled. So could Gabrielle, for that matter. Only one other person would *really* suffer from the revelation that Maximilien Sauveterre underpaid Jews for their art and then lied to cover it up."

Magda looked at her, first disbelieving and then, slowly, accepting. She said, "Are you sure this is about Maximilien Sauveterre forging receipts? Are you absolutely sure?"

Rachel held her gaze. "I am absolutely sure." She swallowed. "But to prove it"—she leaned across the coffee table—"we need to get into the archive. We need to go through the receipts we saw, again. If there isn't one for Ütz and we can write down a few more of the names and check to see if there are living relatives we can contact, then I'll be sure." She closed the computer and started to stand.

Magda put a hand out. "Tomorrow."

"What?"

"Wait until tomorrow. What are you going to do today, go bursting in there demanding to look at their archive? They're going to ask you why, and what are you going to say? But tomorrow is the memorial service. Everyone from Sauveterre will be at the Église Saint Roch. The building will be empty. No one will be there, and we'll have all the time we need. Just you and me, your collection of lock picks, and time to go through the files. Then we can take what we find to Boussicault, and he can question her."

Alan had come out of the bedroom, his hair standing in spikes on his head. He came into the *séjour*. "Have you finished? Are you ready to tell your husband, now? Who is 'her'?"

They looked at him. Together they said, "Antoinette."

Chapter Thirty-Three

~

There passed for Rachel one of the most unpleasant afternoons and nights of her life. She imagined breaking into 21 Rue la Boétie only to discover that the reception for the memorial had been moved there, or arriving at the building only to see that it was under police guard. She imagined her lock-picking skills suddenly deserting her, and just to be sure of herself, she spent the hours between supper and bed picking her model lock, relocking it, then angling it or herself so she could pick it again in some more difficult position. When she finally fell asleep, she dreamt that she did successfully pick the locks on the front door and the door to the archive, only to discover Roland Guipure himself waiting for her in the file room, skeletal and icy pale at having been hidden underground for a month.

At two o'clock the next afternoon, she and Magda came out of Miromesnil station and crossed over to the Sauveterre headquarters. No *clochard* today, Rachel noticed. She gave thanks for small mercies.

Trying to calm herself, she bent over in the doorway of 21 Rue la Boetie, pretending to tie her shoe. From this low vantage point, she could see that the building's glass and metal front doors had two locks, one above and one below the handle. Both appeared to be simple tumbler locks. As she leaned in to look a little closer, she noticed that the white paint on the art deco grille had been allowed to peel away, and the gray iron was beginning to show.

"Stand behind me," she said to Magda.

"What? Why?"

"So no one will see that a middle-aged woman is trying to pick the lock of Maison Sauveterre while everyone who works there is at the memorial service!" She reached into her jacket pocket and unzipped her picklock holder, choosing the ones she needed by feel.

"Oh, right, right."

Magda stood behind her, facing the street, so close that Rachel could feel her body warmth through her own jacket. Rachel took one of the thin lengths of metal out of her pocket and slipped it into the top lock. Willing her other hand into steadiness, she inserted the second pick on top of this first one and began gently moving it up and down, feeling for the edges of the pins so she could ease it under. No, no, n—yes! One, two, three pins clicked up, and the bolt slid back. She felt what she always felt at this moment, a powerful rush of euphoria and disbelief. It flashed across her mind that this must be how a gambling addict felt when a bet paid out—or a heroin addict when the needle went in.

She pushed that thought aside and moved the picks to the lower lock.

"Stop!" Magda's voice was a bullet.

Rachel froze. She heard the sound of approaching heels.

"Pretend to throw up."

"Wh—"

"Pretend to throw up!"

Rachel made retching noises. The heels stopped for a moment and she heard Magda say, *"Çe n'est rien, madame. Mon amie a mangé une mauvaise huître."*

The heels hurried away. Rachel no longer felt like an invincible gambler; she took several deep breaths to stop herself from actually vomiting. Slightly calmed, she managed to release the second lock despite her shaking hands.

As she slipped into the foyer of the building, she felt cold sweat breaking out all over her. "Quick," she said to Magda as she shut the door behind them.

Eleven steps across the foyer, another ten to descend the stairs to the basement, and each one seemed to Rachel to ring out like a pistol shot. At last, though, they faced the steel door with its ugly deadbolt, the protruding knob that seemed simple but was actually more secure than any digital lock. Or so Gabrielle said.

"Hold the knob," she whispered to Magda, "and pull when I say."

Magda held the knob. Rachel's hands shivered only a little as she repeated the movements she'd executed at the front door. The pick slipped under one pin, then another, then smoothly under another two. "Pull the knob! Pull the knob!"

Magda pulled the knob just as the pick slid under the last pin: the door swung open.

Once more the fluorescent lights flickered on as they crossed the threshold. The room looked exactly as it had on their last visit, or perhaps slightly more sterile. The boxes of gloves seemed to have been centered with a ruler on the tables; the Formica tabletops gleamed like mortuary slabs. Rachel had the strange feeling common to those performing illicit actions in empty rooms: that some hidden person was watching, or someone was about to walk in and catch her.

She quashed this sensation by striding over to the fourth cabinet along the wall and opening its top drawer. It was empty. She opened the one underneath it, then the one underneath that. They were filled with folders, all arranged by date and then keyword, but none were the folders that held the Galerie Sauveterre receipts.

She opened the top drawer of the fifth filing cabinet. Empty. It rattled as she pushed it shut. The drawers below were just like those in the fourth cabinet: packed, but not with what she needed.

"Shit." She bit her lip. "Shit." She put out her hand to open a drawer in the sixth cabinet, then dropped it. She knew she wouldn't find what she wanted.

But beside her Magda straightened up and turned back toward the door. "Fine. We'll just have to look upstairs."

"Upstairs?" Why did "upstairs" sound so much more dangerous than "downstairs"? But Rachel knew why. "Downstairs" matched the instinct to burrow, to hunker down and stay safe. "Upstairs" represented windows that people could see through and a literal inability to put her feet on the ground. Upstairs was endless white space with nowhere to hide.

"Yes, upstairs." Magda was brisk. "You just broke and entered, and I just aided and abetted you. We didn't do that to end up finding nothing. We need to check upstairs, to be sure."

She was right. They needed those receipts to prove their case, and they needed to find them before a triple murderer came back from the memorial service and found them there.

"Okay." But still she asked, "What time is it?"

Magda checked her watch "Three. They'll be halfway through the service. And then there's the reception until five thirty."

Rachel lifted her heels in an effort to avoid making noise as they climbed the marble stairs. Up they went, past the couture fitting rooms and the *ateliers* behind them, past the storage rooms and across white landing hung with white-framed mirrors that reflected blankness back at itself. Finally they reached the business offices on the third floor. Rachel nudged Magda. The framed receipt that had hung on the wall was gone.

The door to the reception area was open, the white desk and chair unoccupied. They walked through to Gabrielle's office. Once again Rachel's eyes were drawn to the giant button, the knife-edge hem, but only for a moment before she switched her attention to Gabrielle's desk. Its surface was empty.

She drew a deep breath and let it out, crossing the room to the doorway to Antoinette's office. The carpet in the two outer offices had muffled her footsteps, so the sound of her first step across the threshold, clacking on the naked wood, surprised her. She started, then gave a little snort at her own foolishness. Tossing her head, she crossed the threshold and entered the room.

"Hello," said Antoinette.

Chapter
Thirty-Four

The shock of seeing her there was so great that Rachel actually staggered back. Antoinette stood behind her desk, the eternal fire burning in her fireplace. They had come upon her in the act of warming her hands at its flames, and her arms were still outstretched as she turned to face them.

"Madame Field, Madame Stevens. Come in. I left the memorial service early. I told them I found it too emotional to stay, but really"—her voice became confidential—"I had some work I needed to do. And I was just finishing up when I saw the two of you from the window. I guess you wanted to take advantage of the empty building to do some work of your own." She smiled at her joke, then gestured at the chairs in front of the desk. "Please, sit."

Shit. Rachel looked over her shoulder at Magda, who made a helpless gesture. There was nothing for it but to do as they were asked.

They crossed to the desk and sat in the chairs in front of it. The scene was like a replay of their first encounter. Once again Antoinette was dressed all in black, and once again Rachel saw that the skin around her eyes was swollen from crying. The only difference was that this time she sat down behind the desk rather than coming out in front of it.

"You figured it out."

It wasn't a question, but Rachel nodded anyway. Out of the corner of her eye, she saw Magda do the same.

"Yes. I worried you might be coming close when you came to see me the second time, but I hoped I'd steered you in the wrong direction. Ah, well."

Antoinette turned her head and stared out the window for a moment, her eyes losing focus and looking at nothing. It was a bit like being called into the principal's office, Rachel thought: the same amorphous fear, the same terrifying wait. She shifted her bag from the left side of her lap to the right.

At last Antoinette spoke again.

"The war." She sighed as if the word itself were a disappointment. "You can never get away from the war. Resistance, collaboration . . . you'd think it had all happened yesterday." Another sigh. "Did you know that France trained and armed militias that participated in the Rwandan genocide? In the war in Algeria, the French killed seven hundred thousand people. That's more than ten times the number of French Jews killed in the Second World War. But no one is destroyed by the revelation that his grandfather fought in Algeria, or that he works for Nexter Systems making the weapons France sells to half the world."

Rachel didn't speak. She didn't disagree with Antoinette's assessment. It was true that France had its own arms manufacturers selling death around the globe, and it was also true that every day groups of people were being killed senselessly by other groups, in Paris and everywhere else. But she wasn't sure how to respond to a monologue on relative morality delivered by a murderer.

"It was all that man Ochs's fault. God!" Antoinette snarled. "He wrote to Rolé in February, saying that he was trying to track down a painting his grandfather sold to Grandpère to raise money to go to America. He'd found the receipt inside a book. He thought Sauveterre might have some idea of how to locate the painting, but when Rolé went into the archive to see if there was anything useful he could tell him, he found Grandpère's copy of the receipt. And when they compared them, the receipts didn't match." She smiled thinly. "As I assume you already know."

Rachel nodded. "Your grandfather's receipt showed a much higher price paid than Ochs's did."

Antoinette nodded. "And the serial numbers didn't match either. Every receipt and its carbon had the same identifying number," she explained, "but Grandpère's copy of the Ütz receipt was numbered much higher than the one Ochs sent. It showed a one hundred thousand franc difference in price."

Rachel let out a breath she didn't know she'd been holding.

"Roland wanted to tell everyone," Antoinette said. "He wanted to *make amends*." She folded her hands on the desk in front of her; Rachel could see the pressure from her fingers turning her knuckles pale. "I wore the white. I paid for him to redecorate this whole building to achieve equilibrium. I supported the daily hourlong meditation and the meetings every afternoon with his sobriety counselor. I found that nightclub for his party and paid when he demanded it be redecorated. He was a genius, an absolute genius, and anything he needed to produce his art, I was willing to do. But this . . ." She faded off, then focused again. "He explained that one of the twelve steps was righting your wrongs. I said he hadn't *done* anything wrong. But according to him, since Grandpère's wrongs had funded the business, they were Roland's wrongs too."

Not an entirely unreasonable argument, Rachel thought. After all, a similar rationale had prompted German reparation payments to Israel in the 1950s and 1960s.

From the mystified way Antoinette shook her head, though, it was clear she felt differently. "I said, 'But what about the people who work for us? Should people lose their livelihoods over something they had nothing to do with?'" She looked at Rachel. "Do you know how many people the *ateliers* employ? Never mind those who work in the shop, in the office, in our factories worldwide. Should a man's *employees* have to pay for his grandfather's wrongs?" She stopped as if she expected answers, but when none came she kept going. "Roland didn't care. He was going to meet Ochs to verify his receipt, and then he would announce to the press that our grandfather had made his money by cheating Jews and forging evidence to cover it up. Sauveterre would have been ruined." She put out her hands, asking for consideration. "*Everyone* knows the story: Maximilien Sauveterre paid fair prices for Jewish art sold in desperation, then held onto the pieces in case the sellers came back. When they didn't come back, he sold the pieces at the same prices he bought them for. What did Roland think would happen once people found out that Maximilien *really* waited until he was sure those sellers weren't going to come back, then forged receipts so he could sell the works at an inflated price?" She took a huge, ragged breath. "No one is going to buy from a fashion house founded on blood money! And you saw how many receipts our grandfather forged. The heirs of all those people could have sued for reparations. We would have spent a fortune on court costs alone. And what for? What does it matter now what one dead person did to some other dead people nearly eighty years ago?"

What did *it matter?* Rachel thought. Hadn't she struggled with that very question? What possible purpose could it serve now to unmask one man as a cheater of Jews, especially a man who couldn't be punished for it? It wouldn't bring anyone back, or right any wrong.

Yet it did matter. She couldn't explain how it mattered, but she felt the knowledge of injustice like an instinct. She said, "Your grandfather died in his bed when he was eighty-six. But my great-uncle Paul died at Buchenwald when he was twenty." That was the closest she could come.

Antoinette only sighed, exasperated by the obstinacy of other people. "Roland didn't understand either. I'm not saying our grandfather didn't do anything wrong. Of course he did. But trying to make it all better would be impossible, and it would only have hurt more people. Roland refused to see that."

"So you killed him."

Antoinette looked down at the desktop. "I loved my brother." Suddenly she began to cry. "Do you know what it means to be a twin? What it really means?" She wiped her eyes. "It means reassurance. He was always there. I could take his existence for granted. And now—" She stopped.

"But you killed him." Magda spoke slowly and clearly, as if pointing out a logical flaw to a five-year-old.

"And do you have any idea how hard that was for me?" Antoinette bit her lips. "I had to inject him, and then I had to stand there and wait. Not for a short time, either. Stand there and watch and act like nothing was wrong, and then force myself not to follow him when I finally saw him go outside."

Rachel was almost breathless with disbelief at this description. How to respond to such egotism?

The response came: *by exploiting it to get the details of the crime.* "But how did you do it? With the club so crowded, how was it possible to manage the injection without being seen?"

A brief expression of pride flashed over Antoinette's face. "I counted on its being crowded. I hid the syringe up the sleeve of my coat and waited until late to come to the party, so it would be crowded. Then, when I hugged him, I just slid the needle into my hand and stuck him. He felt it—of course he felt it!—and I said I'd probably just scratched him accidentally."

Rachel could feel Magda beside her, stiff with disgust and disbelief, and she knew that if she turned to look at her, she wouldn't be able to keep her composure. Instead, she took a deep breath to keep her voice level. "And Ochs?"

"Oh." Antoinette sniffed. "That was a pleasure. After the trouble he stirred up."

"You shot him."

She nodded. "With the Luger Grandpère got as a present during the war. I made sure Rolé's assistant saw me supposedly take a sedative and fall asleep, and when she left I went to Rue la Boétie and called Ochs from Lellouch's office."

"You told him your brother couldn't make it."

"No. I didn't know if he would have seen the news on TV. They announced Rolé's death right after I identified him. So I said he had died, but I knew the meeting had been important to him, so I wished to come in his place. Could he find somewhere quiet for us to go to talk? I said I would pick him up at his hotel room and we could go from there. It all went very smoothly. No one argues with a grieving woman." A sigh. "Only I was nervous. I'd never shot anybody before. He turned to reach for something, and I thought—well, I don't know what I thought, but I grabbed a cushion and shot him through it." She made a little clicking sound of irritation. "Afterward, I realized he must have been reaching for the receipt. But I couldn't find it, and I was worried about the noise. So I left without it. I threw the gun in the Seine on the way home, and the next day I came in before anyone else and took the forged receipt out of the archive. I figured if the police showed up with Ochs's version I could just pretend not to know what was going on. After all, I wouldn't be lying if I said I'd never seen it before."

Rachel closed her eyes. She swallowed hard before opening them. "And poor Cyrille?"

"Poor Cyrille? Please, he was a parasite. From the moment Rolé decided to cut him off, I told Gabrielle not to put him through to me if he ever called trying to whine his way back in. Which he did for a while. Then a couple of weeks ago, she told me that he'd started trying to contact me again, and she'd been putting him off. By sheer luck, last week he tried one day after she'd left, and I picked up my own line. He said he wanted to discuss something I might find very valuable, something that I would want to keep within the walls of Sauveterre." She gave a little sneer. "Always so obvious. That's when I knew he knew about the receipts."

Rachel wasn't going to stop Antoinette's flow of words to tell her that she was wrong, but she did spare a pitying thought for two men killed because of what Antoinette Guipure thought she knew. Ochs shot when he was about to give her the very receipt she wanted, and Cyrille reaching for the *croquis*, thinking his ship had come in, not knowing that in a few minutes he would be dead.

"So you arranged to meet him at his apartment?"

Antoinette nodded. "I had the *carte couteau* I always carry in my bag. As soon as we were in the room, he bent to get something from under the bed. I was very quick. Once in each kidney, and when he straightened, once in each lung."

"And what about us?" Magda's voice shook a little. "We're not here for money. We're just going to take what you've told us straight to the police."

But Antoinette gave a little shake of her head. "I don't think you'll be doing that." Her voice was calm, but it was certain.

Did she have another gun? Had she told them what she had because she'd been planning to kill them all along? But Rachel could see that Antoinette's hands lay softly folded on the desktop, unmoving. There was no weapon in sight.

Still, the other woman seemed unconcerned. She turned to look out the window for a moment, gazing into the distance, before turning her attention back to them. Then she said conversationally, "Do you think the police will believe the claims of two women who broke into my company headquarters when they knew everyone would be out at a memorial service, ransacked my files, and made their way upstairs to do further damage? That will be my version of events. They're more likely to arrest two self-proclaimed amateur detectives than they are the head of a highly successful company, a respected woman of business now shaken all over again after the terrible recent loss of her beloved brother."

It was Rachel's turn to be unfazed. "Except that there's evidence to back up what we say. They'll have to search the building, just to be sure our story isn't true, and when they do, they'll find your grandfather's receipts."

"Oh, the receipts!" Antoinette raised her eyebrows. "The evidence of the inciting scheme."

"Yes."

"There's no need for the police to search for the receipts. They aren't very far away."

The two women exchanged a look. Was this some new plan, Antoinette pretending to give them the evidence as a way to rope them in to something else? Magda spoke before Rachel could. "Where are they?"

Antoinette moved her chair sideways. She stretched out a hand behind her. "There."

In the space behind her the two women saw the fire, now a pile of red and orange embers with a heap of ashes beneath.

Chapter Thirty-Five

~

"I'm so sorry," Alan said.

They were gathered in Bistrot Vivienne for their usual end-of-investigation debriefing. This time, though, they weren't celebrating. Rachel had ordered a cup of watery French tea for herself as a penance, and now she sat taking tasteless sips as she waited for what her husband would say next.

"Maybe you could find some comfort in the knowledge that this isn't a unique occurrence? I mean, if news reports and cold cases are anything to go by, there are a lot more murders than there are murderers captured."

He looked over at Capitaine Boussicault, who had invited himself along when Rachel telephoned to tell him what had happened. The capitaine nodded reluctant confirmation. "Although this particular instance is unusual. We don't normally have them confessing and still getting away with it."

"Was it really a confession? What exactly did she tell you?"

Alan was looking for a way to make her feel better, Rachel knew. If there hadn't been a real confession, perhaps she could pretend that Antoinette hadn't really triumphed.

But there was no way around it.

"It was a confession," Magda said. "She started with Ochs's first letter and told us everything Rachel just told you."

"But why not just pay Ochs reparations?" Alan took a sip of his whiskey. "Just speaking purely practically, Sauveterre is very successful. They could afford to quietly give him the money he was owed."

"Guipure wouldn't do it," Rachel said. "He felt this was a wrong that the steps of his recovery program required him to right. His label literally couldn't have existed without the money his grandfather made from reselling those paintings, and therefore he felt that he was complicit. He was going to make his amends by going to the press."

"But she chose an incredibly risky way to circumvent that." Alan frowned. "Injecting him at a party, in public . . ."

"No," Rachel shook her head. "She needed it to be that way. It was part of her plan. The party meant he wouldn't be paying as much attention as he would be if they were alone. And it meant there were two hundred witnesses to say they hadn't seen anything out of the ordinary, just a man being hugged by his sister. And the very boldness of the way she did it made it so unbelievable that no one would even think of it as a possibility. It made her safe." She smiled at him. "You told me she had a brilliant financial mind, and this has all the hallmarks of brilliance. It was risky, and it was audacious, but its risks and audacity were carefully calculated."

"But it didn't pay off," Alan pointed out.

"No, but that was because of something she didn't factor in. She thought that because Guipure was a former addict, the police would dismiss it as an accidental overdose. She didn't expect them to investigate further."

"Don't underestimate the Paris police," Boussicault said with satisfaction.

But Alan was still unsatisfied. "And did she say how she managed to persuade Gabrielle to buy the heroin?"

"Gabrielle didn't buy the heroin."

"But the security video showed her passing it to Thieriot!"

"No." Rachel gritted her teeth. "The security video showed her bumping into Thieriot. We were the ones who assumed it must be a handoff. We saw what we wanted to see, just like we assumed that a woman in a white dress with red hair buying heroin must have been Gabrielle. We forgot that anyone can fake someone's most memorable characteristics. It's easy to buy a red wig and wear a white dress."

"Or sneak into an office," Magda added.

"No, that was my fault." Rachel bit her lip. "You realized that anyone could have used Lellouch's phone without his knowledge."

Magda patted her arm. "But we were both so determined to make Gabrielle guilty that we decided it must have been her."

"And did she kill Thieriot using some audacious plan too?" Alan took another drink of whiskey.

"No, that was very straightforward, just as the police report said. But I think after she did it, she must have started to worry that someone might put it all together. Otherwise, why remove the rest of the receipts from the archive? And then," Rachel said, grinding her teeth, "burn them in her fireplace, leaving us with no evidence admissible in court."

"And she just *told* you all this?" Alan's tone was incredulous. "About impersonating Gabrielle, and her grandfather's Nazi pistol? She just told you right out?"

"She couldn't *wait* to tell us. She had nothing to worry about." Magda shook her head. "She could just sit back and enjoy the big reveal, leaving us to live our lives knowing that there's a triple murderer running around free and that one of France's secular saints is actually just the opposite."

They all looked at Boussicault, the representative of law and order. He took a sip of wine, taking a long time to drink it before he delivered his verdict. At last he said, "Certainly you could accuse her of what you say she admitted to doing. There's nothing to stop you. But equally certainly a *juge d'instruction* would decide you had insufficient evidence to support a case. And if she followed through on her threat, she would respond by demanding of that same *juge* that you be prosecuted for breaking and entering. And for that charge there *is* evidence." He looked at Rachel, then at Magda, then back again. "I'm sorry to say this, but I think in the future it might be wise for you to pick fewer locks and make more calls to the police."

"The future! What future?" Rachel pushed her cup and saucer away petulantly. "If this is private detection, you can keep it."

"I wouldn't be so quick to reach that conclusion." Boussicault scraped a thumb across his jaw. "If I remember your excellent dossier correctly, you have a contact at *Quelles Nouvelles*—well, you have *the* contact at *Quelles Nouvelles*. And some people—not the police of course, but *some* people—might argue that in today's world the real punishments are handed out by the court of public opinion, not a court of law."

The two women looked at each other. "Foucher did make us promise to bring him any interesting revelations," Rachel said.

"And it's not just the internet that loves to believe the worst of others." Magda tapped her fingertips on the tabletop. "We could send copies of the receipt to *Vogue*, and *WWD*, and even some newspapers, along with the details of what we know. We wouldn't even have to put our names on it."

There's more than one way into the square. Hadn't a fashion designer said that? Rachel couldn't remember which one, but that didn't change the value of the observation. Justice was justice, no matter how it came and no matter how long it took. Smiling across the table at her best friend who smiled back, she pushed her cup of cold tea away and turned to Alan.

"Let's order some champagne. Maybe this investigation won't end so badly after all."

Useful French words and phrases

accord de non-divulgation— nondisclosure agreement.
appartement—a grand apartment.
absolument—absolutely.
atelier—studio.
allo—hello (used only for answering the telephone).
alors—so, then.
bal—ball.
bandante—hot (literally, "making something bend").
bon—good.
ça va?—How's it going?
carte couteau—a knife that folds inside a credit card,
    extremely sharp but short.
carte d'identification/d'indentité—*the identification* card all
    French residents carry.
*Çe n'est rien, madame. Mon amie a mangé un mauvaise
    huître*—It's nothing, ma'am. My friend ate a bad oyster.
c'est bon—that's good.
chef—chief, head of department.
chef modéliste—head pattern cutter.

chevalier—a knight or member of a French order such as the Legion of Honor.

clochard—homeless person.

Coke Light—the European equivalent of Diet Coke.

commérage—gossip.

commerçant—merchant.

compagnon—life partner.

compétence—area of responsibility (in this case, geographical area).

couturier—fashion designer.

croquis—fashion sketch.

culotté—bold.

d'acc—okay; short for *d'accord*.

d'accord—okay.

de rien—it's nothing.

défilé de mode—fashion show; *défilé* for short.

désintoxification/désintox—rehab.

drogué—drug addict, druggie.

élégant—dashing.

emmerdeur—trouble-maker (literally, shit-stirrer).

et aussi—and also.

fils de pute—son of a whore.

flic—policeman.

flou—a fashion workshop in which light fabrics are sewn.

galant—charming.

garçon de table—waiter.

gérante—manager.

giton—slang for a freeloader supported by a more mature gay man.

grande investigatrice—great investigatrix.

guillemets—the pointed quotation marks used by the French: " ».

hein—eh?

indemnité de licenciement—redundancy payment.

je vous en prie—you're welcome.

juge d'instruction—examining magistrate, who determines
   whether there is a case worth prosecuting.

les detectives privés pour les nuls—private detection for
   dummies.

louche—sleazy, seedy.

maison—a fashion house.

maison particulier—a grand townhouse.

mannequin—model.

maquisard—resistance fighter (the plural is *maquis*).

maquillage—makeup.

marque—brand.

mise en scène—smokescreen.

morceau—piece.

ne touche pas—don't touch.

partenaire sentimentale—romantic partner.

pathologiste—forensic pathologist.

pommes frites—French fries.

portable—cell phone.

poulet roti—roast chicken.

poussette—stroller, push chair.

pressing—dry cleaner.

recherche google—Google search.

remerciements—acknowledgments.

rusé—sly.

salope—bitch.
séjour—living room.
s'il vous plait—please.
toile—an early version of a finished garment that can still be
    altered and tweaked.
une moule serrée—literally means "a tight mussel."
vraiment?—really?

Acknowledgments

First, as always, enormous thanks to my agent, Laura Macdougall, who is responsible for my writing career and to whom I am permanently grateful. Second, profuse thanks to Olivia Davies, who shepherded me through moments of crisis, then made sure I was happy with the results. Thanks also to Chelsey Emmelhainz, who gave me some of the soundest writing advice I've received, and to Julian Isaacs, who provided invaluable guidance on the (literal) ins and outs of heroin usage, as well as rock 'n' roll anecdotes that impressed and cheered me when I was down. And many thanks to James Bock, who had the unenviable task of editing me and performed it with grace and perspicacity.

Thanks to Andy Peers, my first listener; Jennifer Piddington, my first reader; Ashley Bruce, my weekly supporter, and Kirsty Martin, my soothing and relaxing confidant. I give special thanks to and for Stephen Dineen, the very first person to introduce me to strangers as "a novelist."

Even more than usual, this book wouldn't have been possible without Google Maps and Google Street View. In pandemic times, these made it possible for me to walk the streets of Paris. And thanks to the Paris France Hôtel, which I stayed in on the brief research trip I was able to manage before COVID changed everything. It was the first time I stayed in a hotel on a research trip, and I felt *classy*.

The art market in France during and after World War II is a complex and difficult subject, one that's still being unraveled today. For help understanding it, I used Hector Feliciano, *The Lost Museum: The Nazi Conspiracy to Steal the World's Greatest Works of Art* (Basic Books, 1997); Julian Jackson, *France: The Dark Years, 1940–1944* (Oxford University Press, 2001); "Art Life in Occupied France, 1940–1944," *Modern Art Consulting*; Lynn H. Nicholas, *The Rape of Europa: The Fate of Europe's Treasures in the Third Reich and the Second World War* (Alfred A. Knopf, 1994). Any inaccuracies in this book are mine, not theirs.

Rachel's puzzling over the morality and worth of bringing ancient Nazis to trial are my own, as is the great-uncle. It's a topic I've long wrestled with, and in the writing of this book I had some help from Elizabeth Kolbert's article "The Last Trial: A Great-Grandmother, Auschwitz, and the Arc of Justice," in the *New Yorker*'s February 16, 2015, issue; Eva Mozes Kor, "'Bookkeeper of Auschwitz' guilty of accessory to 300,000 murders" (https://www.itv.com/news/update/2015-07-15/auschwitz-survivor-disappointed-by-groening-jail-term/); Eliza Gray's "The Last Nazi Trials" (https://time.com/nazi-trials/); Melissa Eddy, "Why Germany Prosecutes the Aged for Nazi Roles It Long Ignored" (*New York Times,* February 9, 2021); and the wonderful film, *The Eichmann Show* (BBC TV, 2015).

Acknowledgments

In the more mundane but integral area of private detection, particularly private detection on the web, I used Kevin Beaver, *Hacking for Dummies* (John Wiley & Sons, 2018); Jean-Emmanuel Derny and Samuel Mathis, *Les Detective Privés pour les nuls* (Editions First, 2016). I also consulted Benjamin Sobieck's *The Writers Guide to Weapons* (Writer's Digest Books, 2015), and Eugene Vidocq's *Memoirs of Vidocq* (Whittaker, 1859). To understand, at least to a degree, the cut-throat world of fashion design, I consulted *Fashionary: The Fashion Business Manual* (Fashionary, 2018); Oriole Collin and Connie Karole Burks, *Christian Dior* (V&A, 2018); Lesley Ellis Miller, *Balenciaga: Outside In* (V&A, 2017); Désirée Sadek and Guillaume de Laubier, *Inside Haute Couture: Behind the Scenes at the Paris Ateliers* (Adams, 2016); and André Leon Talley's absolutely riveting *The Chiffon Trenches: A Memoir* (Penguin Random House, 2020).

As always, I made extensive use of Pekka Saukko and Bernard Knight's *Knight's Forensic Pathology*, 3rd edition (Arnold, 2004). This terrific book has given me more hours of enjoyment than its title might suggest.